ALS

DI Ruth Hunter Crime Thriller

The Snowdonia Killings

The Harlech Beach Killings

The Dee Valley Killings

The Devil's Cliff Killings

The Berwyn River Killings

The White Forest Killings

The Solace Farm Killings

The Menai Bridge Killings

The Conway Harbour Killings

The River Seine Killings

The Lake Vyrnwy Killings

The Chirk Castle Killings

The Portmeirion Killings

The Llandudno Pier Killings

The Denbigh Asylum Killings

The Wrexham Killings

The Colwyn Bay Killings

The Chester Killings

The Llangollen Killings

DC Ruth Hunter Murder Cases

Diary of a War Crime

The Razor Gang Murder

An Imitation of Darkness

London, SE1 5

The Anglesey

The Dark Tide

In Too Deep

Blood on the Shore

The Drowning Isle

Dead in the Water

LAST NIGHT AT VILLA LUCIA

SIMON MCCLEAVE

Storm
PUBLISHING

Copyright © Simon McCleave, 2024

Ebook ISBN: 978-1-80508-606-2
Paperback ISBN: 978-1-80508-608-6

Cover design: Lisa Horton
Cover images: Shutterstock

Published by Storm Publishing.
For further information, visit:
www.stormpublishing.co

For our beautiful Emma

PROLOGUE

CERYS

I'm sitting in my favourite spot. I lean forward on the wicker sofa with soft plum-coloured cushions, which is carefully positioned in the shade, just to the left-hand side of my villa.

My villa? It still sounds peculiar and rather grandiose. Even after nearly two years. You'd think I'd have got used to it. I guess it's all part of my imposter syndrome. It's my default position for most things.

The sofa has that little creak as I shift my weight. The tightly wound bamboo readjusting.

And though it's not even 8 a.m., the blazing Tuscan sunshine is already blinding and the air temperature oven hot. A fly buzzes past totally oblivious to what's happened this morning. Or maybe it's a sign. An omen.

I gaze out at the view which I've been looking at every morning for two years. The crest of the hill. The expansive vineyard and then beyond that, sprawling fields, a wood and low rolling hills for as far as the eye can see. It's breathtaking. A spectrum of colour. A landscape speckled by a handful of caramel-brown terracotta roofs of distant villas and farmhouses. Over to my right, an olive grove, golden fields and rows of umbrella-shaped trees. To say that it is idyllic doesn't do it justice.

One of the guests at the villa a few months earlier brought paints and sketch books. He told me about the nineteenth-century Italian artist, Giovanni Fattori, a leading figure of the Macchiaioli. Apparently it referred to a group of Tuscan painters whose use of natural light and colour when painting the landscape of the area was highly influential on the French impressionists. I pretended to be fascinated as he waffled on. And his attempts to capture this view – *my view* – were less than impressive. Better than I could do, granted. But then again, I don't paint anymore, nor would I make a big show of landscape painting if the result was on a par with the work of an eight-year-old. I'm being bitchy. My head is throbbing.

However, this morning, I'm unable to take any of this astonishing view in.

My mind is spinning and out of control.

'My view' has taken on a whole new significance today. I've no idea how all this is going to end. But I am starting to realise that this view may not be 'my view' for very much longer.

I take my Chanel sunglasses which have been pushed up into my hair and pop them on the bridge of my nose. I spotted them on a stall in Portobello Market in Notting Hill about six years ago. The stallholder assured me they were vintage. I thought they looked like the kind of sunglasses I'd seen Brigitte Bardot or Sophia Loren wearing in the seventies and parted with the best part of £200. I've had enough compliments to know that they were worth the investment.

I move a strand of my dirty-blonde hair from my face, tuck it behind my ear and notice that my hand is shaking. It's not surprising after the events of the past half hour. For a moment, I hold my right hand out and watch it quiver. I take a deep breath and try to let it out in a long, slow, controlled stream but the shaking doesn't stop. I need a drink.

By this time of the morning, I would have usually completed my sunrise kundalini yoga class for the guests before making sure that everything is in order for their breakfast. Kiwis, bananas and mangos would have been peeled and chopped. A selection of pastries taken from the freezer to be baked. The coffee machine primed with Melozio pods that are a glorious golden colour. The packet claims they're a harmonious blend of Italian Arabicas with a distinctly sweet note. The split roast adds to the smooth taste and a touch of milk develops a biscuity note.

I'm not sure about any of that. I just know it tastes bloody lovely. I wish that caffeine was my only drug of choice.

And after breakfast is prepared for the guests, I usually wander up to this sofa with my phone, a book and a large glass of cucumber water.

Then it's a ten-minute meditation with a lovely Canadian man called Mike on an app on my phone. He has a comforting, chatty voice that I find very alluring. In fact, until I saw a photo of him, I had imagined him to be a beautiful, dark, handsome man with a beard, in his forties, sitting in white flowing clothes by a lake. Unfortunately, Mike is in his sixties, with a pointed, weaselly face and glasses. I regret ever looking him up on Google now.

Sometimes, I can find the peace and serenity that I strive for in these guided meditations. Other times, my mind is whirring with anxiety.

And this morning I don't have a glass of cucumber water, a book or my phone.

I'm feeling overwhelmed. Completely overwhelmed by a dread that is making my stomach muscles tighten like a clenched fist. A nasty ball of terror deep inside.

Breathe, Cerys. Just breathe, I tell myself.

So I begin the breathing exercises that I was shown back in

those dark days in London. Days when my life was dominated by panic attacks and fear. Before I came to my villa.

In for five, hold for seven, breathe out for eight, I say to myself. *In for five, hold for seven, breathe out for eight.*

It doesn't seem to be working. My pulse is racing.

In for five, hold for seven, breathe out for eight.

I feel like I'm hanging on to my sanity by my fingertips. I close my eyes to steady myself.

In for five, hold for seven, breathe out for eight.

It's no use.

I need to move and not sit still.

I stand up, take a few steps onto the grass and gaze over at the beautiful infinity pool.

I can hardly dare to look – but I force myself.

Oh God.

For a second, I wonder if I had some perverse hallucination when I came out of the villa to lay out guest towels on the sunloungers.

But it's as real as the sun beating down on this terrace.

I go back and sit on the edge of the sofa.

The wind picks up and the air smells of pine.

And then the sound of a police siren fractures the tranquillity.

I wait for them to arrive.

I wonder how this has all happened and how it's all going to end.

Because floating in the middle of my infinity pool, there is a dead body face down in the water.

ONE

ZOE

Two days earlier – Saturday, 8 July 2023
9.28 a.m.

'Listen, *mate...*' Harry Collard's public school accent booms across the desk in the car rental office at Florence Airport.

Here we go, Zoe thinks as she looks at Harry's side profile. She has a flashback to the first time she'd seen him at Shoreditch House – his classic chiselled features and a slightly pointed chin. She fell for him instantly.

'I booked a four by four, so I'm not taking the BMW,' Harry says firmly. 'You need to find me a four by four right now.'

Harry looks at her and shakes his head with a withering expression. 'Jesus,' he says loudly enough for everyone to hear. 'How difficult can it be? I booked the car six bloody months ago.'

Other customers and staff look over as he raises his voice.

Zoe's heart sinks.

'Can you believe it?' Harry snaps to her and their nineteen-year-old son, Charlie.

'Does it really matter?' she says quietly with a shrug, feeling the uncomfortable stares of everyone in the rental office.

Charlie has large wireless Beats headphones on and is purposefully oblivious to what's going on.

'Oh no, you're right, Zoe,' Harry growls sarcastically. 'I should be grateful for any car they give us. Why don't I just bend over while I'm at it.'

The harrassed-looking young Italian man comes back to the desk and Harry starts up his complaints as Zoe walks away with folded arms. It's the same every time they go anywhere – holiday, restaurant, concert or club. Why should she think Harry was going to be any different today? He has spent his entire life getting everything he's ever wanted. And if he doesn't, he raises merry hell until he does. It's highly embarrassing and exhausting.

Zoe knows that as the hugely successful Director of A&R at Kismet Records, Harry believes he is entitled for his every want and desire to be gratified. That's what happens when you went to Marlborough, one of England's most prestigious boarding schools, Zoe assumes. The dark irony is that not only has such privilege set him up for life, it has also left him emotionally damaged for life.

'What's going on?' Charlie asks with a frown as he removes his headphones.

'They've given us the wrong car,' Zoe explains with a sigh. Despite a couple of fans, the rental office is hot and her skin is becoming clammy.

'I bet that's gone down well,' Charlie says sardonically. Charlie calls Harry out on his behaviour and his bullshit on a regular basis. Often it spills over into explosive arguments. And a couple of times, they've had physical fights.

'I'm sure it'll be sorted in a minute,' Zoe says now, thinking that all she wants to do is get into an air-conditioned car. Any air-conditioned car. 'He's insisting on a four by four.'

'Why? I'm pretty sure we're going to just drive to the villa, aren't we?' Charlie groans and then gestures to his father. 'And he's going to spend 90 per cent of his time walking around the pool on his phone. Me and you might pop to a local supermarket. That's it. Unless we're planning on doing some off-roading across the vineyards.'

Zoe gives him a smile and shrugs. 'You know what he's like.'

'Yeah, he's a cock.' Charlie gives her a knowing look. 'He's always a cock.' And with that look comes a certain element of *I told you so...*

Charlie is their only child. She and Charlie are very close and he's told her on numerous occasions that she needs to leave Harry. But there have been moments when Harry has shown a more vulnerable, sensitive side. He's told her about his horrible time at boarding school. She's seen the lasting psychological harm it has inflicted on him. And at times like these, when he's behaving like a complete prick, she sees flashes of a young, frightened and homesick Harry and she convinces herself she can't leave him, however bad it gets.

'Right, sorted at last,' Harry says with a withering roll of his eyes as he strides over waving the car keys. 'Let's get going.'

Pulling their Louis Vuitton luggage, they walk behind Harry as he marches along the long line of rental cars. Other families are doing the same or are stopping to load their cars.

Zoe looks over at a couple in their forties laughing as they open their car doors. Their children are already in the back of the car.

Christ, they look so happy, she thinks to herself. *Were we ever that happy?* She doubts it.

Harry stops by a white SUV. 'Alfa Romeo Tonale. Top spec. Looks nice,' he says but she's not really sure who he's talking to. She has zero interest in cars and Charlie is currently listening to Stormzy's 'Vossi Bop' on his headphones. Maybe Harry is saying it in the hope that someone else will hear and form some kind of positive opinion of him in that brief second. He just can't help himself.

'Right,' Zoe says as she delves into her large Mulberry hand-bag. She found it on a pre-loved website in case Harry complained about her buying yet another handbag. 'I'll just find the postcode of where we're going.' She rummages for the details that she printed off the night before.

Harry's phone rings. Looking at the caller, he instantly gives her a furtive glance.

'Work,' he says, gesturing to the phone as he walks away out of earshot.

He's lying.

For someone who seems to have spent most of their adult life lying, Harry isn't particularly good at it.

As Zoe wheels their luggage towards the car's tailgate, she glances over at Harry. His arms are muscular in his sky-blue Lacoste polo shirt. He's been hammering the gym in recent months. He's lost weight around his middle too.

With a slight groan, Zoe lifts one of the cases into the boot and then stands to one side as Charlie does the same.

She glances over at Harry again who is smiling as he talks.

She's not stupid.

He's having an affair.

TWO

LOWRI

10.17 a.m.

'When are they coming?' Lowri asks as she and her mother, Cerys, put the last of the small scatter cushions on the king-size four-poster bed in the villa's master bedroom.

'About an hour,' Cerys replies as she glances at her phone. 'Bloody hell,' she then mutters under her breath as she crouches down on her haunches and retrieves a large, black plastic hair-grip from under the dark wood bedside table.

Lowri feels the cold of the cream-coloured marble flooring under her feet. The room is tastefully decorated with painted wooden furniture. Light-blue mosquito nets are draped over the ends of each corner of the bed. Her mum really does have a good eye for interior dressing. Lowri's told her she should do it professionally.

Opposite the bed there is an old-fashioned, white, free-standing, roll-top slipper bath with antique brass legs. On either side are vintage rattan chairs with peacock-shaped backs and apricot-coloured cushions.

Lowri frowns as she watches her mother. Her face is taut. She gets like this on changeover days. Snappy and anxious.

Lowri raised a quizzical eyebrow. 'What is it?'

'This.' Cerys groans in exasperation as she shows her daughter the hairgrip. 'I've told her to move stuff when she cleans. But she still cleans around everything.'

'It's not that deep, Mum,' Lowri says with a smirk.

'Deep?' Cerys glared at her. 'I charge a fortune for this place so it has to be perfect.' She held up the hairgrip. '*This* isn't perfect. One bad review and I'm screwed.'

'You could have a word with Lucia.' Lowri shrugs.

Cerys marches around the room to give it a final inspection. 'No, no. She's worth her weight in gold.'

For a second, Lowri's thoughts turn to Lucia's husband, Lorenzo. He might be seriously old, but he's also fit for an older man. Even Mum agrees. She called him 'the Italian stallion' the other day!

As they walk out of the master en suite, Lowri feels the soft cool draught of the air-conditioning. She has no idea what people did before air-conditioning. Her mum explained that back in the seventies and eighties, no villas or holiday homes would have it. It blows Lowri's mind.

They come down the wide stone staircase. The sound of her mum's shoes reverberates around the large hallway with its high ceilings.

Lowri goes over to the sliding doors that lead out onto the patio, the dark grey wooden decking and down to the infinity pool. She's instantly shrouded in the intense heat of the morning but she's now used to it. And it'll be hotter this afternoon.

'Where are they from again?' she asks, even though she's already seen the booking form.

'London,' Cerys says with a wary tone. 'Dulwich Village.'

They get to the stone staircase that leads down to the pool.

There is a lush green lawn that stretches the whole width of the property, with palm trees for shade and benches looking out across the view beyond.

'What's wrong with London?' Lowri says as they walk down to the poolside. 'You used to live there. I was born in London.'

'I know,' Cerys replies quietly.

Lowri regrets her comment. She knows why her mother hates London so much. She knows what happened to her mum four years ago. It's why she came to Tuscany.

'The last family we had from London were entitled wankers,' Cerys remarks.

'They were from Islington,' Lowri says. 'What do you expect? North London chattering classes.'

'Get you,' Cerys says with a mocking grin. 'Sarf London girl, are you? Keepin' it real?'

'Mum?'

'What?'

Lowri gives her a one-finger salute.

'That's nice.' Cerys laughs.

The smells of the outside are invigorating. The summer heat baking the earth mixes with the scent of pine and eucalyptus. The garden is bordered by neatly tended box hedges.

The water of the infinity pool is a smooth, perfect blue stretching to the edge of the terrace, surrounded by azure-coloured sunloungers and umbrellas. There is a wonderfully soothing sound of the water lapping against the tiled walls of the pool.

Cerys moves around straightening the sunloungers so that they are exactly perpendicular. Then she fusses with the big white towels that have been laid out for the guests while removing a couple of rogue leaves that have floated onto the loungers. Her mum needs to have everything perfect. As if arranging a set for a photo shoot.

'Haven't they got a teenage son?' Lowri asks. Again she knows the answer but she just wants to check.

Cerys narrows her eyes. 'Ah, there it is,' she says with a knowing grin.

Lowri gives her mother an innocent look as though she has no idea what she's referring to. 'What?'

'No.'

'What?'

'No.'

'Mum, you can't keep saying the word "no",' Lowri insists.

'I do not want anything going on between you and a guest,' Cerys warns her. 'Please. It could end in disaster.'

'Okay, okay,' Lowri says with a conciliatory smirk. 'I'll leave him alone.'

'Good.'

'Unless he's really fit.'

'Lowri!'

They turn and begin to make their way back to the villa from the pool.

'Dad called me earlier,' Lowri says quietly.

'What did he want?' Cerys asks. She sounds suspicious.

Lowri doesn't acknowledge her mother's wariness. She is well aware of how bad her father's behaviour was in the past. She lived under the same roof. There are things you cannot unhear. Her parents have been divorced for nearly a year. It had been an acrimonious and bad-tempered affair. But then again, so had much of their marriage. She remembers hearing her dad screaming down the phone at her mum over the details of the divorce. Lowri is just thankful that at least they are on speaking terms now, even if she does feel that she is the grown-up sometimes.

'He was just ringing for a chat.'

'That's nice,' Cerys says sardonically.

Lowri looks at her. She can see the effect that talking about her dad has on her. Her mum seems to withdraw into herself. It's as if all that pain shrinks her physically at the mention of his name. Lowri wishes she hadn't told her about the phone call.

'You know I don't have a problem with your dad,' Cerys says. She's trying to sound reassuring but Lowri can hear how unsettled she is.

'Sorry, I shouldn't have said anything,' Lowri mutters.

'It's fine. Don't be silly.' Cerys pulls her into a hug as they walk across the decking but Lowri can see her mum is uneasy.

'It's just that I don't want to keep stuff like that secret from you,' Lowri explains.

'It's fine. I just said it was,' Cerys snaps as she walks away.

Maybe it really would be better not to mention Dad's name again, Lowri thinks.

THREE

ZOE

10.29 a.m.

Zoe looks out of the passenger window. They have been driving south from Florence for about an hour. The Tuscan sky is a deep, rich blue. Vineyards are heavy with the black Sangiovese grapes that are the main ingredient of the regional Chianti wine.

There is a strange silence in the car. It's not tense or uncomfortable. But for some reason, she and Harry feel as if they've slowly become strangers in recent years. It hasn't been helped by her continual feeling that Harry is cheating on her.

For a moment, Zoe is taken back to when she and Harry first got together. They'd go for weekends away at Babington House or Hotel Tresanton in the beautiful south Cornish village of St Mawes. Their journeys would be full of loud music, singing, laughter and constant chatter. And while away, they'd get drunk, make love outdoors and lie in each other's arms. It makes her feel so very sad as she thinks of how they are now and her certainty that he's having an affair.

What happened to us? she wonders. *We used to be so happy, didn't we?*

'We'll have to go wine-tasting,' Harry says out of nowhere from behind his Ray-Ban Aviators. He sounds like this is just something to say to fill the silence.

'Yes, that'd be nice,' Zoe agrees and they fall into silence again.

She turns her head for a second. Charlie is now dozing in the back – his mouth open by about half an inch, headphones still placed over his ears. She can still see the little boy he'd once been before the hormones had kicked in. They'd had their fair share of problems with Charlie in the last two years. He'd been caught smoking weed at school in the first year of sixth form with two friends. The school had a zero-tolerance policy when it came to drugs so they were all politely asked to leave. Harry had kicked up a tremendous fuss, accusing the school of overreacting, contacting lawyers and threatening to sue. They'd managed to get him into a private sixth form college in Hammersmith and he'd scraped three A levels. However, after six weeks at Reading University, Charlie had suffered a nervous breakdown and returned home. He's a bit lost but she's glad he agreed to come away with them. She worries about him being on his own for too long. Maybe her helicopter parenting hasn't helped him. Deep down, she fears she's to blame for her son not being able to cope in the world.

Zoe goes back to staring out of the window at the lush vineyards, dark grapes ripening in the summer heat. Off in the distance, the clock tower and white steeple of an old church stands out against the crisp blue skyline.

The hire car's air-con is just about keeping the blazing mid-morning heat at bay. She grabs her phone, hits an app and looks at the GPS roadmap that appears on her screen.

She feels something on her thigh. It's Harry's hand. She flinches.

In the old days, she wouldn't have flinched. His hand touching her thigh would have been exciting.

'Sorry,' he says, noticing her reaction. He looks almost disappointed.

'It's okay,' she says with a reassuring smile. She doesn't know why she wants to reassure him. It's just what she does.

'We're going to have a lovely holiday,' he says, looking over. 'It'll be good for us all to spend some time together.'

Why is he saying that? It's deluded bullshit.

But there's also part of her that is so incredibly desperate for him to actually mean it.

She points to the road ahead. 'We turn off here in about two miles. Then it's a track up to the villa.'

'Didn't you hear what I just said?' Harry says, sounding upset.

'I did... I just...' She doesn't know what to say. She feels the familiar swirl of dread in her stomach.

Silence.

Zoe looks out of the window.

'Don't ignore me, Zoe,' Harry snaps menacingly.

'What?' She looks over at him with a frown as her pulse quickens.

Harry digs his fingers hard into her thigh with a vice-like grip. It hurts.

'Sorry,' Zoe apologises, trying not to wince. 'I just didn't want us to miss the turning, that's all.'

FOUR

CERYS

10.38 a.m.

I'm in the kitchen and look up at the old-fashioned clock on the
wall. By my calculations, the new guests will be here in ten
minutes. I'm feeling overwhelmed. My head is spinning but I
can't seem to focus. I've wondered recently if I've actually got
undiagnosed ADHD. I'd always thought it was something that
naughty teenage boys had when they were unable to sit still in
class and got into trouble. Then I read a couple of articles. Boy,
did I get that wrong! I'd put my growing forgetfulness down to
brain fog, assuming that I was beginning to get the symptoms of
the perimenopause. But then I read the other symptoms of
ADHD, which apparently can become heightened in women in
middle-age. Issues of time management, anxiety, low self-
esteem, impulsiveness. *Tick for all of the above.*

I look around the kitchen and move the place mats, the
coffee machine, a guide book to Tuscany. Everything has to be
at right angles and perfect. My attention to detail drives others
mad. Sometimes it drives me mad. They don't seem to under-

stand that unless it's like this – neat, tidy, ordered and perfect –
I feel anxious. It feels compulsive rather than a choice.

I notice that the little voice in my brain is yabbering away in
the background with something else. I'm trying my best to
ignore it but it's getting louder and louder. Insistent.
Demanding to be heard.

*It's fine, Cerys. You'll feel better. Just do it. What's the
problem?*

I distract myself by opening the fridge to check for the third
time that I've put everything inside. Water, milk, orange juice
and a welcoming bottle of Italian Prosecco.

My breathing is getting shallow and quick. My hands are
twitchy and my whole body is starting to tense. It might be the
start of a panic attack, I'm not sure. My guests are about to
arrive so I'm not going to take any chances.

So, I finally give in to the voice. To the insidious craving. I
grab a glass and pour myself four fingers of vodka. Then I stop
to listen. I don't want Lowri to catch me. My drinking has been
a source of conflict between us for several years now.

Then I swallow the vodka in three large gulps. Even the
very process of drinking the alcohol calms me. It doesn't make
any sense. The alcohol hasn't even hit my stomach yet, let alone
my bloodstream or brain, but I'm feeling relaxed. Sometimes, I
only need to go into a shop and have the bottle in my hand for
my anxiety to dissipate. Another alcoholic once told me, when I
was going to AA meetings, that the brain produces serotonin
and endorphins in the anticipation that it's about to receive a
shot of alcohol.

My throat burns and I get the grainy hit of vodka in the
back of my nose. Then my stomach warms and glows. And I let
out an audible sigh.

Phew, thank God for that.

I've started early today but I justify it in my head. Today is changeover day. It's stressful. It's reasonable for me to have a drink to calm my nerves. It's total bullshit, of course. But the devious little alcoholic voice in my head is so bloody persuasive. It's the sneaky voice that tells me that next time I drink it will be different. That my drinking will suddenly be controlled, convivial and fun. Not a fucking blackout car crash.

'Mum?'

It's Lowri.

Oh shit!

My heart jumps like I'm a naughty child.

For a moment, I don't turn. I'm trying to assess from the tone of her voice if this is an innocent greeting or whether she just saw me neck a quadruple vodka at 11 a.m.

'Hello, darling,' I say in as breezy a tone as I can muster. 'Final checks. You know what I'm like.'

Lowri peers at me like a hawk. 'Are you all right?'

Oh God, is she on to me?

One of the provisos of her coming out to stay with me for a few weeks was that I wasn't drinking. So far, I've managed to hide it from her. Just.

I'm avoiding eye contact. It's that slight disconnect between the eye and the conscious that gives us problem drinkers away.

And my daughter and my ex-husband both seem to have a laser-guided instinct when that's taken place – however small the amount.

Fuck, fuck.

Lowri glares at me. 'You've had a drink.'

I frown as if this is a ridiculous suggestion. 'No, I haven't. It's eleven in the morning.'

'That hasn't stopped you before,' Lowri snaps. 'Jesus, some-times you woke up and drank in bed before even getting up.'

I pull a shameful face. 'Not any more. I promise.'

From her expression I can tell that she believes me.

I can feel the relief in my body.

I've managed to get away with it this time.

A noise from outside distracts us both. We both know what it is. The familiar sound of an approaching vehicle on our dusty track.

'Come on,' I say with a smile. 'They're here.'

FIVE

ZOE

10.41 a.m.

It has been about ten minutes since Google Maps directed them off the main road south and up towards where Villa Lucia is located. Zoe had looked out at the ancient stone buildings and narrow streets of the sleepy Tuscan villages that went past. Old men sat in the shade drinking or playing cards. It looked like the film set from *The Godfather*. As they peeled off again, the road became narrower and eventually single track. Its surface had gone from smooth tarmac to dusty ground full of bumps and potholes.

'This road would have taken the exhaust off that BMW,' Harry says, raising a conceited eyebrow. 'I'm glad I stood my ground and got this Alfa.'

Zoe nods and gives him a half smile. What does he want her to say? *Well done, darling. You were right again. But then again, you always are.*

Instead, she points at the map on her phone. 'Five minutes up here,' she says in a jovial tone, trying to placate him. She doesn't want any more of his angry outbursts.

'Great,' Harry says but he doesn't sound like he means it. These days, she has no idea what makes her husband happy. However, she is sure of one thing – it's not spending quality time with her or Charlie. She was surprised when Harry didn't wheedle out of the holiday with some spurious excuse of having to work. Last year he had pulled out of the trip to Croatia, claiming he had to fly to LA. If she was honest, she and Charlie had a lovely time sailing down the Dalmatian coast without him.

As the single track steepens, a whitewashed wall flanks them for a few seconds. Then the landscape opens up.

Wow, it's beautiful here.

Zoe glances at Harry, hoping to share the moment, but she catches the distracted and unhappy expression on his face. As far as she can see, no amount of money or professional success – or even looking at a stunning Tuscan landscape on a family holiday – seems to bring him any sense of satisfaction. His inability to be present, to experience pure joy, makes her sad for her and for him.

Glancing over to their right, Zoe sees a huge villa perched on top of a flat plateau.

'That must be us,' she mutters under her breath.

The dirt of the track crunches softly beneath their tyres as they spot a small carved wooden sign – VILLA LUCIA – with a small arrow.

The track gets steeper. The driveway is flanked by tall cypress trees, pruned and straight. Lush lawns of deep green grass stretch out on both sides. A man in his forties – tanned, handsome – uses a sprinkler hose to water the plants and grass.

He looks nice, Zoe thinks, and for a moment her mind races away into some erotic tryst that she could have with the attractive Italian gardener, before she tells herself not to be so stupid.

Pulling into the shaded carport, Harry stops the car. Taking the keys, he turns and gives Zoe a wink. In the old days, she thought Harry had the sexiest wink of any man on the planet. Now she actively hates it. It's probably the wink he gives every available woman he ever encounters.

'Wakey-wakey,' Zoe says as she turns and looks at Charlie who is asleep with his black hoodie pulled up over his head and headphones still clamped to his ears. 'We're here.'

Charlie stirs and squints at her. 'They'd better have decent Wi-Fi,' he mumbles incoherently.

Off to a good start then, Zoe thinks drily to herself.

She opens the car door and steps out. The chill of the air-conditioning is instantly replaced with a hot blanket of air. She stretches out her arms and arches her back. Then she leans down towards her toes. She's aware that her hamstrings are tight. In fact, everything feels tight and it's something she's hoping to rectify in the sunrise yoga sessions that the owner, Cerys Williams, offers. Charlie had pulled a face when she'd suggested that he join her.

Taking a deep breath, Zoe gazes at her surroundings. The air is scented with pine, olive, rosemary and that redolent smell of hot, baked earth that takes her back to childhood holidays on the Costa Brava.

The villa is magnificent. Modernist, whitewashed with huge glass windows. She wants to say it's in the style of Le Corbusier but she's not sure. Maybe she'll look it up.

'Hi there,' says a woman's voice. 'Welcome. How was your trip?'

An attractive woman in her forties approaches. Her expensive-looking sandals click on the stone pathway. Her vintage Chanel sunglasses are pushed up into blonde hair that's pinned in a loose knot and she wears a turquoise maxi dress.

'I'm Cerys,' she says, coming over to shake Zoe's hand. 'You must be Zoe.'

'Yes,' Zoe replies. As usual, she's done all the planning, booking and comms of this holiday. 'What a beautiful place.'

'Thanks.' Cerys beams. 'I really hope you're going to love it.'

Pushing up the car's tailgate, Harry is pulling out suitcases as Charlie slowly emerges from a rear door looking like he's slept the sleep of the dead.

'This is my husband, Harry,' Zoe says. 'And our son, Charlie.'

'I'm guessing there's no concierge,' Harry says with a grin. Zoe doesn't know if he's joking or making a complaint.

Cerys frowns, then catches Zoe's eye and smiles. Zoe gives her a knowing look as if to indicate that she doesn't find her husband amusing.

'Right, let me show you around,' Cerys says in a breezy tone.

'Great.' Zoe is feeling buoyed. She likes Cerys already and it'll be great to have a woman her own age nearby.

Walking up the path, Zoe notices the neat array of cacti on either side. The front door looks solid, made from dark wood with a heavy iron knocker and letter box.

'Here we go.' Cery holds the door open for Zoe, Charlie and Harry, who is carrying two suitcases rather than pulling them on their wheels. Zoe doesn't know whether it's so he can show off his newly honed biceps or just to demonstrate how strong he is, but either way it's pitiful.

The air inside the villa is refreshingly cool. The interior is beautifully decorated with the right mixture of high spec and rustic charm. It's all smooth stone walls and white marble, full of light and exquisitely decorated with tasteful landscape paintings. It is one fashionably furnished room after another. Like something out of *Vogue Interiors*.

I've been to my fair share of villas, but this is stunning.

'And this is the kitchen,' Cerys says.

Rolled marble tops and bespoke cupboards. There's an expensive-looking coffee machine, a huge fridge, and a central island surrounded by dark wooden stools.

Perfect.

They've paid for bed and breakfast. The rest of the time they're self-catering which suits Zoe just fine. Especially as she looks around the spacious kitchen. It's actually bigger than the one they have in their home in West Dulwich.

'Oh, this is lovely,' she says with a smile.

'Thank you,' Cerys replies warmly before continuing, 'There will be a breakfast buffet laid out from 7.30 a.m. and we'll clear it away at 10 a.m. We can do that earlier if you want. And if you have any special requests for breakfast, I can get those in for you.'

Harry is lurking in the background. He has no interest in cooking and never had. He prefers to pay people to do it for him.

'Granola?' he says, sounding as if he's trying to catch her out.

Cerys nods. 'Yes, we've got granola.'

'And none of that manufactured stuff that's full of salt, sugar and wood shavings,' Harry says tersely.

Cerys stops for a millisecond and blinks. Zoe imagines that she's not used to anyone being quite that rude on arrival.

Christ, everything he says makes him sound like a pompous twat.

Cerys then gives Harry a disarming smile. 'Actually, I make my own. Walnuts, dried fruit, oat flakes, grated coconut, chia and pumpkin seeds. But if you want me to adjust that to your taste, just let me know.'

Zoe gives Cerys an amused look. It's the perfect riposte to Harry's rudeness.

Charlie looks at Zoe with a grin. 'Wouldn't mind a bacon sarnie as we're on holiday.'

Zoe loves her son's utter lack of pretension and gives him an affectionate smile.

'We can arrange for a chef to come in and cook dinner if

you'd like that. I can let you have a menu but I find that guests normally like to have a mixture of local Tuscan cuisine.'

'Great,' Zoe says. 'Can we book that in for tomorrow night?'

'Of course,' Cerys replies.

'Anything that you'd particularly recommend?' Harry asks.

'The *panzanella* is incredibly good,' Cerys says enthusiastically. 'It's a Tuscan summer salad. But if you're looking for something a little more substantial, then the *pappardelle al ragù di cinghiale* is great. Tuscan wild boar stew served with either pappardelle pasta or polenta.'

Harry raises an eyebrow. 'Wild boar stew? Now you're talking.'

Zoe nods and then looks at Cerys. She looks a little flushed. Maybe it's the heat. 'And where is the best place for us to go to get food and drink?'

'Montespertoli is about a ten minute drive from here,' Cerys explains.

'Oh yes, I saw it on the map,' Zoe says.

'There's a couple of supermarkets there, plus some nice shops if you fancy a wander around,' Cerys says. 'The next market day is Tuesday so that's always worth checking out too.' Cerys then gestures to the huge glass sliding doors that lead out to the patio. 'I'll show you the outside.'

Sliding open the door, Cerys waits for Zoe, Harry and Charlie to walk out onto the decking before closing it again.

'Try to keep this door shut in the middle of the day,' Cerys explains. 'Despite the air-conditioning, if you leave it open, the villa will still get hot.'

Putting on her sunglasses, Zoe looks out at the view across the infinity pool and beyond. Vineyards and rolling hills. It's exactly how she had dreamed Tuscany would look but it's more wonderful now she's here.

'The pool is cleaned every morning and kept to about thirty degrees,' Cerys says.

'This view is just stunning,' Zoe says quietly.

Harry pops on his sunglasses and points. 'Looks like olive groves over there.'

Cerys nods and gestures with an element of pride. 'This is all the Valdarno Valley. They say that the olive groves over there date back six thousand years and they produce the most wonderful extra-virgin olive oil. I can arrange a tasting if you like.'

'Yes, that would be great,' Harry says and looks at Zoe enthusiastically. 'And as we're in Chianti, we should get some wine tasting in too.'

'Yes,' she agrees. 'That would be lovely. I like a nice Chianti.'

Harry grins. 'I ate his liver with some fava beans and a nice Chianti,' he says, doing an impression of Anthony Hopkins' Hannibal Lecter from *The Silence of the Lambs*.

'That was terrible.' Zoe laughs at Harry and sees his boyish face light up. And for a moment, she sees the man that she fell in love with.

'Sorry.' He smiles back at her. 'I can do my Sean Connery,' he suggests.

'That's even worse.'

Cerys smiles at them both and then points over to their left. 'There's a couple of fantastic vineyards over that way. I can organise that for you whenever you want to go.' Then she looked at Charlie and Harry. 'And at the risk of being sexist, we have a games room down those steps. It's got a pool table, dart-board and Bluetooth speakers.'

Zoe smiles at Charlie who is being his usual awkward self. 'Great. It would be great for you and Dad to play pool together.' She's aware that there is a hopeful tone to her voice. There has been a gigantic chasm between Charlie and his father for the past few years. Harry's idea of parenting often relies heavily on the philosophy of trying to toughen Charlie up so he can survive out there in 'the big, bad world'. However, it often just comes over as bullying. Charlie has rebelled against everything his father believes in or is interested in. Harry is an ardent Arsenal fan and has season tickets. Several years ago, Charlie had refused to accompany Harry to the games and instead follows American basketball, much to Harry's annoyance.

'Yeah. Fancy a few games of pool with the old man, Charlie?' Harry asks brightly.

Zoe can see the hope in Harry's face. He's trying his best to join in and make an effort.

'Not really,' Charlie replies and wanders away.

And for a moment, Zoe can see that Harry is crestfallen. Even though she knows it's his fault, she feels sorry for him. He looks like a hurt little boy.

'Scared of losing,' Harry mumbles defensively. 'That's his problem.'

No, Harry. His problem is you.

There's an awkward silence.

Over to their right, Zoe can see another part of the villa that runs perpendicular to the main building. Keen to move the conversation, she points. 'And what's that over there?'

'Oh, that's the annexe where I live,' Cerys replies.

A figure appears on the terrace outside the annexe.

'Lowri?' Cerys calls and beckons her over. Then she turns to Zoe. 'My daughter, Lowri, is staying with me at the moment.'

Zoe watches Lowri walk towards them. She's wearing cut-off denim shorts and a sky-blue bikini top. She's tanned and has an incredible figure.

'Hi,' Lowri says brightly as she tucks a strand of golden blonde hair behind her ear. She's pretty, with big eyes, high cheekbones and full rosebud lips. She can't be more than twenty, if she's guessing.

She's stunning, Zoe thinks to herself.

'These are our new guests. Zoe, Harry and Charlie,' Cerys says. 'This is my daughter, Lowri.'

'Pleased to meet you,' Lowri says with a friendly smile.

Then Zoe sees Harry's face. His eyes are out on stalks.

Jesus, Harry. Put your tongue away, for God's sake.

Zoe feels a sense of unease in her stomach. She hadn't factored in that there would be a beautiful young woman at their villa.

And with Harry's track record, she fears the worst.

SIX

LUCIA

12.03 p.m.

It's midday and the sun is blazing down on the small ramshackle cottage that Lucia De Nardi shares with her husband, Lorenzo. Lucia uses wooden pegs to secure a bedsheet to the long washing line at the back of their cottage. It'll take less than thirty minutes to dry in the heat. Plus the sheets take on the smell of the nearby pines and olive trees. For Lucia, this is the smell of home. She grew up here.

Lucia's attention is broken by the sharp sound of banging. However, it doesn't bother her as she looks over at the small workshop and shed. She knows Lorenzo is repairing a chair from Villa Lucia that has been broken. She wasn't surprised it broke. The man who had rented the villa three weeks earlier had been about twenty stone. Fat bastard! She had watched him waddle around the pool like a beached whale. His stomach was so enormous that it had virtually covered his swimming trunks so that from a distance it looked like he was naked. Hideous. Lucia can't stand such gluttony. There is no need for it. It shows laziness and a lack of discipline. Imagine having all that money and allowing yourself to look like that, she thinks. He should have gone to one of those expensive clinics where they can suck all the fat out.

As Lucia stretches out and pegs another bedsheet, she pauses. She can hear a sound. A car is approaching. She calculates from the volume it's about two or three minutes away down the track.

She feels her stomach clench and her pulse quicken. The only two places up this track are her cottage and Villa Lucia. There's nothing else up here. She also knows that the new guests have arrived up at the villa about an hour ago. A middle-aged couple with a son who looks like he's in his late teens. She thinks that Cerys told her they were from London.

For a second, she glances up at the home security camera that Lorenzo has mounted high up on the front wall of their cottage. He's linked it to his laptop inside and records what's going past. That way he can see if anyone is snooping around their cottage at night or if there are any strange or unfamiliar cars around. At first, Lucia thought he was being paranoid but she can see that having it keeps him calm.

The banging stops. Lorenzo's anxious face appears at the doorway to the workshop and he looks at her questioningly.

Even though they've been married for nearly fifteen years, she still finds him incredibly attractive. Having just turned forty, Lorenzo is very masculine-looking – heavy brow, wide jaw and strong Roman nose. His thick dark hair is peppered with grey at the temples and his skin is a caramel brown. He has a vee of sweat on his grey T-shirt, which is sticking to his skin and emphasising every single muscle. Not the muscles of some vain gym-head. They are the lithe muscles of a man who does manual labour for a living.

'Just stay in there,' she hisses at him.

Lorenzo nods and disappears back inside anxiously.

Taking a nervous swallow, Lucia continues to peg out the washing as the noise of the approaching vehicle gets louder.

And then a loud crunch of gravel as a black 4x4 car pulls into the entrance to the track that leads to their cottage.

The car is only about twenty yards away.

Lucia puts down the washing, frowns and begins to approach the car. Her heart is now hammering against her chest.

Have they found us? she wonders. *After all this time, have they finally tracked us down?*

As the driver's window slides down, Lucia holds her breath. She braces herself to run and make an escape.

Instead, she sees a woman in her forties with black hair and sunglasses looking out at her with a smile.

'I'm so sorry,' the woman says with an apologetic expression. Her accent is British. Maybe it's Scottish. Lucia can't place it. 'I think we're lost. We're looking for...' Then the woman looks at the man sitting in the passenger seat with silver hair who is evidently her husband.

'Villa Rosa?' the man says, looking at a printed document.

Lucia lets out a sigh of relief. *Thank you, God.*

'Oh yes,' she says with a friendly smile. 'If you go back to the main road, it is the next turning on the right. And you find Villa Rosa maybe five minutes up that road. It is very close.'

'Thank you,' the woman says shaking her head with embarrassment. 'I knew we were close.'

She turns the car around and the 4x4 trundles back down the track the way it came.

Lucia crosses herself. She looks up and says a little prayer of thanks to St Michael the Archangel for his protection.

'Have they gone?' asks Lorenzo in a virtual whisper.

He's holding a shotgun.

'Yes,' she reassures him. 'And put that bloody thing away.'

She looks at the dark tattoos on Lorenzo's forearms – a gun, a Catholic cross and a rosary. The symbols of Lorenzo's dark past.

She and Lorenzo are terrified that his past is going to catch up with him some day with terrifying results.

SEVEN

LOWRI

12.13 p.m.

Lowri scrawls through her TikTok videos. Her homepage shows her singing her own songs which she plays on a twelve-string acoustic guitar. She's had hardly any views and feels a familiar swell of disappointment in her stomach. She knows songs often only go viral when they get attached to a trend or a message, sometimes taking on a whole new meaning. Like how Tom Odell's 'Another Love' blew up when people started using it as a protest song for videos about the war in Ukraine. Lowri sighs. It's impossible to predict what will catch on or when. Plus, TikTok culture is so anti-self-promotion, which makes it hard to get her music out there.

Lowri swipes away from her TikTok page. She's been working on new music since she arrived in Tuscany. That's what she wants more than anything else in the world, to make a living writing and playing her music. When she was little, she'd raid her mum's CD collection and marvel at the sounds of Joni Mitchell, Carole King and Joan Armatrading. By the time she was twelve, she'd taught herself to play the guitar. But she's kept her musical ambitions to herself for years. It had always felt silly and self-indulgent somehow.

Then her mother had heard her singing one of her own compositions in her bedroom one day and told her it was fabulous. Lowri didn't give her mother's words much credence. She was her mum. What else was she going to say? But her mum insisted Lowri showed her everything she'd written and then showed her father. She remembers the first time she'd played her songs to her parents. She had felt sick with worry and embarrassment. What if they laughed at her? What if they told her that they weren't very good? She needn't have worried. She remembers the smiles of joyful surprise on both their faces. It was as if they couldn't quite believe what they were hearing. Her mum said that her songs were 'beautiful' and 'transcendent'.

Her father had told her that her music had a slight country feel and reminded him of Bonnie Rait. Lowri had never heard of Bonnie Rait but was flattered when she did listen to her. Lowri had started to show her compositions to friends and her music teacher at school. She was amazed by their positive feedback. Especially as she was convinced that one day she was going to be found out. One day someone would tap her on the shoulder and tell her that she was a fraud with no real talent and should give it all up. Imposter syndrome is a bitch.

However, in sixth form college, she'd plucked up the courage to play a couple of very small gigs. Just a couple of pubs in South London. The reaction had been amazing. Then she completed her A levels but was now lost. Her mum suggested that she come over to Tuscany to live with her while she decided what to do next. She'd toyed with doing a songwriting degree at London's Institute of Contemporary Music Performance. But music wasn't something that could be taught. A degree in songwriting was a bit artificial. Lacked credibility. She doesn't know what to do going forward and, to be honest, she's a bit stuck.

Lowri looks out of the shutters of her bedroom over at the infinity pool. She sees the son of the family that have arrived a couple of hours ago. Charlie, wasn't it? He's wearing long shorts and a Converse skating T-shirt. He looks a little gangly and awkward but he's good-looking. They've had a couple of boys his age at the villa before. The last one, Jack, an entitled public schoolboy from the Home Counties, clearly spent too much time in the gym and swanned around like a peacock, clearly aspiring to be on some terrible reality TV show like *Love Island*.

She glances over at her guitar and thinks about working on her latest song.

The phone rings and she sees the caller ID – *Dad*. Her stomach muscles instantly tighten and she takes a breath. Lowri loves her father but she's still scared of him. His explosive temper and booming voice used to put the fear of God into her as a child. Sometimes he'd slam doors so hard they sounded like gunshots that made her jump out of her skin. Even now, she can't seem to shake off her nervous reaction to him calling her or the sound of his voice.

'Hey, sweetie,' her dad says in an upbeat tone.

She doesn't like 'sweetie'. It makes her sound young and immature. It feels a little patronising.

Why can't he just use my name like any other human being?

'Hey, Dad,' she replies in a light, carefree tone, taking her phone as she wanders across the stone floor of her bedroom and heads out of the annexe. The sun's heat hasn't managed to penetrate yet so the stone flooring is still nice and cold on the soles of her feet.

'How's it going in paradise?' he asks with a slight tone of sarcasm.

She's not going to rise to his comment. Her parents' move to Tuscany over two years ago was meant to be a new start for them but it only lasted a year. Her dad said that her mum's drinking and behaviour had become unbearable so he returned to London. Lowri suspects he's jealous that her mother seems to have rebuilt her life in the glorious Tuscan landscape without him since he left. He has that kind of arrogance and pettiness.

'Nice,' she says as she walks outside and lets the hot sun warm her face and body. It feels lovely. 'It can be a bit quiet sometimes but I'm getting a lot of writing done.' She's irritated by her continual need to placate or please him.

'Great,' he says indifferently. 'That's great. Did you ever hear back from that A&R bloke?'

Her father's friend knew someone at Arista Records and had passed on a demo of her work to him. That was six months ago and she hasn't heard a thing, so she isn't holding her breath.

'No,' Lowri admits. Then she spots her mum walking down the stone steps that lead to the pathway over to where she's standing. 'It was a long shot anyway.'

'I guess. He'll be kicking himself one day.'

'Maybe,' she says, brightened by his optimism.

God, why do I need his bloody affirmation so much? she asks herself frustratedly.

Then Lowri sees her mum stumble a little on the pathway.

'Shit,' she mutters under her breath. She can't help herself.

'What is it?' her dad asks suspiciously.

'Nothing.'

'Lowri?' her dad says, sounding concerned.

She's watching as her mum pushes up her sunglasses.

For a moment, Lowri feels angry that her mum might have been drinking. But then she remembers the trauma of the assault. It had changed her mum forever. She had never been quite the same person again. And her reliance on alcohol to self-medicate grew to the point where she was a functioning alcoholic. That was understandable, wasn't it? Lowri can feel her pulse quicken as she recalls the terrible rows, listening anxiously to the shouting and screaming from her bedroom. Her mum hiding a black eye under thick make-up and making breakfast as if nothing had happened. She knew that her dad had hit her mum on the odd occasion but no one ever talked about it. And Lowri was too scared to confront him about it. It was just this horrible family secret that they all shared.

'Lowri?' her dad snaps angrily.

'Sorry,' she apologises, getting in a flap. 'It's just... Mum stumbled and I thought she'd had a drink but it's fine. She's fine. Honestly.'

As soon as the words leave her mouth, she regrets it.

'WHAT!' her dad thunders down the phone. 'Jesus fucking Christ, Lowri! I'm flying over today to get you then.'

Lowri felt sick with anxiety.

Why did I say that? I'm an idiot!

'No, no, no,' she insists in a panic. 'She's fine. Honestly. My mistake. Please. You don't need to come over here. I can see her now and she's fine.'

There's a tense silence.

Her heart is racing at the thought of him flying over.

'Sure?' he asks.

'Yes. It's my fault. Honestly.'

'Okay... Well, just so you know, I put £250 into your account this morning.'

'What? You didn't need to do that, Dad,' she says, making sure that she sounds suitably grateful. 'That's really kind.'

'You're my daughter and I miss you,' he gushes.

'I miss you too.' Lowri feels disingenuous saying it but what else is she going to say? She doesn't miss him really. He's love-bombing her. Grand, generous gestures to try to win her over and manipulate her against her mum.

'I've got to run, sweetie,' her dad says. 'Call me if you're worried about your bloody mother. I'm always here for you.'

'Thanks, Dad.'

Lowri ends the call. A queasy feeling pitches up in her stomach and she watches her mother again. She seems to be walking okay now.

Maybe it was just a stumble? Maybe I'm just being hyper-vigilant? she thinks.

But Lowri can't help but be anxious. Not only has the phone call with her dad made her feel uneasy, once her mum starts to drink, it's always a disaster. And if her dad finds out, World War III will break out!

EIGHT

ZOE

Sunday
5.57 a.m.

The following morning Zoe sits cross-legged on her blue yoga mat.
The cool morning breeze seems to whisper as it brushes over her
and through her hair. Cerys had taken her and Lowri on a brisk
fifteen minute uphill walk to the east of the villa to a high plateau
of ground. Stretched out before them in the distance are the
famous, but now abandoned, Bajarra marble quarries which
gleam white in the early morning sun. Over 200 million years old,
Cerys tells Zoe. Legend has it that Michelangelo obtained the
marble for his David from this very quarry. To their right, an old
brick viaduct dissects the landscape. From where they sit, it is a
two-hundred-foot mountainous drop to the bottom of the quarry
but they're far enough away from the edge not to worry about that.

The early start and walk has been worth it just for the
incredible view. Added to that, Zoe has just completed her first
taxing but wonderful session of kundalini yoga with Cerys.

I don't think I could be any happier or feel more peaceful, she thinks to herself. Lowri is about six feet to her right on an identical mat. Cerys puts her hands together and looks over at Zoe and nods.

'Namaste,' she says very quietly.

Zoe puts her hands together and nods back. 'Namaste.' She feels a little silly as she doesn't really know what 'Namaste' means.

After a few seconds of tranquil silence, Cerys gets up slowly as a signal that the sunrise yoga session is over.

Zoe takes in a long deep breath of the cool, early morning air. She arches her back and stretches out her arms.

Wow, that feels so good.

Then she looks out at the canyon below. When they had first arrived over an hour ago, the sky had still been a dark, sapphire blue before soothing to a scarlet and purple hue. Now that the sun has peered over the horizon to their left, a strip of cloud is coloured a dark, rich orange as though the sky itself is on fire.

'How did you find it?' Lowri asks her as they roll up their yoga mats.

'Oh, great,' Zoe says with a smile. 'Just what I needed this morning.'

It's true. The stretching and breathing seems to have removed every twinge of anxiety from her body. Her mind feels calm and clear.

'Have you done kundalini yoga before?' Cerys asks as they begin the walk back to the villa.

'No.' Zoe shakes her head. 'I did some hatha yoga just after Charlie was born but I never kept it up. I wish I had. Is there a big difference?'

'Kundalini is more spiritual,' Cerys explains. 'It can feel more emotionally intense. Hatha is more gentle all round. I like kundalini because it focuses on the energy centres of the mind and body. It's very effective at rebalancing and unblocking your chakras.'

Zoe grins. 'Well, my chakras definitely feel buggered at the moment so anything that helps that will be great.'

Cerys and Lowri laugh.

'I know it all sounds a bit woo-woo,' Cerys admits. 'But it's really helped my mental and spiritual health. I was in a very dark place a few years ago and yoga and meditation have really helped me.'

They continue their walk downhill for a few minutes.

Zoe looks at Cerys. There's an honesty and intensity to what she has just said that feels very powerful.

'I'm wondering if you've got any books here?' Zoe asks as they reach the villa.

'Yes. Lots,' Cerys replies, pointing to a small bookshelf that's nearby with a dozen or so books on it. 'Help yourself.'

'Great. I had a pile of books ready to bring with me and then I managed to forget them. That's the perimenopause for you.'

'Oh God. Brain fog and memory,' Cerys agrees, rolling her eyes.

'I'll see you later,' Lowri says as she turns and heads over to the annexe.

Zoe watches her go. Her hair, skin and figure are all incredible and she feels a little pang of envy.

After a second, she looks at Cerys. 'She's lovely,' she says, gesturing to Lowri.

'She has her moments,' Cerys replies with a knowing smile. 'But yes, we get on very well. And I'm loving having her here with me.'

They arrive at the decking and Cerys pulls open the large glass doors that lead into the kitchen and living area of the villa.

'I always wanted a daughter,' Zoe admits and then corrects

herself. 'I mean, I love Charlie but...' She feels a little silly for being this candid with a virtual stranger.

'I know,' Cerys says with a kind smile. 'I would have liked to have had a son.'

'I guess I need to remember to be grateful that I have a healthy son,' Zoe says.

'Cultivate an attitude of gratitude,' Cerys says with a smile.

Zoe laughs. 'Ooh, I like that. I'm going to use that.'

Zoe feels as if she's making a connection with Cerys. She really likes her. She seems so down to earth compared to some of Zoe's friends that she has in and around Dulwich Village. In fact, it makes Zoe cringe when she thinks of some of the vacuous and materialistic conversations she gets drawn into.

'What kind of book are you looking for? We've got a couple of great psychological thrillers. But we've also got some more spiritual and self-help books,' Cerys explains.

Zoe thinks for a moment. 'You know what, I had intended to read some crime books. But now I've done the yoga, something more spiritual might be good.'

'Ever read *The Power of Now* by Eckhart Tolle?' Cerys asks.

Zoe shakes her head. She's pretty sure she's never read anything remotely spiritual in her life. 'No.'

'Great,' Cerys says as she strides over to a small bookshelf and retrieves a book with an orange cover and hands it to her. 'One of the best books I've ever read.'

'Thanks.' Zoe gets a little tingle of excitement. Sunrise yoga and now a book on spirituality.

From somewhere, there is the sound of footsteps and deep breathing. As they look up, Harry appears. His grey Nike T-shirt is covered in sweat from running and he has white AirPods in.

'Morning,' Harry pants as he goes to get a bottle of water from the fridge. He opens the fridge abruptly, grabs the bottle and swigs from it noisily.

His appearance seems to have fractured the serenity in the room.

Cerys looks at Zoe. 'I'll leave you guys to it. Anything you need, just come and ask.'

'Thank you,' Zoe says with a grateful smile as she watches Cerys go out of the glass doors and close them behind her. She can't help but feel that she would like more friends like Cerys back in London.

'How was yoga?' Harry asks after another thirsty gulp from the water.

'Lovely,' Zoe says with a smile.

Harry nods and smiles. 'Good for you,' he says and Zoe can see that he really means it.

Maybe he really is going to make more of an effort on this holiday.

'I'm going to get a shower.' Harry gestures towards the huge master bedroom with its en suite. Charlie is upstairs in one of the two double bedrooms on the first floor.

'I'm going to read in bed,' Zoe says holding up her book as she follows Harry out of the kitchen and along the cool airy hallway to their bedroom. The back of his T-shirt is dark with sweat. He never used to run. In fact, Harry used to poke fun at anyone that went running or went to the gym.

Going into the bedroom, Harry places his phone down on the bedside table, takes out his AirPods and puts them into the small white charging case.

Zoe sits on the bed, moves the pillows and then manoeuvres herself back so that she is sitting up. Harry kicks off his trainers, takes off his sweaty T-shirt and looks around for a towel.

Silence.

Zoe watches Harry for a few seconds. As usual he is lost somewhere in his own head.

This is what we do. We just exist, she thinks to herself. *We don't have a relationship. We don't talk, we don't laugh and we haven't had sex for nearly two years.*

Zoe lets out a disappointed sigh as she turns to look at the book that Cerys gave her.

The bathroom door closes as Harry disappears to have a shower. A few seconds later, the noise of the running water from the rainfall shower starts.

Maybe it's her imagination, but Zoe feels as if something has shifted since her yoga session and conversation with Cerys that morning. A small but significant thought that things in her life need to change.

Her train of thought is broken by the eletronic beep of a mobile phone. It's the sound of a new message. She glances down at her iPhone that's resting on the bed.

It's not mine.

The beep sounds again.

Where's that coming from?

Looking over at the bedside table, she sees that Harry's iPhone has disappeared from where she saw him put it.

That's weird.

For some reason, she is suddenly compelled to find it.

Jumping up, she moves around the bed and scours the room for Harry's phone.

She can't see it.

Then it beeps again. She can hear the direction from where it's coming.

The bedside table.

It has a drawer.

She finds herself opening it. The iPhone is sitting inside where Harry has clearly hidden it while he was in the shower.

Jesus, Harry! Could you make it any more suspicious?

The screen hasn't yet moved to lockscreen.

There's a new message via WhatsApp from someone called Alex.

Zoe hesitates. Should she just look away, shut the drawer and pretend she hasn't heard it? That's her instinct. That's the sort of thing she's done before. In the past, she's convinced herself that she just doesn't want to know. Bury her head in the sand.

However, this morning, for whatever reason, she does want to know.

So, she grabs the phone and reads the message that's still sitting on the screen.

> Can we talk later? I know you need to be
> discreet so let me know when you're on your
> own and we won't be disturbed.

Suddenly, Zoe feels like she's falling. Head spinning. Her heart starts thumping against her chest. Her breathing is quick and shallow.

She reads the message again to check that she hasn't misread it. And then reads it again.

Jesus! the voice inside her head screams.

Her eyes fill with tears.

Don't cry, she scolds herself. *You knew this was happening. Why are you so bloody surprised?*

Taking a deep breath, Zoe places the phone back into the drawer. Her hand is shaking.

For a few seconds, she just stares at the wall. She can't work out how she feels. Hot or cold. Angry or crushed.

She quickly wipes her face, moves back onto the bed and leans against the propped up pillows.

Now what do I do?

The noise of the shower stops.

Zoe picks up the book. *The Power of Now*.

The bathroom door opens and Harry comes out with a towel around his waist.

'That's better,' he says as he takes off the towel and rubs his blond hair.

Zoe looks at his penis. She can't help herself after what she's just read. For a few seconds, the images of Harry having sex with another woman fill her head.

She pretends to read the book as he gets dressed. The pink Ralph Lauren polo shirt that she bought him for his birthday. The Hugo Boss shorts she helped him pick at the airport. Then out of the corner of her eye, she sees Harry go over to the bedside table and surreptitiously open the drawer and take the phone in one swift move.

Harry looks over at her, comes around the bed and gives her a quick kiss on the lips. 'Love you.'

'Love you too,' she replies.

Then he holds up the phone. 'I've got to ring the office in LA. Won't be long.'

'Okay,' she says.

Harry frowns. 'You all right?' he asks.

'Yes, I'm fine,' she reassures him.

He nods, turns and leaves the bedroom, closing the door behind him.

NINE

CERYS

2.33 p.m.

The afternoon sun is strong and the air is thick with heat as I walk away from the annexe. Earlier, I had emptied a green soft drink – Arnone *limonata*, Italian lemonade – down the sink. Then I'd retrieved the bottle of vodka that I keep hidden in my wardrobe and carefully poured it inside. It is something I've become fairly proficient at these days. I'd taken a good mouthful, swallowed it, shuddered at the taste and burning sensation in my throat, before screwing the cap back on.

After about five minutes of traversing the pathway downhill, I come to the edge of the nearby vineyard. My top is starting to stick to my back with sweat. The vodka has softened the edges and numbed my anxiety. When I was still living in London, Nick and Lowri had insisted that I attend meetings of Alcoholics Anonymous when my drinking got really out of control. They weren't for me. I was told that if I was an alcoholic like them, then total abstinence is the only solution. I didn't like the sound of that one bit. I just wanted to go back to the time I could drink with a degree of control. My twenties, where I could sit in a pub garden, have a few glasses of chilled rosé and wander home with Nick in a lovely, relaxed fuzz. It seemed that those days had gone. Instead, I'd wake and then gauge from Nick's reaction how bad my drinking and behaviour had been the night before. If he smiled and said 'Morning,' then I knew I was in the clear. If he glared and asked, 'Do you remember what you did and said last night?', then I would be overwhelmed by a sinking anxiety as I'd have no memory. I drank to blackout and couldn't recall a thing.

I unscrew the top of the bottle, take another mouthful of vodka and pop the bottle back in my backpack. If I'm truly honest, I know that I'm an alcoholic and that I need to attend AA meetings. But there's another little voice in my head that convinces me that one day I'll regain control of my drinking again. I'll go back to those halcyon days of my twenties. I suppose that's the Holy Grail of all alcoholics. Get control back. And when I think of the bottles of vodka I have hidden in the annexe and the green plastic bottle in my hand, I guess the days of control and sociable drinking are now gone. But I decide I'm not going to think about that at this precise moment.

At the edge of the vineyard there's a dirt path leading on through the trees. The path winds around a pair of towering umbrella pine trees –*pino l'ombrello*. They get their name from their shape and are where pine nuts come from. I come here from early July onwards to collect them for cooking or to make hummus or pesto.

I walk past tall, slender cypresses and olive trees that crouch low to the ground. The trees thicken as the path drops into a dip, curving away, then up and around again. To one side is an old tree trunk covered in creepers and moss.

I sit down here, under the shade, where it's cooler. The occasional call of birds – the blue rock thrush or a Sardinian warbler – is the only sound above the whispering leaves in the canopy of the trees high above me.

A little more vodka seems to be acceptable. My head is nicely fuzzy now. My limbs a little heavier and softer. And, most importantly, the tight fist of anxiety deep inside my guts has evaporated.

I can hear a man's voice.

I strain my hearing to listen. At first it's inaudible but it seems to be getting closer.

'I'm quite aware that I'm looking for external affirmation. But when I get it, it doesn't work, does it?' the voice says. 'It's fucking soul-destroying.'

It's Harry. He's clearly talking to someone on the phone.

I freeze. I don't want to encounter him. He's one of those men that makes my flesh crawl. Even though I haven't had much to do with Harry, I know what men like him are like. Arrogant, entitled and deeply misogynistic. Since #MeToo and the backlash against the predatory nature of certain men, their behaviour has had to be more covert but it's still there.

'We've been through this.' Harry groans. 'The job, the house, the car, the family, the holidays. None of it works. None of it makes me feel better, Alex.'

Harry's voice is getting closer.

I put my hands down to get my balance and get slowly to my feet. I know it's stupid, but now I've made the decision to avoid Harry, I need to move. Having to talk to him is making me feel anxious.

'Okay. Yes,' Harry says. 'I'll come and see you when I get back, I promise.'

I creep forward, trying to tiptoe away and head for the cover of the nearby undergrowth.

A twig snaps loudly under my foot.

I freeze. This is ridiculous. *I'm* being ridiculous.

'Oh, hi,' a voice says.

It's Harry. He's behind me.

I stop, turn around to look at him and smile innocently. 'Oh hi, Harry. How's the villa?'

My heart is beating nervously. I'm not sure why.

'Yeah, it's great,' Harry says in a detached tone as he approaches. He looks me up and down and then his eyes rest for a few seconds on my breasts.

For fuck's sake. Do you want to take a bloody photo? I think angrily.

'Anything you need?' I ask curtly.

'I don't think so,' he says as his eyes eventually move up and meet mine. I'm not sure what he's thinking but I'm now feeling uneasy being on my own with him in this secluded wooded area. 'But I'll ask the memsahib when I get back.'

Memsahib? You really are a cock.

There's a few seconds of awkward silence.

Harry is still looking directly at me.

'Great,' I say with an uncomfortable titter.

'You look hot,' Harry comments with a knowing smirk.

'Yes,' I say with a nod and then touch my sweaty forehead as if to acknowledge what he's said. I need to make my excuses and get back to the villa annexe without appearing rude. 'Right, well, I'd—'

'I could do with a massage while I'm here.' Harry moves his shoulders slightly as if to imply that they're stiff. 'I wonder if you or your daughter... Laura?'

'Lowri,' I correct him.

'Lowri. Well, if you'd be able to oblige.' Harry's eyes are twinkling as if he's being charming or amusing. 'You look like you'd give a good massage.'

Is he actually attempting to flirt with me?

'Sorry,' I say with a shrug. 'We're not trained and it's not something that we offer here.'

'That's a shame,' he says putting his hand to the back of his shoulder. 'I'm feeling a bit tense and I thought you might be able to help me relax.'

'But I can definitely arrange for someone to come up to the villa if you'd like,' I suggest.

'Maybe,' Harry says.

'Okay, well, let me know,' I say. And then I feel a little unsteady so I gesture. 'I'd better get back.'

He doesn't react but instead frowns.

I turn to go. Being with him in this secluded area is making me nervous. I feel compelled to get away.

'Where did you live in London?' he asks.

'Clapham, then Balham,' I reply.

'Nice,' he says. 'Not far from where we are in Dulwich.'

'No,' I agree but my need to be alone is overwhelming. 'Anyway, I'd better get going.'

I turn and begin to march away.

Once I'm out of sight, I break into a little jog.

I need a drink. It's the only thing that's going to stop me having a full-blown panic attack. I can feel it building. Heart racing, chest tightening, head spinning. I can't breathe.

I reach into my backpack as I go, grab the green plastic bottle and take a large mouthful.

Better. That's much better.

And then another mouthful.

As the annexe hoves into view, I can almost feel the alcohol zipping through my neural pathways, soothing my poor, fretful brain.

My phone rings.

I take it out and see that it is Nick calling.

Even in my drunken state, my body instantly reacts with fear.

What the hell does he want? I wonder uneasily.

I know that I have to answer it. If he wants to speak to me, then he won't stop calling until he does.

'Hi, Nick,' I say as breezily as I can.

'Lowri thinks you've been drinking,' Nick snarls down the phone.

Not even a hello. He's such an ignorant twat.

His accusation instantly puts me on edge.

'I don't know what she's talking about,' I reply, trying desperately not to let my drunkenness show in my voice. But I know that Nick has a razor-sharp ear for when I've had a drink.

'Really?' he snorts.

'Are you sure she said that?' I ask, sounding confused as my heart thumps and my breathing quickens.

Silence.

'She said she thought you might be... Are you?' Nick snaps.

I get a flashback of Nick slapping my face and pushing me to the floor.

'No,' I protest anxiously. 'Of course I'm not. Don't be silly.'

'If I think for one second you're drinking again, I'll be on a plane out there and I'll be taking her home,' he says angrily.

His arrogance is astounding but I'm getting scared. It sits deep in my stomach. His voice does that to me. I'm starting to feel shaky.

'Well, you don't have to do that because I'm not,' I reassure him. I hate myself for not being able to stand up to him.

'You'd better not be,' Nick thunders down the phone and then ends the call.

Taking a deep breath, I try to calm myself. My hands are a little shaky but at least Nick didn't notice my drunkenness.

In the old days, that would have resulted in my hair being pulled and a slap.

TEN

LOWRI

3.07 p.m.

Lowri sits on the far side of the villa's estate on a small wooden bench that is hidden from view by a couple of dark green olive trees. The trees give the area a little welcome shade from the midday sun. She holds her acoustic guitar and shapes her left hand and fingers to form an A minor chord. Her nails are painted a dark pink and bangles and bracelets hang from both wrists. She looks down at her iPhone and presses the screen. The song 'Karma Police' by Radiohead from their seminal album *OK Computer* begins to play. Lowri is teaching herself to play the song. The verse is A minor, D, E Minor and then G. She's only just discovered Radiohead after seeing her mum's playlist on Spotify. She thinks they're incredible and like nothing she's ever heard before. It's a discovery that's excited her.

Lowri loves this little bench. It's her sanctuary. It seems cooler here, with a slight breeze that rolls up from the vineyards below. It's also wonderfully quiet. The occasional call of birds is the only sound above the whispering leaves of the canopy created by the olive trees above. Just across from where she sits, there is a dusty track that leads uphill through the trees all the way up to the Bajarra quarry.

She presses play on her phone and glances out from where she is sitting. She pushes her sunglasses up into her hair so that the view isn't washed out by the darkness of the lenses. She knows that she's starting to take this breathtaking view for granted – and she mustn't. The azure sky is wide open. It feels almost as if it could consume you with its vastness. The vine-yards and then the rolling fields are a deep and vibrant green which is flecked only by the deep orangey-ochre colour of the roofs of the farmhouses in the distance.

Wow. It really is perfect, she thinks to herself.

Then a shadow falls across the space to her right.

It startles her for a moment.

Radiohead are blaring through her Beats headphones so she can't hear anything. It makes her feel a little vulnerable.

She squints and pulls down her sunglasses to see who it is.

It's Charlie, the young man who has just arrived at the villa with his parents.

He moves his lips and says something to her.

'Sorry,' she says apologetically as she removes her head-phones. 'I was wearing these. What did you say?'

Charlie looks a little embarrassed. 'I was just saying that it's stunning here.'

Lowri smiles and looks at his dark eyes and floppy fringe. *He's really cute.*

'I was just reminding myself of that actually,' she admits. 'I don't want to take it for granted.' Then she points. 'Have you been up to see the marble quarries yet?'

'No.' Charlie shakes his head.

'You must go and see them while you're here. Although don't go at night.'

'Why not?' Charlie asks.

'One of our German guests drank too much, wandered up there one night and fell half way down the ridge,' Lowri explains, pulling a face. 'It took a rescue team three hours to get him out.'

'Oh God,' Charlie says. 'Was he all right?'

'He broke both his legs.' Lowri shakes her head. 'Their first night here and the whole family had to fly home.'

Silence settles between them as she looks at him and their eyes meet for a second too long. She gets a little fizz of excitement.

Charlie then points to her guitar. 'Sorry, I didn't mean to interrupt you,' he says apologetically.

'You're not.' She gestures to the bench. 'Do you want to sit down?'

Charlie shakes his head. 'It's all right. Looks like you're busy.'

Lowri still has imposter syndrome in buckets. It makes her cringe if she has to tell anyone that she's sitting writing music. She's scared that someone might laugh at her although Charlie doesn't look like that type of person.

'Oh this.' Lowri shrugs and then gestures to her phone. 'I'm just teaching myself a couple of songs.'

Charlie takes a step towards her and looks interested. 'Oh, what are you listening to?'

Lowri pulls a face. 'Radiohead,' she says uncertainly. It's hardly music at the cutting edge of 2023. She thinks he's going to judge her.

Charlie's face lights up. 'I love Radiohead.'

'Do you?' Lowri grins in delight.

'Of course,' Charlie says. 'I've even got an original "Kicking Squealing Gucci Little Piggy" T-shirt.'

Lowri's eyes widen. 'Really? Wow!'

'Kicking Squealing Gucci Little Piggy' were lyrics from the

song 'Paranoid Android'. And the T-shirts were produced in the late nineties and so were vintage and very rare. She's impressed. And Charlie is even more attractive.

'Actually it's my dad's,' Charlie admits as he comes over hesitantly and sits down at the end of the bench.

'Your dad must be cool, then,' Lowri says. She can see that Charlie is starting to feel more relaxed.

'God, no,' Charlie snorts and looks at her. Their eyes meet again. 'My dad is *not* cool. He's the opposite of cool.' He says it in a way that implies there is a lot of tension or even anger between them.

'Sorry, I...' Lowri feels a little awkward.

'Are you good?' Charlie asks her, pointing to the guitar again. He's clearly keen to change the subject.

Lowri shrugs. 'I don't know.' Then she decides to bite the bullet. 'I write and perform my own songs, actually.'

'Really?' Charlie says. He seems genuinely interested and impressed.

'Are you at uni or something?' Lowri asks.

Charlie hesitates in answering. 'Gap year, sort of.' He sits forward for a second. 'I had a few mental health issues after my A levels. I tried uni but... Mum and Dad thought I should have some time off before I think about going back.'

I love the fact that he's so open and honest.

'Sorry to hear that,' Lowri says. It's so refreshing that there's no ego or pretension to Charlie. 'Sounds sensible to take some time out.'

'Yeah. I haven't really done very much so far,' Charlie admits. 'What about you?'

'Same. Gap year,' Lowri replies. 'I did my A levels. I'm looking at some music and songwriting courses.'

'That sounds great,' Charlie says encouragingly.

For a moment, their eyes meet and Lowri smiles.

He really is lovely. This is unexpected, she thinks to herself, feeling a little pulse of excitement.

She reaches into her pocket, pulls out a spliff and holds it up. 'Want some of this?'

'Yeah.' Charlie laughs. 'I'm not meant to. Doctor's orders. But fuck that.'

He smokes weed too.

Lowri gets her lighter, lights it, takes a deep drag and then exhales a long stream of bluish smoke up into a narrow shard of sunlight that's coming through the trees.

She hands it to Charlie and their hands touch for a second. It feels exciting.

'Thanks,' he says.

Then she rummages in her rucksack. She pulls out two cold bottles of Moretti beer and an opener.

'Want one of these?' Lowri asks him.

'Now you're talking.' Charlie grins, nods and takes the beer. 'Cheers.'

He has a slightly lopsided smile that is incredibly cute.

'*Salute*,' Lowri says as they clink their bottles.

'Oh right, yes. *Salute*,' Charlie says and then takes a swig of the beer.

I wonder if he likes me, Lowri thinks. Her parents have told her on numerous occasions how beautiful she is. And she's had her fair share of boyfriends and male admirers. But she would never presume that someone is attracted to her. In fact, quite the opposite, actually. And if someone is, it always feels like a huge surprise.

'Your mum seems nice,' Lowri says and then drinks her beer. It's lovely, cold and the bubbles fizz in her mouth and throat.

'She is,' Charlie agrees. Lowri passes him the spliff again.

'Do your mum and dad get on?' she asks.

'No... Not really,' Charlie replies as he blows a smoke ring from his mouth.

Nice trick, she thinks. Then she gives him a quizzical look as if to encourage him to say more.

Charlie's eyes narrow. He looks angry. 'My dad is a nasty, arrogant prick. He treats her like shit and she puts up with it. I've no idea why. I've told her to leave him loads of times. I've seen her in tears about his behaviour but she just buries her head in the sand.'

There's a beat and Charlie looks embarrassed that he's been so candid.

Lowri glances at him with an empathetic expression. She knows exactly how that feels. For a second, she wants to tell him about her own experience of having a father like that. But then she decides against it. She's never really talked about it with anyone before.

'It sounds difficult.'

Why didn't you just tell him?

'Yeah... Sometimes I just want to...' Then Charlie stops himself from saying whatever he was about to. He drains the rest of the beer. 'How would you feel about playing me one of your songs?'

'Oh God, no,' she says, shaking her head and feeling embarrassed. However, the spliff and the beer have mellowed her a bit.

'Go on,' Charlie says.

'No, I...'

The breeze picks up and she can smell Charlie's aftershave or body spray. It smells musky and sexy.

Then he locks eyes with her. 'Please.'

Shit, how can I say no?

'Okay,' Lowri concedes, picking up her black plastic plectrum. She's played in pubs, a couple of arts centres and at a school concert. But it feels a little awkward sitting on the bench just with Charlie. 'This is just something I've been working on so it's a bit all over the place.'

She takes a breath and begins to pluck the strings. The song is called 'Happier Times'. In her head, she thinks it's got echoes of everything from James Taylor to Olivia Rodrigo.

'There's a shadow on the side of the mountain, there's a hawk with prey in its eyes,' Lowri sings.

Charlie watches her intently. Frankly, she's relieved that he hasn't laughed or pulled a face. He seems to like it. She hopes he does.

After playing the song, which in its current form is just over two minutes long, she stops.

'That's all I've got at the moment.' Lowri shrugs, feeling a little awkward.

'Wow. That's beautiful,' Charlie says, nodding. 'Seriously, I mean it.'

'It's a bit rough around the edges but...' Lowri pulls a face.

'No, it's not,' Charlie says, shaking his head. 'And I should know. I've spent my whole life at gigs and listening to music. Even though he's a prize cock, you should play it to my dad.'

'Why? What does your dad do?' Lowri asks. She's got the impression in the past two days that Harry is a big shot. He waltzes around as if he owns the villa and spends most of his time talking loudly on his mobile phone as he paces around the pool.

'He's Director of A&R at Kismet Records,' Charlie says. 'He signed a couple of Britpop bands back in the day. Since then he's signed four major artists. Which is why he thinks he's the Master of the Universe.' He looks at her. 'Seriously. You have to play it to him.'

She shakes her head. 'It's fine. I'd be too embarrassed, especially if he's worked with big acts.'

'Please,' Charlie insists. 'And if he oversteps the mark, I'll keep him in hand.'

She doesn't quite know what Charlie means by that.

'I don't know,' Lowri says. She knows that it's too good an opportunity to turn down.

Charlie sits back and smiles. 'Christ, I thought this holiday was going to be really boring until I met you.'

Lowri feels her pulse quicken a little. She's not sure what to say.

ELEVEN

ZOE

3.26 p.m.

Zoe has hardly touched the lunch that she'd prepared for Harry and Charlie. Bread, hummus, olives, cured meats and cheeses. She doesn't feel hungry. Her head is spinning and her stomach churning after the message she'd read on Harry's phone. She swings between the desire to confront him and completely ignoring it.

She lies back on the lounger by the pool and closes her eyes. The bright sunshine glows orange behind her eyelids. However, every time she closes her eyes, a little voice inside her head keeps scolding her as though she were a child. *You're such an idiot, Zoe. You've known what he's like for years and you've allowed him to get away with it. Why?*

Round and round, and then round and round again. And then a carousel of negativity and self-loathing. Every inadequacy as a woman, a wife, a mother and a daughter. *God, I really am pathetic.*

The voice sounds remarkably like that of her mother, Sarah. That's how she spoke to Zoe and her sister, Emma, as they were growing up. A constant negative stream of critical, even bitchy comments about their intelligence, appearance and then, as they got older, life choices. To say that such a start in life had damaged Zoe's self-esteem would be a huge understatement. Their mother was a cold, controlling, petty bitch.

Zoe's wonderful father, Peter, died from a heart attack when she was only ten years old. Zoe had been devastated by the loss. She still is. She had been so close to him. Her mother lives in Harpenden, a commuter town in Hertfordshire. It's where Zoe grew up. She rarely visits and Charlie has only met his grandmother a handful of times. Zoe refuses to expose him to her toxicity.

Zoe looks down at the book that lies unread on her lap. *The Power of Now*. Every time she picks it up and tries to read a few lines, her mind slides off into the darkness. Her husband's infidelity. Her sham of a marriage. She thinks that maybe she should try and read the Welsh-based crime book that she found sitting on a shelf inside the villa. Maybe getting her head into a dark whodunnit set in Snowdonia will distract her. It probably won't.

Then Zoe's mind turns and she wonders who the message to Harry was from. Somebody he works with? It must be. She knows that there's a new girl in the office. Was her name Alex? She's sure that Harry says she's in her twenties. How can she possibly compete with that?

Zoe has just read on her phone an article about how to make difficult decisions in life. The article said to think of yourself in seven years' time. Then ask your future self to give you advice about what to do in the present. *What does my fifty-five-year-old self tell me to do? Leave Harry? Probably. Confront Harry? Definitely. Slap his face very hard? Yes, he deserves it.*

There is a soft gust of wind which brings the smell of pine and the baking ground. The water in the pool ripples and makes a delicate swishing sound.

Fuck my life, Zoe thinks to herself. *I'm getting a bottle of wine and I'm getting in that pool. I don't care about my make-up or my hair. What bloody difference does it make?*

Putting on her sandals, she traipses up to the villa from the pool, slides open the doors and heads into the kitchen and living area. It's so lovely and cool and smells of fresh fruit and herbs. She goes to the fridge, grabs a bottle of rosé and then heads to a cabinet where she takes two large wine glasses and a steel wine cooler. She has no idea where Harry is but she's taking him a glass just in case. It's a force of habit.

Going out of the doors again, Zoe pads down to the pool and sits on the blue lounger. She twists open the bottle of rosé, pours herself a decent glass and drinks a mouthful before reclining in the sun.

Out of the corner of her eye, she spots two figures in the distance. Charlie and Cerys's daughter, Lowri, who is carrying a guitar. Charlie has a black rucksack slumped over his shoulder. She doesn't recognise it. Maybe it's Lowri's and Charlie is carrying it for her. *How chivalrous,* she thinks. The two are deep in conversation. Zoe gives a half smile. It makes her happy to see Charlie smiling and looking content. He's really struggled in recent years.

Her mind drifts to a chilly Saturday morning watching eight-year-old Charlie play football. His cheeks and nose red with cold, a quiet determination in his eyes as he ran around the pitch. Her heart does a leap for that little boy. Then she remembers Harry spent the entire time berating him from the touchline. While she would be nothing but encouraging, Harry picked holes in everything Charlie did. Harry even resorted to filming Charlie's matches on his phone so he could show him afterwards where he'd gone wrong. Her quietly confident son who'd enjoyed a kick-about at the weekend suddenly lost any joy for the game. He looked lost on the pitch, his shoulders drooped, too scared to ask for the ball. And unsurprisingly, the football didn't last more than one season before Charlie flatly refused to go anymore.

Charlie and Lowri are still chatting away. His eyes are sparkling with delight and for a second this transports Zoe back to reading bedtime stories to him. His delight as she did the different voices for the Gruffalo and the big bad mouse. It was often just the two of them as Harry was always working late. It feels as if that was only yesterday rather than sixteen years ago.

A shadow looms over her.

Even though she's wearing her black Gucci sunglasses, she still has to shield her eyes from the sun to see who it is.

It's Cerys.

'Hi, Zoe,' Cerys says. She is smoothing down a lovely flowing pink maxi dress and she has her hair tied up.

She always looks so effortlessly chic and well put together, Zoe thinks to herself.

'Sorry to interrupt. I've spoken to Lucia and Lorenzo,' Cerys says. 'They're aiming to serve dinner at 8 p.m. if that's still okay? Lorenzo is an incredible cook.'

'That's great,' Zoe says with a friendly smile and then gestures to the bottle. 'Do you want a glass of wine?'

'I'm fine,' Cerys says, shaking her head.

Zoe feels a little disappointed. What she really wants to do is drink a few glasses of rosé by the pool with a woman her own age and have a natter and gossip... or whatever.

'Sure?' Zoe asks, pulling a face.

She sees Cerys waver for a second.

'Come on,' Zoe says encouragingly. 'I won't take no for an answer.'

'Okay.' Cerys gives a little laugh as she sits down on the adjacent lounger. 'But just one glass.'

'We'll see,' Zoe says with a little cackle as she reaches for the bottle, pours Cerys a glass and hands it to her.

'Thanks,' she says and she reaches over to clink glasses. *'Salute.'*

'Salute.' Zoe is buoyed that Cerys is joining her.

'Harry not around?' Cerys asks.

'No,' Zoe replies with a knowing roll of her eyes. 'He's probably out there on the phone to someone. I don't know why he bothers coming.'

Cerys nods and takes a sip of her wine.

Zoe wants to launch into a tirade about Harry but she doesn't know Cerys well enough. She doesn't want her to think that she's a psychopath.

Charlie is approaching. Zoe can see that Lowri is wandering back to the villa's annexe over to the right.

'Hey,' Charlie says.

'You two seem to be getting on well,' Zoe says. The wine has given her a bit of glow and relaxed her.

Charlie nods but looks awkward. He sits down on a nearby lounger. 'Lowri sings. And she writes her own music. She's really good.'

'Oh wow,' Zoe says as she looks over to Cerys.

'I know I'm her mother,' Cerys says almost apologetically, 'but I think she's talented.'

'Yeah, she played me a song,' Charlie says. Zoe hasn't seen him this animated in months. It's lovely to see.

Zoe and Cerys share a look and then smile.

'Hey, can Lowri come and have dinner with us tonight?' Charlie blurts out.

'I don't see why not,' Zoe says immediately. Then she turns to look at Cerys. 'In fact, you must both come.'

'No, I can't do that,' Cerys says, shaking her head adamantly. 'It's one thing having a glass of wine but dinner...'

'Please,' Zoe says with a pleading expression. She knows that as soon as they've finished eating, Charlie will slope off somewhere, leaving her and Harry sitting alone. How is she meant to do that with all that she knows? Having Cerys and Lowri there will change the dynamic. 'You'll be doing me a favour.'

'It's true,' Charlie agrees. 'It's always a bit awkward when it's just the three of us, to be fair.'

'I'm just not sure that it's appropriate,' Cerys says wavering.

'It's only dinner,' Zoe says with her best winning smile.

'Erm... I...' Zoe spots a momentary hesitation in Cerys's resolve.

'Right, that's settled, then,' Zoe says with an excited clap of her hands. 'You and Lowri will join us for dinner.'

'Great,' Charlie says.

'Oh, okay,' Cerys concedes. 'You've twisted my arm.'

Zoe reaches over, takes Cery's glass and fills it again with rosé. 'Here you go. I think I'm going to enjoy this holiday more than I thought I was.' She clinks her glass on Cerys's. '*Salute.*'

'*Salute.*' Cery laughs.

TWELVE

LUCIA

7.12 p.m.

The afternoon sun is beginning to set and the sky is glowing with a burnt orange towards the horizon. A line of hills cuts across the view with a smooth undulating line. There is the soft, rhythmic tone of cicadas which signals that daytime is nearly over. A patch of beautiful purple irises lines the pathway to the right.

Lucia makes her way up the dusty track from her cottage up to Villa Lucia. The stones crunch underneath her feet as she goes, as they did when she was a child. She and Lorenzo have been asked to prepare an authentic Tuscan supper.

It's been fifteen years since the original Villa Lucia had been repossessed from her father; it still sometimes makes Lucia angry. After all, it is *her villa*. It's her birthright.

As a little girl, she had watched her father and uncle toil away for nearly two years to turn the top of that hill into a small rustic holiday cottage. She remembers the utter thrill of being told that it was going to be named after her. And then the sheer exhilaration of watching the wooden sign that her father had carved in his workshop being erected outside. VILLA LUCIA.

'It's for you, *mia piccola principessa*,' her father had told her. My little princess. That's how her father referred to her most of the time. 'One day, it will be yours.'

For the next two decades, Villa Lucia was a popular destination for families who wanted to holiday in Tuscany. Many were from Britain, but also Germany and even the US.

But after Lucia's mother died from a pulmonary embolism when Lucia was twenty-five, her father started to drink. And Villa Lucia became tired, worn and rundown. Her uncle and his family moved to Florence, so it fell on her father to maintain the property – but he just wasn't interested. So, the holiday bookings dwindled and then stopped. And then local property taxes went through the roof and finally Villa Lucia was repossessed.

Her father blew his brains out with a shotgun the following day.

And then the villa was pulled down and redeveloped into a huge monstrosity with a pool!

In the years since then, Lucia hated having to do the washing, cleaning and cooking for the guests. Deep down, she still thought of it as her villa and having to act like a virtual *domestica* – servant – made her angry. It didn't seem right. But she and Lorenzo needed the money so she had to swallow her pride and do the work. And she has grown to like 'the Welsh lady' Cerys in the past two years. Cerys is not arrogant like the previous owners. She treats her and Lorenzo very well and is generous. And she also watched how Cerys was abused by her ex-husband, Nick. Lucia remembered how Cerys used to go for an early morning swim before anyone was awake. She knew why. Her arms were often covered in bruises and Cerys didn't want anyone to see. But Lucia saw. Once, she saw Nick pulling her off a sunlounger by her hair.

No woman should ever have to put up with behaviour like that. Lucia is glad that Nick has gone back to London. There were moments when she had to prevent Lorenzo from intervening and teaching Nick a lesson. With Lorenzo's background, she knew they couldn't afford any trouble, especially with the police.

Lucia stops for a moment to get her breath. The air is still thick, dusty and hot. She wipes the sweat from her top lip with the back of her hand. As she glances up the steep pathway to the villa, she can see a figure watering the grass and gardens.

It's Lorenzo.

She smiles at the sight of her husband. She can't help it. He reminds her of her father in many ways. They have the same temperament. Strong and quiet. Lorenzo keeps things to himself most of the time and isn't a man to talk about his emotions. He has a simple dignity. That's how Lucia likes her men. She doesn't understand this sudden need for people, particularly men, to talk about their feelings. She sees it as a sign of weakness.

Like Lorenzo, her father also had an explosive temper, especially if he felt that his honour, or the honour of his family, had been insulted. She remembered a family trip to the coast, just north of Pisa. A lorry driver cut them up and her father beeped his horn in annoyance. The lorry driver gave him a hand gesture and told him to *vaffanculo a chi t'e morto*. It meant 'Go and fuck the dead members of your family' and was one of the worst insults anyone could say.

As they continued the journey, Lucia could see the anger building in her father. She and her mother had tried to calm him down. Twenty minutes later, they had stopped at a road toll. The same lorry driver had parked up and was smoking a cigarette. Lucia's father pulled their car over, grabbed a baseball bat from the boot and attacked the driver, beating him to the ground. As the driver lay bleeding and groaning, her father had spat at him, telling him that he had now avenged his and his family's honour. That's just who her father was and part of her was proud that he had defended their family's honour that day. The lorry driver had brought it upon himself.

Lucia takes a deep breath as the pathway now levels off and the villa and its grounds hove into view. The grass is a luscious green and bordered by colourful plants and box hedges. She can't see Lorenzo now but she can hear the water from the hose from behind a row of cypress trees.

The husband of the family that is staying marches out of the villa, down the stone pathway and heads for the shaded car parking area. She remembers that his name is Harry, like the British prince that she has seen in the news. The one with red hair.

Harry talks loudly into his phone and doesn't give her a second look. Lucia has already made her mind up about him. He's a *stronzo*. A pompous moron. She's watched him striding around the pool, talking loudly into his phone as if he owns the world. He's rude to his wife and aggressive towards his son. She knows about men like Harry. They are just frightened little mama's boys – *mammoni*. They have to spend their lives proving to the world how strong, powerful and successful they are, because deep down they are terrified that they are none of these things.

Harry continues to talk loudly as he rummages in the car, before grabbing a pair of sunglasses, slamming the driver's door shut and heading back up the path.

Out of the corner of her eye, Lucia spots a figure appearing from behind the trees.

It's Lorenzo.

He grins at her as he holds the hosepipe that he's been watering the garden with. With a little laugh, he flicks the hose so that water flies up into the air in her direction. It's their little game and she usually gives a little squeal of delight as she tries to avoid the water.

However, almost in slow motion, Harry strides past them at that very second. Lucia watches as the drops of water from the hose fly through the air and land on Harry. He jumps back and then glances around in utter fury.

'What the fuck!' he shouts. Then he looks at his phone and says, 'Mate, I'm going to have to call you back.' Then he glares at Lorenzo. 'Some fucking peasant has for some reason doused me in water.'

'*Mi scusi*,' Lorenzo says with an apologetic expression.

'You fucking idiot!' the husband snaps. 'Didn't you see me here? What the fuck were you doing?'

Lucia hates seeing this man talking to Lorenzo like that. He had no need to call him a peasant and an idiot. Who does he think he is? She knows she must keep calm and takes a few steps forward. 'My husband is very sorry. It was an accident,' she says gently.

'Doesn't he speak English?' Harry asks with an incredulous expression.

'Not really,' Lucia explains. 'But I can dry your clothes for you.'

What she really thinks is that she doesn't know why this man is so rude and angry. If he sits in the sun for five minutes, his clothes will be dry again. Why all the fuss?

Harry glares at her. 'I'm not worried about my clothes.' He points to his mobile phone. 'But if this thing gets wet and doesn't work, my fucking holiday is ruined.' The man turns and points to Lorenzo. 'And Luigi, or whatever his bloody name is, needs to watch what he's doing. Jesus!'

Harry mutters to himself as he storms away.

Lucia can see that Lorenzo is about to explode with anger at the way Harry spoke to them both.

'It's okay, Lorenzo,' she tells him, putting a reassuring hand on his shoulder. She can feel that he is shaking with rage. His breathing is shallow.

'No,' Lorenzo tells her with gritted teeth. 'No. I not let him speak to you like that.'

She looks at him. It scares her when she sees Lorenzo this angry. She knows what he's capable of.

'You mustn't say anything,' she says, trying to pacify him. 'We need our jobs here. Please. *Fai un bel respiro* – take a deep breath.'

After a few seconds, Lorenzo gives a slight nod, takes the hose and walks away. But she can see that he is full of anger.

THIRTEEN
CERYS

8.33 p.m.

I sit back and look with pride at the dining area to the rear of my villa. The little fairy lights and lanterns are all lit and it looks magical, even if I do say so myself. My head is fuzzy from drinking all day and I'm worried that I'm starting to slur my words. However, I haven't had 'the look' from Lowri yet to signal that she's on to me. Zoe has put on an Ibiza chilled playlist which is playing on the Bluetooth speaker. So far, the conversation has been light and amusing.

'This is gorgeous,' Zoe says, pointing her fork at the *panzanella* starter that Lucia brought to us about ten minutes ago. 'I'm trying to work out what's in it.'

'It's so simple,' I tell her. 'Bread, tomatoes, onion, cucumber, olives, capers, basil and parmesan. It's my favourite summer salad.'

'It's essentially peasant food though, isn't it?' Harry says in a haughty tone. Then he smirks. 'If it's got bread in, it's cheap and for the peasants.'

I feel my cheeks colour with embarrassment for Zoe who is married to this idiot of a man.

Charlie fixes his father with a stare. 'Bruschetta is simple peasant food and you love that. What's your point?'

'It was a joke,' Harry mumbles as he sips his wine. 'I just think it's funny that we've come to a villa like this and we've been served *peasant* food, that's all. I guess it's ironic, no?'

He looks around at everyone for a reaction.

There is an uncomfortable silence.

Lowri gives me a look as if to indicate that Harry is a dickhead.

'I suppose it is peasant food,' I say to keep a lid on things. 'Originally.'

'Well, I don't care,' Zoe says brightly. 'It's delicious and I'll be making it when we get home.'

I smile at Zoe. Like me, she's trying to keep the mood light and upbeat. Then I look at the apricot-coloured dress that Zoe is wearing. 'That's a beautiful dress.'

'This?' she says with a self-effacing smile. 'I got it on one of those vintage websites. It was a steal.'

'I wish I could get away with wearing something like that,' I say.

'Don't be silly,' Zoe tells me. 'You'd look gorgeous in it.'

'Really?' I ask. I know that I'm fishing for compliments but that's fine.

'Of course.' Zoe puts her hand on my arm. 'You'll have to try it on later.'

Zoe takes the bottle of white Toscana Bianco wine and goes to pour it into my glass.

I make a show of putting my hand over the rim. 'I'm all right, thanks,' I say. I've told Lowri before the meal that I'll have one glass of white wine with dinner and that will be it. I can see out of the corner of my eye that she's clocked what I've done and is pleased. What she doesn't know is that the small bottle of mineral water that I have resting close to me is actually vodka. I'd like to admit that I hate deceiving her and feel ashamed. But now there's a substantial amount of booze in my system, I don't care anymore. All I know is that being sober is too raw and uncomfortable. The guilt and shame will come in the morning when I wake.

'What?' Harry snaps as he looks over at Charlie who has been glaring at his father.

'Nothing,' Charlie replies in an unconvincing tone.

'Go on,' Harry prompts him.

Lowri leans forward and looks Harry straight in the eye. 'I suspect that Charlie thought your use of the word "peasant" sounded unpleasant and pejorative.'

Charlie nods at Lowri to indicate they're on the same page. 'I did. But I guess that's what I've come to expect from him.'

I catch the anxious frown on Zoe's face just before she rearranges it into a forced smile. 'Let's be nice and not spoil things.'

Harry raises an eyebrow at Lowri. 'Pejorative?... Right,' he says, sounding very condescending.

I know that Lowri can be argumentative and that this might escalate. However, they are paying guests so I want everything to be just perfect.

'Did you think it wasn't?' Lowri asks.

'I thought it was a throwaway comment that doesn't need to be examined in microscopic detail just in case offence could be taken.' Harry groans wearily.

'Don't be a twat, Dad,' Charlie snarls.

Harry fixes Charlie with a hostile stare.

Zoe turns to me and then says in an upbeat sing-song tone, 'We need to arrange that olive oil tasting with you.'

She wants to change the subject quickly.

'Of course,' I say, glad to move on from the current conversation. 'It's normally busy at the weekends but you should be okay on a weekday.'

'Great.' Zoe takes a swig of her wine. 'It's just so lovely here.'

Lowri is bristling. She looks at Harry. 'That's just your generation's excuse for all forms of casual racism, misogyny and homophobia. It was just a joke,' she says. 'But casual discrimination allows it to continue. And I'm sure George Floyd didn't think it was funny when a white racist police officer knelt on his neck for ten minutes and choked the life out of him.'

'For fuck's sake,' Harry hissed under his breath.

'Harry!' Zoe snaps.

Harry looks at Zoe. 'I'm not going to sit here and be interrogated by the woke police. I made one comment and now I'm a fucking member of the Ku Klux Klan!' He then looks at Charlie and Lowri. 'It's about perspective. And you and your generation have lost all perspective. We fought wars for free speech and you want to take all that away. And you want to put anyone over thirty in some re-education camp like Stalinist Russia.'

'I heard you on the phone yesterday,' Charlie growls. 'You said to someone... "he's probably a bender. You know what they're like." That's not bloody free speech. That's blatant prejudice. And the worst thing is that you can never admit you're wrong.'

Harry stops, blinks and takes a visible breath. It's clear that he didn't know that Charlie had heard him, and it's blindsided him.

'I don't have to listen to this bullshit.' Harry gets up abruptly from the table and takes his phone from where it was sitting and puts it into his trouser pocket.

'Come on,' Zoe says in a withering tone. 'Why can't we just have a nice meal without arguing for once?'

'Because Dad is a fascist wanker,' Charlie says sarcastically.

Harry ignores this, takes a cigar from his top pocket and

looks directly at me. 'I assume there's a decent break before the main course, so I'm going to go and smoke this.'

He walks away.

'He's such a prick,' Charlie mutters.

After a few seconds, Zoe looks at me with a frown. 'Sorry about that.'

'I'm the one that should apologise,' I tell her. 'I think Lowri was being her usual contrary self.'

Lowri ignores me, pulls a vape from her pocket and waves it at Charlie. 'I'm going to sit down there if you want to come with me?'

'Yeah,' Charlie says with a half smile. 'I could do with something to calm me down.'

'I don't know why you have to argue with him all the time,' Zoe says.

'Why do you always protect Dad? Someone's got to stand up to him,' Charlie says caustically. 'And it's not going to be you, is it?'

Silence as Lowri and Charlie wander away.

'Ouch,' Zoe says, pulling a face at me.

I raise my eyebrows but I'm careful not to judge Charlie's outburst. It's none of my business.

In that moment, Lucia arrives to collect their plates. 'Everything is okay?' she asks in her Italian accent.

'Lovely. Thank you,' I say as I reach for my water bottle to take a sip of vodka.

Zoe smiles at Lucia. 'It was incredible. You're so lucky to be married to a man that can cook like that.'

'Yes,' Lucia replies, looking a little self-conscious. 'I am.' She takes the plates and disappears.

'God, I really am so sorry about all that.' Zoe sighs. 'I bet you're regretting having dinner with us? We're so fucking dysfunctional.'

'I think all families have their moments,' I reassure her.

Zoe looks over at where Charlie and Lowri are sitting. 'Charlie is right, of course.'

I frown. I'm not entirely sure what she means. 'Sorry, I...'

'I don't ever stand up to Harry or call him out,' she admits with a resigned shrug.

'Right,' I say. I'm not sure how to respond to this but I'm drunk so I have no filter. 'Why don't you stand up to him?'

'I don't know.' Zoe takes a deep breath. 'I guess I'm scared of him.'

I don't like the sound of that. 'Do you mean you're scared of him physically?' I ask with a raised eyebrow.

Zoe doesn't respond for a few seconds. Then she nods and says very quietly, 'Yes.'

The music has stopped and for a moment there's just the distant chirp of the cicadas.

'He's physically abusive to you?' I ask, feeling my anger growing. I know how this feels.

'Yes,' she replies and then I see her eyes fill with tears.

'Oh, I'm so sorry,' I say as I lean over to her and give her a reassuring hug. 'Poor you.'

'Sorry, I don't know why I'm telling you this,' she sobs. 'I'm so embarrassed.'

I look her directly in the eyes. 'Please. You don't need to be embarrassed. In fact, it's very brave of you to tell anyone. I've been through something very similar so I know how difficult it is to talk about.'

Zoe dabs her eyes and sniffs. 'I haven't even told my friends at home. I don't know why. For some reason, I don't want them to hate Harry. And I don't want them to judge or pity me for being with him.' She blows out her cheeks and takes a deep breath as she tries to compose herself. 'What a bloody mess.'

'It doesn't have to be,' I tell her as I lean forward and put my hand reassuringly on her forearm.

'He's having an affair,' Zoe says and gives an ironic laugh.

She then shakes her head. 'God, now I'm saying all this out loud, I sound completely mental.'

I frown. 'How do you know he's having an affair?'

'I had my suspicions,' Zoe admits. 'But then this morning I found a message on his phone and it wasn't a message that could be misconstrued.'

'Bloody hell, Zoe,' I say looking at her.

'Bloody hell, indeed,' she says with a forced smile. Then she grabs the bottle of wine. 'I think I need a drink.'

I push my glass over towards her. Even though I'm pretty drunk already, I want another glass of wine, although I suspect I won't stop at that. 'I think that we should get drunk, don't you?'

Zoe smiles at me. 'I think that's a very good idea. Thank you for being so nice to me.'

I point to her glass. 'Shut up and drink.'

Zoe laughs.

'Fuck men,' I say as I clink her glass.

'Yes, fuck men,' Zoe says loudly.

FOURTEEN

LOWRI

11.56 p.m.

Lowri washes her face in her sink and pulls her hair back into a ponytail. She looks at herself in the mirror. She takes a make-up pad, applies some remover and then wipes off her eye make-up.

Wow, what a shitshow of a night, she thinks to herself

It's been over an hour since Lowri and Charlie had helped Zoe to bed as she was also struggling to walk in a straight line. Charlie then made his excuses and told Lowri that he was going to have an early night. The row with his father seemed to have rattled him.

No one had seen Harry since he stormed off to smoke his cigar. They'd finished the meal without him. Her mum was hammered. She and Zoe had continued to drink more and more, singing Oasis songs at the tops of their voices. Charlie and Lowri just exchanged glances like two disapproving parents.

Lowri isn't sure what to do. Her mum promised she wouldn't drink while she was staying. It was horrible to see her in such a state earlier. She could hardly speak when she slumped onto the bed.

Lowri comes out of the bathroom and into her bedroom. She clicks her phone and thinks about texting her dad to tell him what's happened. Then she decides to wait until the morning. Maybe it's just a one-off. But Lowri feels like she's been here before. It's always 'just a one-off'. It's always, 'I promise I'm never going to drink again.'

Moving across her bedroom, Lowri takes her phone and clicks it onto the little tripod that she uses to film her TikTok videos. Then she taps the app to record and grabs her guitar.

She plays a few chords and frowns in exasperation. Then she tries it again before giving a frustrated sigh and putting down the guitar.

Lowri clicks her Bluetooth speaker. 'Gorilla' by Little Simz begins to play as she starts to undress for bed.

'Knock, knock,' says a voice.

'Jesus!' Lowri jumps out of her skin.

She glances anxiously over at the open door of her bedroom and sees Harry standing there. He's leaning casually against the door frame with a smirk on his face.

'Sorry, I didn't mean to startle you,' Harry says. Then he points to the Bluetooth speaker. 'Little Simz. She was in my office last week.'

What the hell is he doing here? Lowri wonders, feeling nervous and vulnerable standing in her bedroom with just her bra on.

Lowri doesn't respond.

'I just came over to apologise for what I said earlier,' Harry says as he takes a couple of steps into her bedroom.

'Okay.' Lowri shrugs as she grabs a top to cover herself. 'Don't worry about it.' She turns slightly to indicate that there's nothing more to say and that he can now go.

'That's very nice of you,' Harry says, coming in a little further and then sitting down on the edge of the bed. 'Sometimes I just get a bit carried away, that's all.'

What the fuck is he doing?

'Charlie tells me you're a talented singer-songwriter,' Harry says, his eyes scanning her body. Creep.

'I wouldn't say that,' Lowri replies. She can feel that her voice is a little shaky. 'Look, I'm really tired so if you—'

'Oh right. Of course,' Harry says with a nod, but he doesn't move. 'I guess Charlie told you what I do for a job.'

Lowri nods. Her pulse is racing and her mouth is dry.

'Yeah, my job is to find new artists for the record label,' Harry says. 'You should play me your stuff.'

'Maybe tomorrow.' She shrugs. She just wants him out of there. Her mum is passed out in the other bedroom. She's on her own with him.

'Of course,' Harry says. 'No problem.' Then he puts his hand to his shoulders and rubs them. 'I'm a bit stiff in my shoulders. Any chance you could give me a massage?'

Lowri's stomach clenches.

Did he actually just say that?

'What?' she asks with a frown.

'A massage?' Harry asks as if this is a completely normal request. 'I'm sure you've given someone a massage before.'

'No, I haven't,' Lowri replies. She takes a deep breath. 'Actually, I'd like you to leave, please.'

Harry gets up from the bed.

At first, Lowri thinks it's because he's going to leave her bedroom.

But he doesn't.

'I can pay you, if it's a problem,' Harry says with a smile. 'Shall we say £200? That's pretty good for a fifteen-minute massage.'

'I'm not going to give you a massage,' Lowri says, trembling. 'And if you don't leave, I'm going to shout at the top of my voice.'

Harry pulls a face. 'Come on. You're not going to do that.

Do you know how useful I could be to you getting a record deal?' He clicks his fingers. 'I can get you signed like that. And all I want is an innocent massage. I don't think that's too much to ask, is it?'

'Get out,' Lowri hisses.

Harry is still moving towards her and she's forced to back away from him.

'Why are you being like this?' Harry asks, shaking his head. 'You want people to hear your music, don't you? I know some of the best producers in the world. And I can do that for you. I think you're actually being a bit ungrateful, Lowri.'

'I want you to get out right now,' Lowri shouts.

Harry reaches out and tries to touch her face. 'So pretty...'

She ducks her head away.

'Just fuck off!' she yells. Her head is spinning and her heart is pounding. She can hardly catch her breath.

I can't believe this is actually happening.

Harry grabs her by the wrist and glares angrily at her. 'What the fuck is the matter with you? You need to do what I've asked you to do, do you understand me? Don't make me angry.'

Suddenly, Harry pushes himself against her, forcing her back into the wall. He then thrusts his crotch hard against her torso as he tries to kiss her.

'GET OFF ME!' she screams, moving her head away. His breath smells of booze and cigars.

And then he's reaching down to try and take off her skirt.

Lowri can hardly move as she's now pinned against the wall. She tries to kick out but it's no use.

.   His hands are roaming up her legs, onto her inner thighs and then inside her underwear.

'No, no, no,' Lowri shouts, trying to jerk her body away. 'Get the fuck off of me!'

'Turning me down is a big mistake, Lowri,' Harry says in a virtual whisper as he continues to fumble in her underwear.

'GET OFF ME!' Lowri yells at the top of her voice.

Out of the corner of her eye, she sees a sudden movement.

'What the fuck are you doing?' a voice says. 'Get the fuck off her!'

It's Charlie.

He pulls Harry off her and pushes him across the room.

'You don't understand,' Harry snarls at Charlie.

'I fucking hate you,' Charlie snaps as he throws a punch but misses.

Harry responds by punching Charlie in the face. He crumples to the floor, holding his nose which is bloody.

Lowri attacks Harry, trying to slap him. 'You bastard! You sick, fucked-up bastard!'

Harry backs away and shakes his head with a smirk. 'Don't be so bloody naive, Lowri,' he spits before sauntering out of her bedroom.

Lowri crouches down beside Charlie. 'Are you all right?'

Charlie glares at the doorway. 'I'm going to fucking kill him.'

'Come on,' Lowri says, helping Charlie back onto his feet. 'Let's get you cleaned up. And you need to get some ice on that.'

FIFTEEN
CERYS

Monday
6.55 a.m.

Wow, my head hurts, I think as I come out of my bedroom. I've already seen a text at 5 a.m. from Zoe apologising for her behaviour the previous evening and cancelling our dawn yoga. *Thank God!* Zoe texts that she needs to sleep it off.

I haven't had a hangover for months and I'm kicking myself for drinking so much the night before. My head is pounding like someone is hitting it with a sledgehammer. For a moment, I'm tempted to immediately drink vodka. I know a decent slug of vodka will take the hangover away in a matter of seconds. It's incredibly tempting, but also totally alcoholic behaviour. As I try to piece together the events of the previous evening, I realise that the last part is all a bit of a blur. More than a blur, it's blank. A blackout. I remember singing 'Wonderwall' with Zoe. I remember Lowri's look of disgust and her helping me towards the annexe. Then, nothing. I assume that Lowri put me to bed.

Taking a step outside, the sunshine immediately makes my headache ten times worse. I take the blister pack of paracetamol from my pocket, pop two in my mouth and swig them back with water. And this time it is actually water. I then pop my sunglasses on. *That's a bit better.*

I've got to go and set up breakfast but all I want to do is lie in bed. *You are such an idiot, Cerys!* I console myself with the fact that I can return to the annexe once I've laid out all the breakfast items.

As I walk along the pathway towards the villa, I can feel the heat of the day beginning to build. Even walking feels like an unpleasant slog this morning.

Come on, Cerys, you've got this.

I pass the pool, climb the steps and cross the decking to the large sliding doors to the villa. I'm praying that I don't bump into anyone, especially Harry. I haven't seen him since he stormed off from dinner to have a cigar. I'm aware that I don't have the energy or wherewithal to hold a decent conversation with anyone, let alone a twat like Harry.

I reach my hand to the metal of the handle, pull the sliding door back and turn to go back inside.

For a split second, my eye wanders over to the pool which is just below.

Then I'm about to pull the door closed when my brain registers that there is something in the pool.

I take off my sunglasses and look again.

Oh my God. My stomach tightens in shock.

Someone is floating in the pool face down.

I hold my breath. I tell myself that it's okay. Maybe it's Charlie and he's gone for an early morning swim. And he's just floating like that for a second.

But the person isn't moving. They're just floating there motionless.

My whole body reacts with a surge of panic.

I have to do something. I have to go down there.

Oh my God, oh my God, this can't be happening, can it?

As I step out, cross the decking and run down the stone steps, I feel like I'm in a terrible dream. It's all so surreal.

I get to the pool.

I hold my breath as I walk down to the far end.

But I'm not mistaken.

I get closer to see who it is.

I recognise the clothes, the hair and the expensive watch on the wrist.

It's Harry.

Fuck, what the hell is going on?

Then I notice the water around Harry's body. It's a pinky colour.

It's blood.

I go and grab the long aluminium pole and net that Lorenzo uses to clean the pool.

Slowly, I manoeuvre the pole so that it touches Harry's back.

'Harry?' I say.

He doesn't move or react.

'Harry?'

Oh God, he's dead. What do I do?

I wonder if I should try to pull him out of the pool. He's too heavy.

I wonder about the blood. Did he fall in and hit his head and drown? Is that what happened?

Should I call the police?? What would I do if I was in England? I'd call the police.

I reach for the mobile phone in my pocket. My hand is shaking uncontrollably. I dial the emergency number 112.

SIXTEEN

ZOE

7.12 a.m.

Zoe is sitting on the middle of a sunlounger staring at the body of her husband. She's numb with shock. It doesn't feel real. Is it real? It can't be.

How can Harry be lying there in the pool? she asks herself. *It's not possible. This isn't happening.*

She stares at the back of Harry's polo shirt which is a dark shade of pink because it's wet. There seems to be some air trapped under the material so there is a strange little bubble holding the shirt away from his skin.

What the hell happened, Harry?

Putting her hand to her face, Zoe can feel that her whole body is shaking. She's overwhelmed, as if she's having an out-of-body experience.

She continues to watch him float. She wanted to get him out of the pool but Cerys insisted that they leave him there until the police arrive. She knows that's the sensible thing to do but it feels so cruel and callous to leave him in there like that. It's undignified. However Harry behaved on the surface, Zoe knows how much he'd care what people thought of him. Although he would never admit it, deep down Harry was terribly insecure. He would have hated to think that his last moments on earth would be spent floating around in a pool for everyone to see.

The other thought that is nagging away in her head is Charlie. How is she going to break the news to him? They might not have got on in recent years, but Harry was still Charlie's dad. He is going to be devastated.

'The police are on their way,' says a voice very softly.

Zoe turns to look and sees Cerys approaching slowly. She sits down on the sun lounger opposite and shakes her head. 'I'm so sorry.'

Cerys's appearance and words suddenly bring home the reality of what has actually happened. This isn't a terrible dream that Zoe is going to wake from. It is real.

'Do you want me to get you anything?' Cerys asks in a whisper. 'Some water, tea?'

Zoe shakes her head. She blows out her cheeks and bites at her lip but it's all too much. Her eyes fill with tears and she begins to sob again. 'Oh God...'

Cerys gets up slowly and comes to sit next to her. She puts a comforting hand on Zoe's shoulder. 'I really am so sorry.'

'I don't understand...' Zoe weeps. 'What happened to him?'

Then she sobs uncontrollably as her body shudders with her cries.

After about a minute, it subsides a little. Zoe sniffs and rubs the tears from her face with the palms of her hands. The sudden outpouring of grief seems to have had the effect of calming her, as if she's got some of the shock and pain out of her system. She takes a long, deep breath.

'I guess the police will be able to tell us that,' Cerys says. She looks directly at Zoe and gives her an empathetic expression. 'I can't imagine what you're going through.'

Zoe furrows her brow and looks confused. 'Do you think he just fell into the pool?'

'I don't know,' Cerys admits. 'He must have.'

For a moment, they both turn and look over at Harry's body again.

'But Harry can swim. He's a good swimmer,' Zoe says in disbelief. 'And he wasn't blind drunk, was he?'

'I don't know,' Cerys says again. 'I didn't see him after he went off to smoke his cigar.'

Zoe glances at her. 'No, neither did I.'

'He didn't come back to the bedroom last night?' Cerys asks.

'I don't think so.' Zoe looks confused as she tried to recall the events of the previous night. 'I was hammered. I remember Charlie and Lowri helping me to bed. I sent you that text about the yoga a few hours ago. And then the next thing you woke me up.'

Cerys pulls a face. 'I'm really sorry... but when I found Harry I think I saw some blood in the pool.'

'Blood?' Zoe asks, her eyes widening with fear.

'I don't know, but I thought maybe Harry had fallen into the pool, banged his head and drowned.' Cerys pauses. 'Sorry, I shouldn't have said that.'

'It's fine,' Zoe replies. She then looks perplexed. 'Why would he just fall into the pool? Unless he drank lots more booze after we went to bed?'

'MUM?' shouts a voice.

They both glance up and see Charlie hurrying down the steps, a look of sheer panic etched on his face.

'What's happened to Dad?' Charlie asks as he runs towards them.

'Oh, Charlie,' Zoe sobs as she stands to her feet, her body shaking as she tries to put her arms around him.

Charlie snaps. 'What's wrong with him?'

Charlie moves towards the pool as Zoe tries to pull him back. 'There's nothing you can do, Charlie.'

'Dad!' Charlie shouts, his voice breaking into a horrifying sound as his eyes land on Harry's lifeless body.

'He's gone, Charlie,' Zoe says. It's breaking her heart to see Charlie so shocked.

Charlie looks back at them. 'Gone? What are you talking about? We need to get him out of the pool and give him CPR or something.'

'I'm really sorry, Charlie,' Cerys says tenderly as she gets up. 'I think he's been in there all night.'

'What?' Charlie barks. His eyes roam around in total disbelief and panic. 'No, no. We need to get him out of there right now.'

Charlie crouches down and stretches out, trying to grab the back of Harry's pink polo shirt so he can pull him to the side.

'Charlie,' Zoe says in a distraught voice. It's unbearable to watch Charlie try and reach his father's body. She puts her hand gently on Charlie's outstretched arm. 'Please, Charlie. We have to leave him there.'

Charlie doesn't respond for a few seconds. His breathing is quick and shallow. Then he turns to look at his mother. 'Why?'

'The police are on their way,' Zoe says as she crouches down beside him.

Charlie pulls his hand back from the pool as the realisation of what's actually happened hits him.

Zoe reaches and touches Charlie's face tenderly. 'It's okay, darling.'

Charlie's expression twists in shock and pain. 'What are we going to do, Mum?' he gasps as she pulls him close and wraps her arms around him.

SEVENTEEN

LOWRI

8.26 a.m.

Lowri sits forward on the chair outside the annexe and gazes in horror at the villa. It's awash with Italian police officers. It doesn't feel real. She watches as an officer unravels red-and-white police evidence tape – *Polizia Locale*. Then several officers begin to cordon off the whole area around the swimming pool. It's like some terrible film or television series.

How can this be happening? she wonders.

Sitting back in the chair, she can feel a pain on her left shoulder blade. Then she remembers. It's bruised from where Harry pushed her back against the wall last night.

And now he's dead? *What the fuck?*

Lowri's head is spinning. First the attack and now this. She wonders if the two are connected somehow. Did Harry regret attacking her, drink himself unconscious and fall into the pool?

For a second, she can almost feel Harry's body against her. Smell the cigar and booze on his breath. Her heart immediately starts to race.

Lowri looks at the green tea she made herself about twenty minutes ago. She hasn't touched it. It just feels weird to be doing something as mundane as drinking tea. Then she looks down at her phone. Messages and notifications from Whats-App, TikTok and Instagram. It all feels so weird.

As she looks over at the police officers again, who appear to be inspecting the grassy area down from the pool, she sees Charlie approaching.

Oh God, poor Charlie. She wonders how he's dealing with this. Her heart goes out to him. And then she remembers how badly things ended last night between Charlie and his father. None of it feels real.

'Hey,' Charlie says as he gets about twenty yards away.

'Oh God, Charlie,' Lowri says jumping up and going to him. She wraps her arms around him. 'I'm so so sorry.'

'Yeah,' he says with a vacant nod. He looks in shock. Of course he's in shock.

'What's going on?' Lowri asks as she goes back and sits down. 'Do you want a tea or coffee or something?' Then she wonders if that's a stupid question. As if having a tea or coffee is going to make him feel any better.

'I'm fine,' Charlie mumbles as he comes over. 'Mind if I sit down?'

'Of course not,' Lowri replies insistently.

'My mum and your mum are talking to some detective,' Charlie explains.

'Was it some kind of accident?' Lowri asks and then wonders if it's even okay to ask that kind of question.

'I think so. I don't know,' Charlie admits. 'I can't believe he's gone.'

'No,' Lowri agrees. Then she looks at him. 'And after last night...'

Charlie nods, his eyes staring into space as though he's deep in thought. Then he looks at her with a serious expression. 'I don't think we should tell anyone about what happened last night. When my dad came to your room.'

'What? Why not?' Lowri asks. She's confused. Harry sexually assaulted her. Why would they hide that?

'We're in a foreign country,' Charlie explains quietly. 'My dad attacked you. He punched me. I don't know, but what if they think...'

'What?'

'I don't know,' Charlie says as he runs his hands through his hair. 'I can't think straight.'

Lowri gets a horrible sinking feeling in her stomach. 'Don't we just tell the police the truth? We haven't done anything wrong, have we?'

'No, of course not,' Charlie reassures her.

Silence. They are both lost in their thoughts.

Lowri starts to run through various scenarios. Why does Charlie think that they shouldn't tell the police what happened?

Charlie leans forward and looks at her. 'Okay. I'm just thinking of a worst-case scenario here,' he says under his breath. 'What if the police think that someone pushed my dad into the pool, he hit his head and drowned?'

Lowri frowns. Her pulse is racing and her mouth is dry. 'Charlie... you're really scaring me.'

'Sorry.' Charlie reaches over and puts his hand reassuringly on her forearm. She pulls it away.

'What are you trying to tell me?' Lowri says. Her head is spinning as she looks directly at him. 'Is that what happened?' she whispers. 'Did you push your dad into the pool and he drowned?'

Charlie looks horrified. 'No! God, no,' he says shaking his head emphatically. 'I promise you, I didn't see him after he left your bedroom. But if we tell someone that he attacked you, and me and him had a fight, it might look bad for both of us.'

Lowri is feeling sick at the prospect of lying to the police. 'I really don't want to lie to them. What if someone finds out what happened?'

'Who?'

EIGHTEEN

CERYS

8.27 a.m.

Detective Franco Saachi has been interviewing Zoe and me for about ten minutes. In his mid-forties, Saachi is handsome, with ink-black hair that's swept back from his deeply tanned face. He has a scar just above his right eyebrow and a tiny dimple in his chin. In any other circumstance, I might think that he's incredibly attractive. But not this morning.

So far, he's just collected basic information such as names, addresses and phone numbers.

'And you're here on holiday?' Saachi asks Zoe as he scribbles in his black notebook.

'Yes,' Zoe replies. She's still in utter shock. Her eyes are puffy and red from crying.

Poor, poor Zoe, I think. It's such a terrible thing to have happened on holiday – or anywhere, come to think of it.

'And it's just you and your husband that are on holiday?' Saachi says.

Zoe shakes her head. 'My son, Charlie, is with us.'

Saachi frowns and looks at her. 'And where is your son, Charlie?'

'I don't know,' Zoe admits and then gestures. 'He's out there somewhere.'

'I will need to speak to him,' Saachi explains.

'Of course,' Zoe says.

Saachi looks at his notes and then at me. 'And I must speak with your daughter... Lowri.' He trips over the pronunciation of her name as though it's totally alien to him. Maybe it is.

'Yes,' I reply.

My stomach is in knots. Although adrenaline is coursing through my veins, I can still feel the hangover from the night before. I need a drink. God, how I *need* a drink.

Saachi pulls out a mobile phone and shows it to them. 'I am going to record the interviews today. And anything you tell me can be later used as evidence in a court of law. Okay?'

I don't like the sound of that one bit. 'Evidence?'

Saachi puts his hands up in a gesture that is designed to reassure me. 'This is just routine. I would be doing this for any sudden or unexplained death,' he explains.

His words do calm me a little but it feels so strange. To be fair, everything feels strange and dreamlike this morning.

He looks over at Zoe. 'So, you and your family have been here since Saturday morning, is that correct?'

'Yes,' Zoe replies.

'And where do you live in the UK?' he asks.

'London,' she says.

Saachi nods. 'London, right. And you flew from London to...?'

'We flew into Florence,' Zoe explains.

He looks at her. 'Can you remember the flight details?'

'We flew with British Airways,' Zoe says. 'And we landed at eight thirty in the morning.'

'Okay, thank you,' Saachi says. 'And what did your husband do in London?'

'He worked for a record company,' she replies. 'Director of A&R.'

Saachi raises an eyebrow. 'Oh right. He worked with musicians, yes?'

'Sort of.' Zoe nods.

I register the use of their past tense when talking about Harry. It's so weird.

'And what do you do in London, please, Mrs Collard?'

'It's Zoe,' she says, looking a little awkward. 'Erm, I own a café in Dulwich Village.'

'Village?' Saachi looks confused. 'So you don't work in London?'

'Yes. Dulwich Village is in London,' Zoe responds, sounding a little flustered.

I can see why Saachi is confused. I guess I'm just used to the more affluent, pretentious parts of London having that conceit – Wimbledon, Barnes and Hampstead.

'Oh, okay,' Saachi says. 'What kind of café is it?'

'Mainly vegan,' Zoe says.

He nods. 'Vegan, right, okay.'

This seems to faintly amuse Saachi.

'And last night, you were all having dinner together out there?' Saachi asks as he points to the large glass doors that lead to the decking and the outside area.

'Yes, that's right,' I reply.

'What time did that start?'

'About eight, I think.' I look to Zoe for confirmation.

'Yes, eight,' she agrees.

Saachi looks at Zoe. 'And there was you, your husband, your son, Charlie...' He then looks at me. 'You and your daughter, Lowri. Was there anyone else at the villa?'

'Lucia and Lorenzo,' I say.

Saachi gives me a quizzical look. Obviously he has no idea who they are.

'Sorry, they were cooking and serving the dinner for us,' I say by way of an explanation.

Saachi nods and rubs his jaw with his hand. 'They live near here?'

'Yes,' I say. 'In the cottage down the track. Literally a minute from here in a car.'

Saachi seems intrigued by my mention of Lucia and Lorenzo. I've no idea why. 'And they work for you?'

'Sometimes. I mean yes,' I reply, wondering why I can't seem to get my words out properly. Shock, I guess.

Saachi gives me a look to imply that he'd like more details about what Lucia and Lorenzo do for me. He doesn't need to say it. His face and eyes are very expressive. I guess that's because he's Italian and then wonder if that's racist and prejudiced.

'Lucia helps me clean the villa. She washes the sheets and towels. That kind of thing,' I say, glad that I've managed to become lucid again. 'Lorenzo tends the gardens. Cuts the lawn, trims the hedges. He also looks after the pool.'

'Right. Thank you. And do you know their surname?' he asks.

'De Nardi,' I say with some hesitation. 'Yes, I'm pretty sure that it's De Nardi and they are married.' I'm not quite sure why I added that last bit. Nerves.

Saachi scribbles this down, takes a breath, sits back and then looks at them both. 'So, at eight o'clock, you sat down for dinner?'

'Yes.'

'And the last time you saw your husband was around eight thirty?'

'Yes,' Zoe says.

'He went off to smoke a cigar,' I explain.

Saachi frowns. 'And you didn't see him after that?' He sounds confused.

Zoe and I both shake our heads and then say virtually in unison, 'No.'

Saachi narrows his eyes. 'Didn't you think that was strange?' he asks.

Oh God, he sounds a bit suspicious now, I think. It's not good for my raging anxiety. My heart is fluttering and I think a panic attack might be brewing.

I have an idea.

'Would you like a coffee or soft drink, Detective?' I ask him. 'Or a glass of water?'

'Please, it's Franco,' he says in a friendly tone. 'Yes, a glass of water, please.'

I get up and wander away from the living area of the villa and head into the kitchen. I now know that I'm going to get alcohol in my system and that starts to calm me.

Grabbing a glass, I pop some ice in it and go to the fridge. I take a bottle of water and pour it.

With a cursory glance around, I check that no one is looking before going to the bottle of Smirnoff by the fridge. There's no time for niceties. I unscrew the cap, take the bottle and glug two big mouthfuls. My throat burns a little and the vodka fumes go up my nose. I always think it smells like glue. Then I put the bottle back. I have five more bottles of Smirnoff hidden away in the annexe so I can replace this one before Lowri notices.

I take the glass and wander casually back, before handing it to Saachi. 'There you go.'

'*Grazie*, thank you,' he says with a half smile. He has nice white teeth which are made all the more dazzling by his dark, olive skin. Then he puts the glass down on the coffee table and looks at us again with a quizzical expression. 'How was your husband acting last night?'

Zoe looks confused. 'How do you mean?'

'Was he happy, sad, angry, depressed?' Saachi explains.

'He was all right,' Zoe says and then looks to me for confirmation. 'I think.'

'Yes.' I nod. 'He seemed fine to me.' I'm not about to explain that he was acting like a pompous twat and had rowed with my daughter and his son.

'And what time do you think you both went to bed?' Saachi asked.

Zoe pulls a face. 'I'm not really sure. Ten, ten thirty?' She looks at me again for verification.

I nod. 'Yes, I think it was about that.'

'We'd had a few drinks, you see,' Zoe says.

Don't tell him that, I think with frustration.

'You were drunk?' Saachi asks.

'No, no,' I reassure him. 'Just a few glasses of wine, that's all.' I don't think it's a good idea to mention that I have virtually no recollection of deciding to go to bed or getting there.

A female police officer in uniform comes in and begins to talk to Saachi in Italian. There's something about her tone that I don't like. She gestures for him to follow her outside.

Saachi looks at them. 'I must go for a few minutes. But please, just stay here.'

'Of course,' I say. The vodka has done its trick. My whole nervous system has been soothed and I feel fuzzy.

We watch Saachi as he follows the officer out through the sliding door to the patio and down towards the pool.

'What's going on?' Zoe asks me anxiously.

'I don't know,' I reply. 'I'm sure it's nothing.' I'm lying but I want Zoe to remain calm.

Zoe closes her eyes and purses her lips as if she's in pain. Then she opens her eyes and looks at me as they fill with tears. 'How can any of this be happening?'

I move across the sofa towards her and take her hand in

mine. 'It's going to be okay. I'm here if you need anything. And I'm going to be with you every step of the way.'

Zoe squeezes my hand. 'Thank you,' she whispers.

There's a noise and we both look up to see Saachi re-entering the room. He comes over and sits down.

He gives us a dark look that makes me scared.

'I'm very sorry to have to tell you this,' he says quietly. 'But your husband was stabbed.'

'What?' Zoe exclaimed.

Oh God! My stomach lurches with the news.

'He has wounds in his chest and his stomach.' Saachi looks at us. 'Someone has killed him. I'm very sorry.'

NINETEEN

CERYS

Four Years Before – Thursday, 23 May 2019

I stand in the quiet corridor of the Natural Health Centre in Marylebone. My stomach is tight with nerves as I knock on the door of the exams office. For the past nine months, I've been studying for a Diploma in Yoga and Reflexology. If I've passed, I can get insurance to practise as a professional yoga teacher and reflexology therapist. My heart is thumping in my chest.

My husband, Nick, has been less than supportive. In fact, at times he's been downright dismissive. He thinks that anything holistic is 'woo-woo'. His words, not mine. I try to ignore him but it hurts. I feel like we're drifting apart. I think that Lowri can also sense that things aren't right at home. I don't want her to have to experience that. My parents would row and then not speak to each other for days on end. I grew up in a house where the overriding feeling was one of tension and I swore that I'd never allow my children to suffer the same. I'm hopeful that if I get this qualification and bring more money in, it will get our marriage back on track.

The door opens and a smiley woman in her thirties, with curly blonde hair, looks at me.

'Have you come for your results?' she asks me.

I nod. 'Yes.' My mouth is dry.

'Could I have your name?' she asks as she scuttles over to her desk to a small pile of brown envelopes.

'Cerys Williams.'

'Cerys, that's right,' she says under her breath. I've seen her and said hello a few times while I've been attending lectures and seminars. 'Here it is.'

I hold my breath as she comes over and hands me the envelope. 'Good luck.'

I take it with a nervous smile, turn and then walk down the corridor.

Here goes, I think to myself. I prepare myself to be disappointed. In fact, as I open the envelope, I've already told myself that I've failed.

But I haven't.

There it is in printed words:

Candidate: Cerys Elizabeth Williams

Diploma: Yoga Teaching & Reflexology Therapy Grade: Distinction (D*)

I can't believe it. I've bloody nailed it. It's the highest grade possible. My heart is beating now with excitement. I'm so pleased.

I literally dance out of the Natural Health Centre, along the Marylebone Road and down into the Tube station. I feel giddy about what I've achieved and excited about the prospect of a whole new career ahead of me.

Twenty minutes later, I climb the steps of Balham Tube station and head along the high street. My plans have already started. Get some business cards printed. Advertise online. Plus there are various holistic centres in South London that I can now approach and see if they'll take me on. Either that, or I can rent a room from them and see clients there and teach classes.

I pop into the off-licence to buy a cheap bottle of Champagne and a bottle of white wine to celebrate. I figure one bottle isn't going to be enough.

I pull out my iPhone to call Nick and tell him the good news. I want him to be excited and proud of me. I look at the photograph of Nick on my phone. He looks handsome. Lowri is about three years old and she's sitting on his shoulders. We were blissfully happy then. And Nick was so thrilled to be a father in those days. I can't seem to pinpoint when he became so ill-tempered and controlling. But I'm confident that this is going to be a new start for us. I just want us to be a happy family unit again.

I turn into our road. I'm looking forward to necking a few glasses and getting drunk with Nick. I think I have an unhealthy relationship with booze. In fact, I know I do. I've done some pretty crazy things while drunk that I can't remember. But hey, hasn't everyone?

Then I spot something that stops me in my tracks.

Someone's coming down our little path from the front door. It's a woman.

Who the hell is that? I wonder as I get a horrible sinking feeling in my stomach. *And what was she doing in our house?*

I watch her intently. She turns and waves to someone at the front door. I can't see from here but it has to be Nick. There's no one else at home.

The woman is in her forties, slim, brunette and fashionably dressed. She has a light, carefree, even happy spring in her step as she goes to a white Mini Clubman and gets in.

She's just shagged my husband, I think. *I know it. What other explanation can there be?*

I feel sick.

TWENTY

LUCIA

Monday
8.46 a.m.

Lucia uses her hand to shield her face from the rising morning sunshine. It's been nearly an hour since two police cars arrived at the villa. She can see the officers walking around outside on the decking, the grass and down by the pool.

Where the hell is Lorenzo? she wonders. He went up to the back of Villa Lucia to find out what's going on. He still hasn't returned.

Her husband is being unusually quiet this morning. She thinks that the incident with the car yesterday has spooked him. Plus there was a news story on the radio earlier about a judge who was putting members of the Bassilino crime family on trial. The judge had been killed by a car bomb just outside Naples. Lucia knows that such a story will scare Lorenzo. It demonstrates that no one is safe from the Bassilinos.

Walking across the pathway that leads up to the villa, Lucia begins to climb the steep terrain to see if she can get a better look at what is going on. She feels it's her responsibility. It's her villa, after all.

After about two minutes of striding uphill, she can see the decking to the rear of the villa, the steps down and the infinity pool. There are several police officers either looking into the pool or crouched down beside it.

What on earth is going on?

She then sees the officers lifting something out of the pool and putting it down on the ground.

It's a body.

Blessed Madonna.

Lucia crosses herself and begins to mouth a prayer for *anime pezzentelle* – lost souls.

'Are you praying?' asks a voice.

It's Lorenzo.

'Yes,' she replies. 'Of course.' She points up to the villa. 'Someone has died. We both must pray.'

Lorenzo has a strange expression on his face. He's not giving anything away.

'Do you know what happened?' she asks.

Lorenzo gestures with his head up the hill. 'Yes, it is him. That man.'

'Harry?' Lucia asks, remembering his name.

'Yes... And I won't be praying for him,' Lorenzo mutters angrily.

'Lorenzo!' Lucia exclaims and shakes her head. 'The man is dead. We have to pray for him.'

Lorenzo shakes his head and looks at her with a sour expression. *'Vendicarsi dà soddisfazione.'* Revenge is sweet.

Lucia looks horrified. 'Revenge? Why are you talking about revenge?'

'What?' Lorenzo shrugs.

Except for the light breeze that gently swishes a nearby cypress tree, there are a few seconds of silence.

Then she looks at him. 'What did you do, Lorenzo?'

'Nothing,' he replies calmly. 'I did nothing. That man was like some maniac. On the phone, blah, blah, blah. He probably had a heart attack and drowned in the pool. But that is God's revenge for what he was like.'

Lucia gives him a look. She knows how angry her husband was after the incident with Harry yesterday. And she knows about Lorenzo's dark past.

He had been a member of the Camorra Mafia in Naples. As a young man, he had got caught up in La Faida di Scampia – the Scampia Feud in 2004 and 2005. Two rival mafia families who fought each other for the control of drugs and prostitution in the northern suburbs of Naples.

Then she spots the palm of Lorenzo's right hand. There is a long cut along it.

'What happened?' She gestures towards it as a flutter of anxiety dances in her chest.

'When I was fixing that chair in the workshop yesterday,' he replies. 'I told you that. Come on. There is nothing else we can do while the police are there.'

'Lorenzo?' Lucia says in a serious tone. There's something about his manner that's making her uneasy.

'What?' He sounds frustrated.

'If you did something, you must tell me,' she says in a hushed voice.

Lorenzo laughs. 'Don't be ridiculous! Come on.'

He turns and begins to make his way down the footpath back to their cottage.

For a few seconds, Lucia watches him go and then follows.

TWENTY-ONE

LOWRI

9.42 a.m.

Lowri blows out her cheeks. The day is already baking hot. The sky above is cloudless and a flawless blue. She can feel her heart thudding in her chest and sweat on her top lip. Pulling her hair back, she fastens it into a high ponytail. It feels a relief to have it off her face and neck. Normally she likes the heat but this morning it's suffocating.

She's sitting on the stone patio at the back of the villa's annexe and opposite her is Detective Franco Saachi. He's been asking her all sorts of questions about the previous evening. It's making her feel flustered and sick, especially after the conversation she had with Charlie. In her mind, she keeps lurching backwards and forwards. *Tell the truth about Harry attacking me. Lie about Harry attacking me.*

For a second, she makes her decision. *Why should I lie? I had nothing to do with what happened to Harry.*

As far as she's concerned, Harry might have got roaring drunk and fallen in the pool, hit his head and drowned. In fact, it has to be something like that, doesn't it?

Don't lie, you have nothing to hide, she tells herself. *If you lie, you'll just make things worse.*

But then she remembers her conversation with Charlie. Had he told her that they needed to cover up Harry attacking her because he had something to do with what had happened to his father? Is Charlie trying to use her to cover for him?

Lowri squirms in her seat and looks down at her feet which she can't seem to keep still. *Oh God, this is unbearable.*

Saachi is writing in his notebook. His eyebrows are thick and bushy with a couple of longer grey hairs that stick up like spider's legs.

Why doesn't he just cut them? It's so unattractive, Lowri thinks and then reprimands herself for having such a banal thought in such a horrible situation as this.

Saachi stops writing and looks over at her. He seems to have the expression of someone that knows more than he's letting on. Or is that just her paranoia?

'And you and your mother joined the Collard family for dinner last night at around 8 p.m.? Is that correct?' Saachi asks.

'Yes,' Lowri says, noticing that her mouth has gone dry. And then the urge to ask a question gets the better of her. 'I'm sorry, but if Harry fell into the pool and drowned, why do you need to know all this stuff?'

Saachi looks at her for a few seconds.

It wasn't long but it felt agonising.

Oh God, why did I say that? Have I said too much?

'I'm afraid we are now treating Harry Collard's death as murder,' Saachi explains.

What? No. I don't understand.

For a moment, Lowri thinks she must have misheard him. *Murder?* A surge of overwhelming anxiety sweeps through her whole body. *That can't be right.* Everything starts to feel surreal. The pit of her stomach seems to drop. Pulse racing.

'Murder?' Lowri whispers. She can't quite believe that word has just left her mouth.

'I'm sorry,' Saachi says calmly. 'But yes. Can you tell me how Harry seemed at the dinner last night?'

Lowri takes a deep breath to compose herself. Her head is spinning.

Just calm down, Lowri, she tells herself.

If Harry was killed, did Charlie have something to do with it? Is that why he came to her earlier?

What am I meant to do now? Tell the truth.

'Erm, he... he seemed to be fine,' Lowri stammers.

Saachi lifts one of his eyebrows quizzically. 'Fine? I don't know what that means. Was he happy, sad, angry?'

Lowri doesn't know how to respond. She can hardly tell him that Harry had acted like an arrogant entitled twat and they'd rowed.

'It was hard to tell,' she says. 'But he seemed happy enough. It didn't seem like there was anything particularly bothering him, if that's what you mean.'

Saachi nods as if he understands and scribbles in his notebook. Then he looks over at her. It's a meaningful look that concerns her. 'And after Harry left to go and smoke his cigar, you didn't see him again? Is that correct?'

Tell the truth. You have nothing to hide. You've done nothing wrong.

As her pulse thunders in her neck, Lowri can hardly catch her breath. She puts her hand nervously to her face.

'No,' she whispers. Realising that her answer is barely audible, she clears her throat and then says a little louder, 'No. That was the last time I saw him.'

There are a few seconds of interminable, unbearable silence.

Oh God!

She's made her decision. She's lied.

Saachi fixes her with a stare. 'And you're sure about that?'

Oh no, does he know something that I don't? Jesus. What have you done, Lowri? Just hold your fucking nerve.

She feels like she's going to explode with anxiety.

'Yes, I'm sure,' she says in as confident a voice as she can muster. She looks up, and through the kitchen window she sees Charlie walking in the distance.

'And you don't know where he went after he left the table?' Saachi asks.

'What? No...' Lowri shakes her head. 'He just said he was going to smoke his cigar and he walked off.'

Saachi watches her for a second and then nods.

TWENTY-TWO

ZOE

9.54 a.m.

It's been just over an hour since Detective Saachi revealed that Harry had been murdered. Zoe just can't seem to process it. It's like she's trapped in some terrible anxiety dream. She looks down at her engagement and weddding rings and touches them as if this will somehow connect her to Harry. She just doesn't understand how he can be gone and that she won't see him again.

Zoe remembers when Harry proposed to her. June 2000. They were on holiday in South Africa. Just the two of them. They'd started the holiday at Karoo National Park in the Western Cape and seen black rhinos and lions. She recalls the utter thrill of seeing a huge male lion as it wandered majestically past their jeeps, only twenty yards from where they were sitting. In the evenings, they'd eat dinner, drink too much wine and make love in their Dutch-style cottage that had stunning panoramic views of the Karoo landscape. Harry was so engaged in those days. It was the first time that he'd ever really opened up about his childhood and how much he believed it had truly damaged him. He told her that when he was eleven, the day after he'd arrived home from boarding school for the summer holidays, his parents had flown to Kenya to go on a month's safari with friends. They told him he was to stay at home with the housekeeper, Mrs Burridge, as he wouldn't enjoy a safari and would just get under their feet. He recalled the crushing feeling of rejection and abandonment that had made him feel.

After Karoo, they'd flown over to Cape Town. One morning, they got up at the crack of dawn and took the cable car up to the top of Table Mountain. The view from the top was breathtaking as the sun rose over the Lion's Head and Signal Hill. Cape Town stretched out to their right and Robben Island, where Nelson Mandela had been incarcerated for eighteen years, sat in the sea in the distance ahead of them.

Harry had taken her off the beaten track, dropped to one knee and pulled out an engagement ring. He told her that he'd found his soulmate and that he wanted to spend the rest of his life with her. It was so incredibly romantic and Zoe wept.

Zoe touches the eighteen-carat solitaire diamond engagement ring. She was so happy that day. She can't remember where it all went so wrong. And now Harry is gone. That just isn't possible.

'Here we go,' says a voice.

It's Cerys. She's holding a glass of wine for herself and a large vodka, lime and soda. Normally, Zoe would be horrified by the idea of starting to drink before 10 a.m. even on holiday. But she needs something to change the way she feels. To numb the shock and pain.

'Oh God,' Zoe gasps as she takes a deep breath. She looks at Cerys. 'I forget for a few seconds. And then I remember what's happened and it seems to hit me again as if it's the first time.'

Cerys hands her the glass and puts her hand on Zoe's shoulder for a moment. 'I'm so sorry. It just doesn't feel real, does it?'

'No.' Zoe shakes her head and takes the glass. 'It really doesn't.' Her hand is shaky.

She needs to know what happened to Harry and why he was attacked.

'Maybe a stiff drink will help a little,' Cerys suggests as she sits down.

'I don't know what I'm supposed to do,' Zoe mutters and then she swigs at the drink. It's very strong and she pulls a face.

'Sorry,' Cerys apologises. 'Too strong?'

'No,' Zoe replies. 'Strong is good.'

There's a noise of footsteps and Saachi comes back into the villa and approaches.

He sits down on the big leather armchair and leans forward. Up until now, he has been incredibly supportive, keeping them informed of everything that the police are doing.

Looking down at his notes, he then looks at Cerys. 'Have you noticed anything missing from the villa? Anything valuable? Cash? Or an expensive phone or computer?'

'No, sorry.' Cerys shakes her head. 'I haven't really searched around but I haven't noticed anything yet.'

'Okay,' Saachi says. Then he looks at Cerys again and points in the direction of the kitchen. 'Just one more thing. One of my forensics officers noticed that there are two knives missing from the knife block in the kitchen?'

Cerys frowns. 'Are there?'

'Yes.' Saachi nods.

'Oh, I know that a knife got broken,' Cerys replies. 'Maybe that's it.'

'You mean that a knife got thrown away?' Saachi asks as he furrows his brow.

'I don't think so,' Cerys says. 'I'm really sorry but I just don't know. I don't tend to cook in there. It's either the guests or Lorenzo who use that kitchen.'

'Okay,' Saachi says with a nonchalant shrug. Then he puts

the notepad back into the inside pocket of his navy jacket and looks over at Zoe with a sombre expression. 'I am sorry, but we now must take Harry with us from here.'

Zoe nods but the idea of Harry being taken away in a coroner's van is all too much for her. She dissolves in floods of tears and Cerys goes to console her.

After a few seconds, Zoe tries to get her breath back as she wipes her face. 'Sorry, I...' she whispers.

Saachi holds up his hand and shakes his head. 'Please, do not apologise. This is a terrible shock for you and your son.'

Zoe looks up at him. 'Where are you taking my husband?'

'The University Hospital in Florence,' Saachi explains gently. 'We will take good care of him, I promise you.'

Zoe nods slowly but she still can't believe this is actually happening.

'Should we call the British Consulate in Florence?' Cerys asks.

'Yes,' Saachi replies. 'You must tell them what has happened. They can give you advice as we go forward.'

'How long...' Zoe asks, but she's not quite sure how to finish her question.

'I'm sorry,' Saachi says with an empathetic expression. 'It's hard for me to tell you how long all this is going to take. And I'm afraid that as a precaution, I will need you to hand over all your passports.' He then looks at Cerys. 'And yours and your daughter's, please,' he says politely.

Cerys frowns. 'Why?'

Zoe registers what Saachi has said. Her anxiety worsens. 'I don't understand. I'm assuming that someone came up to the villa last night and for some reason attacked Harry. Maybe they'd come to rob us.'

'Yes, of course.' Saachi nods. 'That is one line of investigation for us to pursue.'

'One line?' Cerys snaps. 'It's the only line, isn't it? You can't think that someone here had anything to do with Harry's death.'

'Oh God, no,' Zoe says. 'That's ridiculous. And horrible.'

'I understand your distress.' Saachi gets to his feet. 'But your husband was murdered at this villa. I have to look at everyone who was here last night. I wouldn't be doing my job properly if I didn't. So, I need your passports and you mustn't leave the area.'

Zoe looks at Cerys, aghast.

'And I need to question your son,' Saachi explains.

'Question him about what?' She can feel the distress rise in her throat.

'I need to speak to everyone that was here.'

'Can I sit with him?' Zoe asks, suddenly feeling very protective.

Saachi raises an eyebrow. 'Is he under twenty-one years old?'

'Yes, he's nineteen.'

'Then yes,' Saachi says calmly. 'In Italian law, an adult can be present so I will allow it. And it will be routine, so there's no need to worry.'

But Zoe is worried. How is Charlie going to cope with all this?

TWENTY-THREE

LOWRI

9.57 a.m.

Lowri has been frantically looking for Charlie for nearly ten minutes. Her anxiety is overwhelming. She has to find him before he's questioned to tell him that she's lied about being attacked by his father. Charlie has agreed to tell the police everything and that will put them both in a very difficult position.

Bloody hell, Lowri. Why did you have to lie?

Looking down at the swimming pool, she can see forensics officers doing a fingertip search of the whole area. One of them takes something from under one of the blue sunloungers with tweezers and pops it into a clear evidence bag. Meanwhile, other forensics officers are pool-side, using small test-tubes to take samples of the water.

Lowri just cannot believe that this is actually happening at her mum's villa. It's like the scene from some Netflix crime thriller series.

Turning quickly, she heads around to the front of the villa where the Collards' car is parked. As she turns the corner, she stops in her tracks.

A blacked-out van is parked at the top of the driveway. The back of the van is open. A metallic trolley is being wheeled very slowly towards it. On top is a black body bag.

Jesus! Lowri takes a breath to steady herself. She can't comprehend that Harry is dead inside that bag. And that someone has killed him.

She turns and jogs back the way she came, scouring the area for any sign of Charlie. Her anxiety is now through the roof.

Looking down, she can see Detective Saachi wandering past the pool, clearly looking for something – or someone. What if he's looking for Charlie?

Then she sees something out of the corner of her eye.

A figure sitting up on a dry stone wall in the distance. He's about fifty yards away.

Charlie.

She glances back to Detective Saachi. He hasn't seen Charlie yet.

The only thing she can think to do is to break into a jog across the grass to the far side of the villa.

It's hot and she's keeping her eye on Detective Saachi. She can hardly call out to Charlie. And even jogging is going to look a little suspicious.

And then Saachi clocks where Charlie is sitting.

Fuck!

Keep it together, Lowri, she thinks as her strides get longer and her pace quicker. Her pulse is racing and now she's breathing quickly.

Saachi is taking his time and hasn't yet spotted her.

'Hey,' she says loudly, trying to attract Charlie's attention as she slows her jog to a march.

But Charlie's wearing headphones and looking down at his phone.

For fuck's sake, Charlie!

She's about ten yards away now but Saachi is heading up directly from the villa.

There can't be more than ten seconds before he arrives.

Putting her hand on Charlie's shoulder, Lowri gives him a little shake.

He takes off his headphones and gives her a quizzical look.

She stares directly into his eyes and gives him an urgent look. Then she hisses very quickly under her breath, 'Don't react to what I'm telling you. There's a detective behind me. I didn't tell him that your dad attacked me. I lied. I said the last time I saw him was when he left the dinner table. Do you understand that?'

Charlie's eyes widen in surprise.

'Charlie?' Lowri whispers frantically. 'Do you understand?'

She can sense that Saachi is right behind her now. And then she can see his shadow fall across the ground to her right.

Shit!

Charlie looks at her and gives her a conspiratorial nod. 'Yeah,' he whispers.

Thank God, Lowri thinks.

'Charlie?' Saachi says.

'Yes?' Charlie replies.

Lowri turns, wearing the best innocent expression that she can muster.

Saachi looks at her with a frown. 'You look a little out of breath?'

'It's very hot. Even when you're walking,' she replies with a shrug.

Saachi gestures to Charlie. 'Charlie, if you can come with me. I need to ask you a few questions. I know this has been a shock for you so it won't take long.'

Lowri sits down slowly as she watches Saachi and Charlie walking back down the grassy bank towards the villa. She wonders how she's managed to get herself into this predicament.

TWENTY-FOUR

ZOE

10.12 a.m.

Zoe plays with a bracelet on her wrist. Harry had bought it from a very fashionable jewellery maker in London called Kirstie Le Marque. The shell bracelet. Apparently it's iconic, one of her friends told her. One of the designers is married to a pop star or a singer but she can't remember who it is.

Detective Saachi has been interviewing Charlie for about ten minutes. All her concern is now focused on her son. Saachi's phone has been placed on the table again as he is recording the interview. The very act of this has made Zoe uneasy.

So far, Charlie has responded to his questions in a soft voice, telling Saachi the same details that Zoe and Cerys told him earlier. Zoe doesn't really see the point in him going over all details again. She knows that detectives get everyone's account of what happened in case there are discrepancies. As far as Zoe is concerned, Harry was attacked by an intruder who he disturbed while trying to rob the villa. There is no other explanation. The police need to be out there looking for that person.

'Okay. And then your father left the dinner table to go and smoke a cigar?' Saachi asks as a way of confirming what he already knows.

'Yes,' Charlie says quietly.

'Did you think that was strange?' Saachi asks.

'Not really,' Charlie replies with a shrug.

'But the dinner wasn't finished,' Saachi continued. 'Why did your father suddenly decide to get up from the table and leave to smoke a cigar?'

'I thought he was coming back,' Charlie says. 'And that's what he's like anyway.'

Zoe takes a nervous breath. No one has mentioned that there was an argument at the table and that Harry had effectively stormed off in a huff. It's not something she wants Saachi to know and she's concerned that Charlie has unwittingly opened a can of worms.

Saachi immediately picks up on what Charlie has said. He arches an eyebrow quizzically. 'That is what he is like? I don't understand.'

Charlie looks at her and then back at Saachi. Zoe holds her breath as she wonders quite what Charlie is going to reveal about Harry. 'He's just a bit moody.'

Well, Charlie could have said far worse, Zoe thinks.

Then it strikes her that Charlie has used the present tense. He should have said, 'He *was* a bit moody.' From now on, Harry will be past tense. She shudders at the finality of that thought.

'Moody?' Saachi furrows his brow. 'What is "moody"?'

Charlie looks at Zoe again.

Zoe pulls a face and shrugs. 'A bit grumpy?' she suggests.

Saachi nods. He clearly understands the word 'grumpy'. 'Right, yes. Grumpy.'

Saachi scratches his nose, frowns and looks directly at Charlie. 'You didn't like your father?'

'No.' Charlie frowns as he trips over his words. 'I mean yes. Sometimes.'

'I see,' Saachi says and leaves a pregnant pause.

Zoe is panicking that Charlie is allowing himself to be taken down a worrying line of enquiry.

'You know. Fathers and sons,' Zoe says, trying to explain and defuse the situation. 'They sometimes didn't see eye to eye. But they loved each other.'

Zoe is aware that she is babbling nervously as if she's trying to overcompensate for Charlie's answers.

Oh God, I think I'm actually making this worse.

Saachi narrows his eyes and looks at Charlie. 'Yes, you loved each other. And of course, your father was your hero. A man you looked up to. And someone you wanted to be when you got older.'

Charlie looks baffled. 'Sorry, I...'

'I'm just asking if your father was your hero, Charlie?' Saachi asks in a nonchalant tone.

'Not really,' Charlie replies.

Saachi looks over at Zoe and studies her for a moment. 'Right, I see.'

TWENTY-FIVE

LUCIA

10.38 a.m.

Lucia takes a glass of cold water over to Detective Saachi who has been sitting at the small table in her kitchen for around ten minutes. Lorenzo taps his fingers together nervously. It's what he does when he's anxious. And having a detective from the State Police – Polizia di Stato – is making them both very edgy.

Above them, the original slanted wooden joists and beams of the roof are exposed. To their right, there is the small cooker and next to that an old wooden dresser that is cluttered with various knick-knacks. Saucepans hang from hooks on the wall and ceramic plates, bowls and cups are neatly stacked on the shelves to the right of the cooker. The walls are grey, exposed stone, and a wooden crucifix hangs to one side next to a commemorative plate of the Vatican City.

'Here you go,' Lucia says politely as she hands the glass to Saachi and then sits down on a rickety stool which rocks a little on the uneven stone floor.

'Thank you,' Saachi says as he takes the glass, sips at it and puts it down on the table next to his phone which is recording their interview.

Lucia catches Lorenzo's eye. With his hunched shoulders and blinking eyes, he looks like a schoolboy who has been summoned to see the *direttore* – headteacher. She wants to give him a shake and tell him to sit up straight. Be a man. He looks guilty of something just by the way he is sitting there. It's stupid.

'Okay,' Saachi says as he scratches one of his thick eyebrows. 'Lucia, you went up from here to the villa just after 7 p.m., is that correct?'

'Yes,' Lucia says and nods.

Saachi turns to look over at Lorenzo. 'But you were up at the villa already, yes?

Lorenzo nods but doesn't say anything.

'And you were watering the lawns and plants?' Saachi says.

'Yes.' Lorenzo nods again.

'Did you see Harry Collard while you were up there?' Saachi asks.

'Yes,' Lorenzo replies but Lucia can see that the question has made him uneasy.

'Did you talk to him at all?' Saachi asks.

Lucia looks at Lorenzo. She knows he's not stupid enough to tell the detective that he accidentally sprayed Harry with water and he insulted them.

Lorenzo shakes his head. 'No.'

Saachi looks back at Lucia. 'You arrived just after 7 p.m. And you went into the kitchen and began to prepare the dinner for the guests?'

'Yes,' Lucia replies.

'And did you have any interaction with Harry Collard while you were in the kitchen?' Saachi enquires.

'No,' Lucia says. 'I only speak with Cerys about the dinner.'

'Did you see Harry before you began to serve the food to them?'

'No.'

'And at around 8 p.m. you began to take the food from the kitchen out to the people seated outside on the decking area?'

'Yes.'

Saachi looks down at the notes in his notebook. 'And out there were Cerys, her daughter, Lowri, Harry Collard, Zoe Collard and their son, Charlie?'

'Yes, that's right,' Lucia agrees.

Saachi takes a few seconds and then asks, 'How did they all seem?'

'Seem?' Lucia frowns as she doesn't understand what he means.

'Were they all having a good time? Were they happy?' Saachi explains. 'Or was there any arguing or bad feeling maybe?'

Lucia hesitates. She knows what she'd seen from inside the villa. Harry rowing with Charlie and Lowri and then getting up and walking away.

'Please, anything, however small you might think it is, it might help us find out who did this to Harry,' Saachi explains.

Lucia doesn't want to lie. After all, the eighth command-ment in the bible is 'Thou shall not bear false witness.' And it's not as if she particularly likes serving food to rich English people who are sitting in what is essentially her villa.

'I saw that there was an argument between Harry, his son and Lowri,' she says.

'Do you know what the argument was about?' Saachi asks.

'I'm sorry but no,' she admits.

Saachi turns to Lorenzo. 'Did you see this argument?'

Lorenzo shakes his head. 'No. I was busy cooking.'

Saachi looks back at Lucia. 'And what happened after this argument?'

'Harry got up from the table and left,' Lucia says.

'He was angry then?'

'Yes.'

'Did anyone go after him?' Saachi asks.

'No,' Lucia replies. 'Everyone stayed at the table.'

'Did you see where Harry went?'

'Yes.' Lucia nods. 'He went down the step to the pool. Then took the pathway that leads down the hill... and so then I couldn't see him anymore.'

'And did you see Harry again that evening?' Saachi says.

Lucia shakes her head. 'No.'

Saachi glances over to Lorenzo who is still fidgeting. 'What about you? Did you see Harry after that point in the evening?'

'Sorry, no,' Lorenzo says.

'And while you've been at the villa, have you noticed any other rows or arguments between Harry and anyone?' Saachi asks them both.

Lucia thinks for a moment. 'No.'

Saachi taps his pen against his notepad and looks at Lucia. 'And you grew up here. Is that correct?'

'Yes,' Lucia says. 'I grew up in this house.'

'Right,' Saachi says with interest. Then he turns to Lorenzo. 'But you're not from here?'

'No,' Lorenzo replies.

Lucia can see Lorenzo's anxiety increase.

'Where are you from?' Saachi asks casually.

'Naples,' Lorenzo replies.

Lucia can feel her pulse starting to quicken.

'Naples?' Saachi raises an eyebrow. 'Long way from home, then?'

'Yes,' Lorenzo says quietly.

'You prefer it here?' Saachi says.

Lorenzo nods. 'Yes. Very much so.'

Saachi frowns as if he's deep in thought.

Lucia's breathing is now shallow and quick. She's scared that Saachi is going to ask Lorenzo more about his background. If he decides to do any checks, then Lorenzo's past might surface. And that would be disastrous.

There is an uncomfortable silence.

Saachi gives them both a polite nod, takes his phone and then gets to his feet.

'Right, that's all I need for now,' he says as he reaches into his shirt pocket, takes out a contact card and hands it to Lorenzo. 'But please let me know if you do think of anything else.'

'Yes, of course.'

Lucia watches as Saachi goes and then glances at Lorenzo. She can see the fear in his eyes.

She feels the same fear.

If they dig into Lorenzo's past, they will discover he is wanted for questioning in connection with a murder.

TWENTY-SIX

CERYS

Four Years Before – Thursday, 19 December 2019

I come out of Earl's Court Tube station and up onto the main road. It's a cold, wet night so I put up my umbrella. The traffic is heavy on the Earl's Court Road and the air thick with exhaust fumes. A double-decker bus hits its air brakes which hiss loudly close to where I'm walking and startle me for a second. Commuters are weaving their way along the pavement in both directions, hurrying to get to their destinations.

Taking a left, I begin to make my way through the side streets. I have my rucksack over my right shoulder. The huge Georgian houses of Kensington loom on both sides of the residential roads. Most are three storey, with steps leading up from pavement level to their grand front doors. I don't know exactly how much they are worth but I do know it runs into millions. Some of the windows have twinkling Christmas decorations. Through others, I can see the tasteful fairy lights on Christmas trees.

Taking the scrap of paper from my pocket, I check the address again. Barkstone Mews. It's a bit of a weird one.

Melanie from the South London Holistic Clinic asked me to go to a party with her. She said that one of her clients from the clinic asked her to go and she didn't want to go on her own. I said that I'd go for a few drinks and meet her there. I like Melanie. She's very down to earth but I fear she's a little naive sometimes.

I yawn. I started the day with a 6.30 a.m. yoga class and I've been back to back since then with classes and reflexology clients. I don't have a choice. We're struggling financially and because my feckless husband swans around like he's Norman Mailer and brings in peanuts, I'm the main breadwinner. And Christmas is just round the corner.

Eventually I turn down Barkstone Mews. It's one of those quaint nineteenth-century London mews that you see in period films or films by Richard Curtis. Apart from the Christmas lights at various windows, the mews is dark. The cobblestones are uneven, wet and a bit slippy. It's also eerily quiet. In fact, it's spooking me out a little.

Number 6 is over in the left-hand corner. Even in the darkness, I can see that it's been painted a pastel blue. The house to the right is a dove grey and the one opposite a powder pink. There's a convertible Mercedes parked outside with its roof up.

I compose myself and knock on the door. I can hear loud voices and music from inside. A few seconds later, an attractive man in his forties – dark hair, twinkly eyes, nicely dressed – answers the door. He's holding a bottle of beer.

'Hi,' he says in a confident public school voice.

'I'm looking for Melanie,' I explain with a polite smile. 'I'm her friend Cerys.'

'Oh right,' he says. 'I'm Jasper.'

There is booming male laughter from down the hallway and a shout.

'It's A Beautiful World' by Noel Gallagher's High Flying Birds is playing. She can hear that the party is in full swing.

'Great, great,' Jasper says and then gestures. 'Come in, come in. Melanie's already here.'

Jasper gives her a smile. 'Can I get you a drink?'

A drink? Maybe the only way to get through this is to have a drink. Soften the edges.

'Vodka and soda, if you've got it,' I reply as I follow Jasper along the tastefully decorated hallway towards what looks like a huge kitchen and living area.

'No problem,' Jasper says.

A woman in a cocktail dress snorts a line of cocaine from a small mirror and hands it, along with a rolled-up £50 note, to Jasper.

'Here you go, darling,' she says, rubbing her nostrils.

I take a deep breath to try and compose myself. I'm feeling incredibly uncomfortable.

As I turn to go and find Melanie, a man holds out a glass. 'You look like you need a glass of Champagne,' he says as he thrusts it into my hand.

I take it and shrug. 'Erm, yes. Great. Thank you.'

TWENTY-SEVEN

CERYS

Monday
2.32 p.m.

It's been an hour since the last of the police officers left my villa. Not for good, obviously. Detective Saachi made that abundantly clear. He told me that the forensics team would be back in the morning. There's various questions that are outstanding. Harry's mobile phone still hasn't been found. Maybe the killer took it? I can't believe that this is what is whizzing around my head at the moment. The murder weapon (although that's not exactly how Saachi put it), is still missing. I can't quite remember what he said now. I've had a few drinks during the day so far to keep me comfortably numb. Comfortably numb? The phrase rings a bell in my head. It's a song or an album by someone, isn't it? I dredge my addled memory for a second or two. Pink Floyd, isn't it?

I used to recall facts like that in a millisecond.

A head full of a million useless facts, Nick used to say in his usual pompous tone. *God, what a prick.* But that ability to pull those 'useless facts' from my cerebral filing system seems to have dwindled in recent years. I blame my 'dwindling' levels of oestrogen. The bloody perimenopause. Brain fog. Sometimes I reach for the simplest of words and it's just not there anymore. The other day I couldn't remember the word 'umbrella'. I ummed and ahhed like a moron, clicking my fingers as if that would help. My mother's generation never even mentioned the word 'menopause', let alone the preceding years of peri-menopause. That generation didn't get much further than whispering, 'She's going through the change, dear.' Jesus!

I look up into the azure sky and feel the heat on my face. I'm sitting up on my favourite wicker sofa. Lowri has brought up a sunlounger and is lying in the shade, although a few shards of sunlight have penetrated the tall, slender row of dark green cypress trees. There's a snippet of light on her face which highlights the troughs and hollows of her beautiful cheekbones, nose and chin. I have a sudden urge to draw her. Not take a photograph. I'd like to sketch her with chalk and charcoal. White chalk for the highlights of her nose, chin and cheeks, charcoal for the hollows of her eyes, her nostrils and around her mouth. I used to love drawing and sketching. I took A-level art but my parents made me promise that I wouldn't go to art college like some of my friends. They said that teenagers who went to art college took drugs, did no work or ended up in bands.

I take a sip of my vodka and tonic. I've made a show of only pouring one measure, telling Lowri that I won't get drunk today. She's heard it all before.

I look over at her and say, 'I'm not sure what I'm supposed to be doing.'

It feels so very strange to be sitting in this beautiful place, with this stunning view, after the terrible thing that's happened.

'I don't think there's anything we can do, is there?' Lowri says in a reassuring tone. 'We've been told to stay put and not go anywhere for the time being.'

'I know,' I say. 'I felt like we were suspects or something.'

Lowri doesn't answer.

'Have you seen Zoe or Charlie?' I ask. 'I was trying to give them a bit of space but maybe I should go and see if they need anything or if there's anything I can do.'

'I saw them walking down the hill a bit,' Lowri replies. 'I'm guessing they just want to be together at the moment.'

'Yes,' I reply and take another sip of my drink. 'Of course.'

'You shouldn't be drinking anything,' Lowri says as she looks over and points. I didn't know she was watching me that carefully.

'Jesus, Lowri,' I sigh. 'You know what's happened today. It's been horrific. If I have to have one vodka to cope, then I don't think you should give me a hard time.'

I feel bad at pretending to be frustrated at her because I've probably had the best part of ten vodkas since breakfast. But I have to keep up the pretence, however exhausting.

Lowri shakes her head at me. 'You shouldn't be drinking anything at all, Mum. You're...' She then pauses as if she doesn't really want to say it. There's still such a stigma attached to that label.

I look over at her. I feel a little sting of hurt as I know what she's going to say. 'An alcoholic? You see, darling, I'm not sure that I really am. I know I drink too much. But I give up for weeks and months at a time. And it's not as if I drink every day or drink in the morning.'

Jesus, Cerys, remember what you once heard in an AA meeting? How do you know when an alcoholic is lying?... Their lips move. Ha ha.

'You know none of that is relevant, Mum,' Lowri said. 'I just wish you'd stop drinking full stop before you make yourself really ill or something terrible happens.'

'For God's sake, Lowri,' I groan. 'I don't think that today is the day to give me a lecture on my drinking... again.' I tap my glass. 'One vodka, that's it. I promise.'

Lowri gets up off the sunlounger. 'Mum, you were completely hammered last night.'

'So was Zoe. And we were having a nice time,' I reply, suddenly aware that I sound like a scolded teenager talking to their parent.

'I got up at one point and you weren't even in your bed,' Lowri says. 'Where the hell were you?'

'I think I was sick a couple of times,' I say, but it's all such a blur. 'Was the bathroom light on?'

'I don't know,' Lowri replies. She's getting tetchy with me. I don't blame her. I'm a terrible mother sometimes and I hate myself for it.

'I think that wild boar stew was too rich for me,' I say. 'You know how weak my stomach is.'

Lowri looks at me. 'Wild boar stew? Yes, that'll be it, Mum. You keep telling yourself that.'

She grabs her things from the sunlounger and walks away with a calm disappointment. It's far harder to see her like this than when she's angry.

'Lowri?' I call out gently with a pained expression. Our roles are now reversed. I'm the child seeking the approval or attention of a parent.

'What, Mum?' she asks with a shrug, trying not to get irate.

'Where are you going?'

'For a nap,' she says as she continues to walk away.

'Good idea,' I say as I reach for my glass again.

TWENTY-EIGHT

ZOE

2.35 p.m.

Zoe and Charlie are sitting quietly on a bench in the shade. Zoe unscrews the cap of the water bottle and takes a sip. Her head feels fuzzy and numb. Everything feels numb. It feels like the time the doctor gave her some diazepam for her back and she walked around in a daze for a few days.

'Are you okay?' Zoe asks Charlie as she puts her hand on his shoulder and then smooths his hair away from his lovely face. For a moment, she can see Harry in his features. The strong nose and jawline. It's heartbreaking.

Charlie nods, sits forward and then looks down at the dusty ground at their feet.

Zoe looks over at him. There's two dark flecks of something on Charlie's thigh, just above his kneecap.

'What's that?' Zoe asks.

Charlie looks at them and shrugs. 'I don't know.' He licks his finger and rubs his skin. They turn a slightly red colour.

'It looks like blood,' Zoe remarks.

'Oh, I had a nosebleed,' Charlie says as he rubs the marks away.

Zoe looks at him. 'When was that?'

'After you went to bed,' Charlie explains. 'It was nothing.'

There is silence.

Zoe looks down at her toes. They're painted a minty blue-green. The girl at the salon told her they looked great but Zoe feared they were a bit too much. They had made her self-conscious but Harry hadn't even noticed. She had just wanted him to say how nice they looked, like any normal husband would. Yet all that seemed pathetically trivial now. He was gone.

Then she thinks of Harry tackling an intruder, being stabbed and then falling into the pool. She can't bear to imagine his last few seconds of life. It's too much. Floundering in the pool, fighting for life...

Taking an audible breath, she feels overwhelmed by anxiety. The stifling, oppressive heat is making her feel suffocated.

Silence.

Zoe's voice drops to a whisper. 'I'm going to have to start telling people.'

'Sorry?' Charlie gives her a quizzical look.

'I'm going to have to start to tell people what's happened,' Zoe says, the words catching in her throat. She can barely voice it out loud.

'Yeah, I suppose so.' Charlie hesitates, then offers, 'I can ring some people if you like. I can ring Grandma and Granddad.'

Zoe's stomach clenches at the mention of Harry's parents, Barbara and Roger. They have very little to do with them, which is no bad thing. Zoe can't stand her in-laws. She finds them emotionally cold, self-absorbed and selfish. Barbara and Roger spend most of the year at their villa on the Algarve playing golf and socialising with their ex-pat friends. Harry had long ago given up trying to arrange for them to visit. Every date he suggested would always prove 'inconvenient' for some reason or another. The rare occasions they flew back, parties and social gatherings always took precedence over seeing their son and grandchild. Empty promises to visit next time had worn thin.

Zoe feels sorry for Charlie. His paternal grandparents are complete strangers to him. And Zoe's difficult relationship with her own mother means that Charlie rarely sees her parents either. Maybe once or twice a year. It used to break her heart when she stood at the school gates of Charlie's primary school and watched the sheer joy of other children's grandparents picking them up or taking them to the park. She wasn't about to claim that Charlie wasn't fortunate to have the chances he'd been given. After all, he'd had everything he'd ever wanted and she had certainly demonstrated her love for him as much as she could. But the lack of grandparents, and an often absent, hostile and selfish father, meant that she and Charlie often looked to each other for support.

'Did you ever want to send me to boarding school?' Charlie asks out of the blue.

'God no,' she replies. 'Your father said they were "fucking barbaric", to use his exact words. And he would know.'

Charlie nodded. 'Good. I don't know how anyone can do that to their child. Why bother having children if you're going to pack them away for weeks on end.'

'I've no idea,' Zoe admits.

Charlie is deep in thought. 'Dad never really talked about his time at school, did he?'

'No,' she agrees sadly. 'He didn't much.'

She knows Harry felt he had been sent to boarding school by his parents because he had somehow been a disappointment to them as a son. He never wanted to question their decision as this would only make their opinion of him worse. As for the abuse he suffered at the hands of the masters and other pupils,

Harry admitted that to survive it a small but important piece of him had to die.

Then Zoe looks at Charlie.

'You know that I've loved having you at home and watching you grow up. Why would I want to miss all that?'

'Even the grunty, smelly hormonal stage?' Charlie asks.

'Oh, I didn't realise that stage was over,' Zoe tries to joke but the image of Harry as a frightened, abused little boy has disturbed her.

Charlie rolls his eyes. 'Ha ha.'

Then, out of the corner of her eye, she spots something on the ground in between two cypress trees. It's a small black shape.

It looks like a mobile phone.

With a frown, Zoe gets up and walks over to the trees, crouches down and retrieves it.

'What is it, Mum?' Charlie asks anxiously.

It's Harry's.

'It's your dad's phone,' she says, lost in thought as she turns and heads back with it.

'Do you think you should be touching it?' Charlie wonders.

'I don't know,' Zoe replies but it seems strange to leave his phone there without taking it. 'He must have dropped it last night.'

Zoe clicks the screen and types in the security passcode. She tries various permutations.

'You don't know Dad's passcode?' Charlie asks looking surprised.

'It might be your date of birth,' Zoe guesses.

'Really?' Charlie says. He looks almost pleasantly pleased by this information.

'It always used to be,' Zoe says as the screen bursts into life. 'There you go.'

Charlie shifts uneasily. 'Mum, should you really be going into Dad's phone? Won't it piss off that detective?'

'It's fine, darling,' Zoe reassures him. She has a sudden, over-whelming urge to find out who Harry was having an affair with and read the messages.

With trembling fingers, she opens Harry's WhatsApp, and immediately finds the string of messages between Harry and Alex.

Using her index finger, Zoe scrolls the messages back to where they start. As she reads, her heart plummets in her stomach.

> Hi Harry, thanks for getting in touch via my website. My initial consultation fee for psychotherapy is £50. My fees from then on are £70 per 50 minute session. Let me know if you'd like to book something in. Kind regards, Alexander Richardson, BACP (accred) BA Hons (Applied Psych)

Zoe frowns in disbelief. *Harry was seeing a therapist!*

'What are you looking at, Mum?' Charlie asks sounding frustrated.

'Nothing, darling,' Zoe says as breezily as she can, closing down the phone and trying to still her shaking hands. 'You're right. I shouldn't have been poking around in your father's phone. I'll just hand it to the police.'

TWENTY-NINE

LUCIA

2.46 p.m.

Lucia has been standing on the dusty road that leads up to Villa Lucia for about fifteen minutes. She has tucked herself behind a couple of cypress trees with a pair of binoculars. They are scratched and old. In fact, they were her father's, *buonanima* – God rest his soul. She still has the lovely old brown leather case which is battered and worn, but retains that redolent leathery smell. Her father used them to watch birds when she was very little. He had a little book and taught her to identify them as they took it in turns to use the binoculars. His particular favourites were the small squacco herons. He thought their brown plumage combined with the dark strips on their heads and blue-black tip to their beaks made them beautiful. He said they were elegant. Lucia's favourite was the tiny scops owl, which were very difficult to spot as their streaky grey-brown plumage allowed them to blend perfectly into the bark of the trees. She loved their little golden-yellow eyes. Her father said that the owls were symbols of wisdom. He bought her a little ceramic owl for her seventh birthday which she still kept on a window sill next to a framed photograph of herself and her father. However, her uncle insisted that owls were a bad omen and would bring them bad luck.

'What are you looking at?' asks a voice which interrupts her train of thought.

It is Lorenzo.

Lucia hesitates but he can see that the binoculars aren't trained on Villa Lucia and the police operation that is going on up there.

Instead, Lucia has been watching an expensive-looking, black Mercedes C-class saloon that is parked about fifty yards further down the track. Inside are three men who have been looking up at the villa for the past fifteen minutes. They don't seem to be talking and she doesn't like the look of them one bit.

Lucia passes Lorenzo the binoculars and gives him a knowing look. It's too late to pretend that she wasn't spying on the men in the car.

Lorenzo takes a look for himself.

After a few seconds, he turns to her. She can see that he is concerned.

'Who are they?' he asks anxiously.

'I've no idea,' she replies.

'Police?' Lorenzo suggests.

Lucia shakes her head. 'No. Why would three detectives be sitting down there, looking up at the villa?'

'I don't know,' Lorenzo replies with an innocent shrug. Sometimes her husband reminds her of a little boy. For someone who was involved in the criminal world of Naples, Lorenzo seems so incredibly naive. But his boyish charm is one of the things that Lucia loves about him.

Lorenzo puts the binoculars back to his eyes and takes another look.

'Journalists? Or photographers,' he says and then looks at her again. 'Maybe they are here because it's a good story?'

Lucia purses her lips dubiously. 'They don't look like press to me.'

'Well, what do they look like to you?' Lorenzo asks, starting to sound impatient.

Lucia thinks about the men's black hair, their deeply tanned faces and their smart clothes. 'They look like southerners to me. *Terroni*.'

Terroni is a derogatory term Italians from the north use for Italians from the south. *Terroni* refers to people who work on the land and so the implication is that people from the south of Italy are poor, peasants.

Lorenzo's face drops. 'Why would they be here? And why would they be interested in what's going on up there?'

Lucia shrugs. 'I don't know. I am just saying what I think. Maybe I am wrong.'

Before they can continue talking any more, there is the distant sound of an engine starting. The driver revs the powerful engine and the Mercedes turns around on the track and speeds away, throwing a huge dust cloud up into the air.

Lucia and Lorenzo share a look. They have no idea who the men were, but their appearance has unsettled them.

And if they're connected in any way to the Bassilino crime family from Naples, that will spell disaster for them both.

THIRTY

ZOE

7.46 p.m.

Zoe sits outside the villa, watching as the sun slowly disappears below the horizon. She's spent much of the afternoon in bed, attempting to rest or sleep – but she can't. She doesn't know how to be, what to think or how to feel. The despair and grief comes in waves. At the moment, she just feels numb. The world is dreamlike.

She takes a long, deep breath of the warm air. She thinks how lovely it is that the evenings are so warm that you sit out in a dress or shorts and never have to duck in to grab a sweater or blanket. Harry had talked about them buying a place over in Ibiza but they'd never got much further than discussing it.

The noise of the cicadas seems to crescendo as the sun throws a deep orange and pink haze across the horizon. It's stunning. A couple of lights in the villas and farmhouses in the distance have come on in the fading light. The air smells of jasmine and honeysuckle.

And as the sun finally disappears, Zoe realises that the day that she found her husband murdered is coming to an end. It's such a horrible, perplexing thought.

She can't seem to get out of her head the messages from Harry's therapist, Alex. She's angry at herself for assuming they were from a woman that Harry was having an affair with. It's filling her with terrible guilt and remorse. Her stomach twists at the thought of it.

What if I'd just confronted Harry and allowed him to explain? Why did I just assume it was a woman? Harry died with me hating him for what he'd done.

Another voice in her head tries to rationalise it. She suspected Harry of having affairs for years. It wasn't a huge stretch of the imagination to believe the message was from a woman he was cheating on her with, was it?

But what if Harry had turned a corner? He was going to a therapist to try to unravel the psychological damage of his child-hood. But I didn't give him a chance to explain. I could see that he was making more of an effort on the holiday.

'How are you holding up?' A voice interrupts her spiralling thought.

It's Cerys.

'I'm okay,' Zoe says but she feels exhausted by the continuous chatter in her head. 'Sort of. You know... I just wish I knew what had happened last night. I keep going over it.'

Cerys nods sympathetically. 'Of course. I know it's probably not much comfort, but so do I.' Cerys has a stainless steel wine cooler with a bottle of rosé in it and two glasses. 'I took the liberty of bringing this with me. Thought you might need it.'

'Yes, that's a good idea,' Zoe replies with a half smile. 'I haven't had anything to drink since the police left.'

'No, neither have I.' Cerys settles into the reclining chair next to her. 'But it's been one hell of a day.'

'Yes,' Zoe says quietly.

Cerys glances over, a flash of guilt crossing her face. 'Sorry, I mean... obviously it's been a million times worse for you and Charlie...'

Zoe shakes her head, mustering a faint smile as Cerys takes the wine and pours her a glass. 'It's okay, Cerys. I knew what you meant. We're all in shock, aren't we?'

'Yes,' Cerys replies as she hands her the wine. 'Here you go.'

'Thank you,' Zoe says. 'You've been so incredibly kind today.'

Cerys shrugs. 'I can't imagine what you and Charlie must be going through.'

Zoe then looks directly at her. 'I found Harry's iPhone.'

'Did you?' Cerys's eyes widen. 'Where?'

'Down by that bench where I think Lowri hides herself away. It was just on the ground between two trees. I'm amazed I spotted it.'

'Have you told the police?' Cerys asks.

Zoe nods. 'I'll give it to them in the morning.'

'Is it still there, or did you pick it up?' Cerys asks.

Zoe pulls a face. 'I picked it up. Charlie told me that I shouldn't. I suppose I should have just left it where it was but...' She hesitates. She's feeling a little awkward.

Cerys waits patiently for her to continue.

'I put Harry's code in and opened up the phone. I wanted to see if there were any more messages from the woman I thought Harry was having an affair with,' Zoe explains, hoping that Cerys doesn't judge her too much.

'Oh right.' Cerys looks surprised. 'And were there?'

'That's the thing,' Zoe says tentatively. 'I got it wrong. The message I saw was from a therapist that Harry was seeing.'

'Oh God,' Cerys says with a frown. 'Really?'

'I feel terrible.' Zoe shakes her head.

Cerys narrows her eyes. 'From what you told me last night, it doesn't sound like Harry was an angel. I know that might not be the right thing to say after today, but...'

'He wasn't,' Zoe agrees sadly. 'But this morning, there were a couple of moments where I actually thought Harry had got what he deserved for treating me so badly and cheating on me.' She takes a breath as her eyes fill with tears. She doesn't know where the emotion has come from. It's as if it's just crept up on her. 'Isn't that a shocking thing to say?' she says with a sniff as she wipes her cheek.

'Hey.' Cerys reaches over and puts a comforting hand on her shoulder. 'It's really not. When I found out that Nick was cheating on me, there were moments when I was so full of rage that I really did want to kill him.'

Zoe sighs. 'Yeah, hell hath no fury and all that, eh?'

THIRTY-ONE

LOWRI

7.55 p.m.

Lowri sits propped up against the pillows of her bed. She's watching a film on her laptop hoping it will distract her but she can barely concentrate. She takes a puff of the minty vape and then reaches for a bottle of beer on her bedside table. It's her third. She needs to numb her head after all that's happened in the past twenty-four hours. It feels like some terrible dream that she's going to wake up from.

Earlier that afternoon, Lowri had called her dad, Nick, to tell him what had happened to Harry at the villa. She felt she had to tell him. It's only a matter of time before he'll see it splashed across the media. She explained that none of them could leave the area until the police allowed them to. She didn't tell him that Harry had attacked her. Despite her reassurances, her dad told her that he was jumping on a plane and would be there soon.

Her heart sank. She didn't want him there. One of the main reasons she had come to Italy was to get away from his controlling, smothering behaviour. He claimed it was him just being a protective father. But he demanded to know where she was and who she was with every time she went out. It was exactly the same as he had been with her mum. She also knows how her mum will react to her dad's arrival. It will put her into an anxious tailspin.

A figure appears at her doorway. It's Charlie. He looks tired and lost.

'Hi,' she says. She just can't imagine what he's going through. She doesn't know how she'd cope if she ever lost her dad like that.

'Hey,' Charlie mumbles. 'Have you seen my mum?'

'I think she's talking to Mum on the far side of the villa.' Lowri uses a hand to point in that direction. 'How are you doing?'

Charlie shrugs. 'I don't really know, to be honest. It's really hard not knowing what happened to my dad last night.'

'Of course it is.' Lowri then holds up a pre-rolled spliff she'd made about an hour ago. 'I've got this if you think it might help a bit.'

Charlie thinks for a few seconds, nods and approaches. 'Yeah, sounds good. I don't think I could feel any worse.'

He sits down at the end of the bed as she lights the twisted paper end, puffs and takes a deep drag.

She looks at him. *He looks broken and so sad*, she thinks as her heart goes out to him.

'I don't know about you,' she says, 'but I don't think I can cope with being completely sober and straight today.'

'No,' Charlie agrees as he takes the spliff from her and takes a long drag. He gestures to the laptop. 'What are you watching?'

'*Rye Lane*.'

'I haven't seen it,' Charlie says. 'Is it any good?'

'Yeah, not bad,' she tells him. Then she shifts over on her bed and points to the space next to her. 'You can sit here if you want to watch?'

Charlie is hesitant. Lowri wonders if she's been too forward.

'Yeah, okay,' he says as he moves across the bed to sit beside her.

Lowri can feel a little pulse of excitement. She wonders if that's at all appropriate on a day like today.

Charlie looks at her. 'I told that detective that I didn't see my dad after he left.'

Lowri nods with a serious expression, drags on the spliff and hands it to Charlie. 'You were right. We shouldn't tell anyone about what happened when your dad came in here last night.'

'No.' Charlie nods and then blows smoke from his mouth. He hands it back to her.

Lowri takes a final drag and stubs it out.

When she turns back to look at him, Charlie's eyes are full of tears.

'Hey, you okay?' She reaches down and touches the back of his hand.

He nods and blinks. 'Sorry, I...'

'You don't need to apologise,' Lowri reassures him.

Charlie shakes his head, his body shuddering as he sobs. 'I didn't mean...'

Lowri frowns. She doesn't know what he's talking about.

Then Charlie turns and looks directly at her with his watery eyes. 'I saw him.'

'Okay.' Lowri is still none the wiser.

'I saw my dad later,' Charlie explains. 'After he attacked you.'

'What?' Lowri frowns. 'Did you?'

Charlie nods. 'He tried to apologise for hitting me but I told him to fuck off.'

'Where was this?' Lowri asks.

'He was sitting by the pool,' Charlie tells her, choking. 'I said some horrible things to him. I told him that I wished he wasn't my father.'

SIMON MCCLEAVE

Lowri nods. 'It's all right...' However, she feels a little conflicted after what Harry did to her last night. Charlie shouldn't feel at all guilty.

Charlie looks scared. 'But I didn't have anything to do with what happened... You know.'

'Of course you didn't,' Lowri assures him.

Charlie's eyes widen as if she doesn't believe him. 'I didn't. I promise. When I left he was just sitting by the pool smoking a cigar.'

'It's okay.' Lowri holds Charlie's gaze, her eyes locked into his. 'I believe you.' Her fingers gently graze the contours of his cheek. She feels her skin fizz as she touches him.

'Do you?' Charlie asks.

'Yes,' she replies.

'I'm just really frightened,' Charlie says. His whole body seems to be shaking a little with the emotion of it.

'Have you told your mum?' she says.

'No.' Charlie sounds even more scared. 'I don't want to. I don't want anyone to know except you.'

'That's fine,' Lowri says gently as her fingers brush against his hair. 'I'm not going to tell anyone.'

'Promise?'

She gives him an earnest look. 'I promise.'

He looks into her eyes, moves forward and kisses her very gently on the lips.

'Oh God, sorry,' Charlie mutters awkwardly as he moves away. 'I don't know why I did that.'

Lowri smiles at him. 'It's fine.'

She leans in and kisses him back, gently then harder.

Then they're moving together, hands around each other as the kissing becomes more intense.

Lowri lifts her T-shirt over her head. She wants to get lost in having sex and she can see that Charlie does too.

And that's fine.

THIRTY-TWO

CERYS

Twelve Months Earlier – Friday, 8 July 2022

Today is the day. Today is the beginning of the rest of my life, I tell myself as I settle in a wicker sofa with soft plum-coloured cushions, carefully positioned in the shade, just to the left-hand side of *my villa*.

Well, it will be completely mine in a few minutes – hopefully.

At the moment, I only own half.

My villa? I can't believe it. I'm so incredibly excited that I can feel the adrenaline coursing around my veins.

I sit back and look at Martina Lenzini, who works for Proprieta Azienda Toscana – the Tuscany Property Company.

The sofa creaks a little as I shift my weight. The tightly wound bamboo is readjusting and I wonder if it's because I'm too heavy. I've always been worried about my weight. It yo-yos and I'm never happy with it. Maybe it's because I'm starting to think that I'm perimenopausal. At forty-three, it's definitely possible. I read somewhere that a woman gains one and a half pounds every year once she's perimenopausal. I feel like I'm gaining double that.

'If you could just sign here, please?' Martina says in her beautifully sexy Italian accent.

'Of course,' I reply in my own accent that still has a hint of the nasal notes of north-east Wales. As far as I'm aware, that's never been a sexy accent. It's a hybrid of the guttural catarrh sound of Merseyside along with the clipped throatiness of a solid North Wales accent. Frankly it's hideous and I'm glad it's virtually gone. I guess the years of mixing with the London chattering classes has washed it away. The accent reminds me of hanging out in Wrexham town centre and hearing badly dressed women pushing prams and greeting each other with 'All right, cock?' with all the subtlety of a foghorn.

Oh God, I sound like such a snob.

'Here we go,' I say softly under my breath as I scribble *Cerys Williams* on the final contracts. I give Martina a friendly smile but she doesn't return it. She's uber-businesslike. In fact, she's intimidated me through the whole process of buying Villa Lucia outright. She makes me feel 'less than'. Not deliberately. It's just that anyone with a modicum of intelligence and attention to detail seems to have that effect on my self-esteem. The story of my life.

Martina tucks a strand of coal-black hair behind her ear. She's in her late thirties. Her hair is chin-length, cut into a fashionable bob that seems to slightly accentuate her pointy face. Her navy trouser suit is immaculate. Nails, jewellery, sunglasses and watch are tasteful. But, if I'm honest, with a different haircut, clothing and accessories, she might be quite ordinary-looking.

I'm being a little bitchy and judgy.

I sit back for a moment. I can feel the tension in my stomach. It's where my anxiety always seems to settle itself. The final contract is signed. Now it's just a question of the money transferring and Villa Lucia will be completely mine.

Grabbing her mobile phone from the table, Martina pushes her sunglasses up on top of her head to look at the screen.

I wonder what she's like in bed. I imagine her having wild, abandoned sex, shouting and shuddering.

Then Martina looks over at me and I feel my cheeks hot with embarrassment. I fear that she knows exactly what I was thinking.

'The money has transferred,' she informs me in her composed voice.

And for a minute, I can't quite believe it.

I should probably give myself a pat on the back. A mixture of inherited money, divorce settlement, savings and a hefty mortgage has bought me this little piece of paradise. Of course, I'm going to continue renting out the main part of the villa in peak season as I've been doing for the past twelve months. I can't live on thin air.

It's been a year since my husband, Nick, and I bought Villa Lucia together and moved out here. A year since I thought this beautiful villa would save our marriage. But it didn't. And now Nick is in London and I'm buying him out of his share and so the villa belongs – lock, stock and barrel – to me.

'That's great,' I say, trying to hide my utter delight.

'Congratulations, Cerys,' she says with a half smile.

'Thanks.' I think I have a slightly baffled look on my face as Martina gets up to go. Of course, I'm excited and nervous. But there's also an element of sadness that I'm having to do this on my own now.

'Good luck.'

I stand up and move towards her. 'Thanks for everything. You've been a star,' I say as we kiss cheeks politely. It's all very European.

I watch her walk away up the stone steps that lead to the shaded car parking area.

Bloody hell, Cerys.

Blowing out my cheeks with the enormity of it all, I take a few seconds.

Martina's white BMW pulls away with a noisy crunching of the dry, stony track.

As she disappears into the distance, a long trail of ghostly dust hangs in the air like a sandy fog.

And then I do a little dance on the grass and, for some reason, I hold my arms out horizontally and spin like I'm a child.

Woo-hoo! Welcome to Villa Lucia. My little slice of paradise.

And for once, I actually believe that I deserve it.

THIRTY-THREE

LUCIA

Twelve Months Earlier – Friday, 8 July 2022

Lucia De Nardi watches the sleek white BMW glide past her on the track that leads down from the villa. She waves away the cloud of dust thrown up by the fancy car and narrows her eyes.

That bitch from the property company, she thinks to herself. *Who does she think she is, driving like that?*

Lucia had heard that Martina wasn't even from Tuscany, let alone Chianti. Someone in the village told her she's from Milan! And she knew what people said about the women from Milan. Cold, unemotional, fake and they only eat polenta.

Lucia gazes up at the villa. She can see a figure standing outside.

Cerys.

If she is honest, Lucia has mixed feelings towards Cerys Williams. Even though she resents Cerys buying the villa, she can't help feeling sorry for her sometimes.

Cerys and her pig of a husband, Nick, bought the villa a year ago. Then he left and moved back to London. And now she is there on her own.

Cerys reassured Lucia and her husband, Lorenzo, they would have the same arrangement as before.

Lucia is in charge of cleaning the villa, changing beds, towels and linen on changeover days and getting them laundered. Responsibility for keeping the garden and flowerbeds neat and tidy, as well as cleaning the pool and making sure that the balance of chemicals in the water is correct, falls to Lorenzo. They have the same arrangement with two other villas in the area and that has kept them solvent. Plus Lorenzo is a fantastic cook so sometimes guests ask her and Lorenzo to come and cook a traditionial Tuscan supper. Most of the guests are rich idiots. But Lucia is happy to take their money even though she resents them being there. It sometimes makes her feel better about what had happened to Villa Lucia.

'So, Cerys owns the villa on her own?' asks a deep male voice.

It is Lorenzo.

There's a curiosity to his expression but it vanishes as he turns his head and his eyes flick towards her. His lips twitch at the edges.

'Yes,' she mutters. 'She does.'

Lorenzo looks at the old watch on his tanned wrist. 'What time are we going up there?'

'Eleven,' she replies.

Lucia looks at him knowingly, raises her eyebrow and snorts. 'I wonder if she knows *il malocchio* is up there?'

In Italian folklore, *il malocchio* is an ancient curse. It means 'the evil eye' and causes misfortune, illness or bad luck.

Lorenzo shakes his head and rolls his eyes. 'It's 2022. I'm pretty sure no one believes in stuff like *il malocchio*.'

Lucia feels her anger rising. She finds Lorenzo's indifference to Italian folklore and tradition irritating.

'Well, Cerys should believe it. Think of everything that's happened to her since she moved in,' she growls.

'Maybe it's a new start for her?' Lorenzo suggests.

'I don't think so. Whatever you say, I know my father still watches over Villa Lucia.'

THIRTY-FOUR

LOWRI

Tuesday
7.55 a.m.

Looking in the mirror in her bathroom, Lowri washes her face and begins to clean her teeth. She has a white towel wrapped around her head and another around her body. She heard her mum shuffling around earlier and she guesses she has now headed over to the main villa to be with Zoe.

As she swills her mouth with water, images from the previous night with Charlie pop into her head. There's a little tingle of excitement. They were up to the early hours. Afterwards, they smoked a spliff and drank beer listening to an Amber Mark playlist on Spotify. For a few seconds when she had woken, Lowri had forgotten about Harry and all that had happened. Then it all came tumbling back in a horrible, gut-wrenching, dark mess.

Leaving the bathroom, she pads across the cold stone floor and comes back into the bedroom. Charlie is now awake and propped up on his elbow. He looks deep in thought.

'Hey,' she says, trying to sound casual but feeling a little awkward.

Charlie looks a little sheepish. 'Morning.' He avoids full eye contact.

His hair is tousled, his eyes sleepy and sexy, and the white sheet lies across his nicely defined chest.

'Sleep okay?' she asks, trying to stop herself blushing.

For a moment, there is a glimmer of a smirk and then he looks at her and nods. 'Yeah. Great, thanks.'

She returns his knowing smile.

Charlie sits up on the bed and puts his fingers through his hair.

'I should go and see my mum,' Charlie says as he gestures in the direction of the villa. 'She's probably wondering where I am.'

Lowri pulls a face. 'Oh yeah... Are you going to tell her about...'

'I don't know,' Charlie says with a shrug as he starts to get dressed.

'Might be best not to with everything that's going on,' Lowri suggests.

'Yeah, maybe,' Charlie replies pulling on his T-shirt.

'How is your mum doing?' Lowri asks, shaking her head a little. 'I can't imagine. It's so hard for the both of you.'

'You know she found my dad's iPhone yesterday,' Charlie says as he pulls on his shorts. 'Did I tell you that already?'

'No.' Lowri shakes her head. 'Where was it?'

'Down by your bench. The one where you write music.'

'What was it doing down there?' she wonders.

'No idea. It was just sitting there on the ground between two trees.'

'Maybe your dad dropped it or it fell out of his pocket,' she suggests.

'Maybe,' Charlie says but he has a quizzical expression on his face.

Lowri looks at him. 'What is it?'

'It's just that Mum went over, took the phone and then used a code to open it.'

'Really?' Lowri pulls a face. 'I would have thought that she should have left it where it was.'

'That's what I told her,' Charlie says.

'Was she looking for something?' Lowri asks.

'I'm not sure,' he admits.

Taking the towel from her hair, Lowri looks over at Charlie as he laces his trainers. Then she notices that he has something underneath his nostril.

It's blood.

Charlie notices her expression.

'What is it?' he asks.

She points. 'You've got blood...'

'Oh right.' Touching it, Charlie looks at the blood on his finger. 'Must be a nose bleed. My dad punched me pretty hard the other night.'

Silence.

Charlie stands, looking flustered.

He's acting really strangely all of a sudden, Lowri thinks.

'Are you okay?' she asks, stepping forward towards him.

'Yeah, fine. Sorry, I'll go over to the villa and get cleaned up. See you later,' Charlie mumbles as he steps back from her, grabs the rest of his stuff and leaves hurriedly.

Lowri watches him go, a feeling of unease washes over her. What is Charlie hiding?

THIRTY-FIVE

LUCIA

7.55 a.m.

Lucia is using her binoculars to watch the villa and see what is going on. It's her villa. It's her birthright so she must find out. Part of her is intrigued by the murder. She can't say that she is very upset that that man has been killed. He was vile. When she asked Lorenzo what he thought about the Englishman Harry being murdered, Lorenzo just shrugged and said, *Credevo che fosse borioso e arrogante* – I thought he was pompous and arrogant. But does that mean he deserved what happened to him? she wonders. Maybe God works in mysterious ways.

Lucia scours the villa and gardens again. She can still see the red and white police evidence tape sectioning off the pool and the surrounding area. The only thing she has seen so far is Cerys and Lowri walking together from the annexe across to the main villa. She wonders how long they will stay there. Although she doesn't like to admit it, there's also part of Lucia that is pleased at the dark chaos that now surrounds the villa. She wonders if Cerys will now have to sell up. And maybe no one will want to buy it because there has been a murder there. And finally the villa will return to her. But she knows such thoughts are not Christian. In fact, it is written in John 13: 'You shall love thy neighbour as thyself.'

'*Ficcanaso*,' hisses a voice.

It's Lorenzo.

She takes down her binoculars and looks at him. *Ficcanaso* means someone who is a nosy busybody.

'Why are you so interested in that place?' Lorenzo asks angrily.

She frowns as if that's a stupid question. 'You know why.'

Something hasn't been quite right about Lorenzo since that night. He seems a little more snappy and agitated than usual. Maybe it was the men in the car yesterday that spooked him. They still have no idea who they were.

Lorenzo gives an audible sigh and gestures to his workshop. 'I have that door from Villa Travicello to fix.'

Lorenzo and she work for the German owners of Villa Travicello. One of the doors blew closed in the wind and all the glass smashed so Lorenzo is fixing it. Jurgen Klose is the name of the owner. He is some big-shot banker millionaire. He is also *borioso e arrogante* like the Englishman Harry.

Lorenzo walks away towards the workshop. Lucia admires his body from behind. She loves the fact that she still finds him attractive even after years of marriage. They are lucky like that.

Wandering up the stony driveway, Lucia enters the cooler darkness of her cottage. Behind the front door is a line of iron hooks. A flat black cap hangs from one of them. It was her father's cap. When she remembers him, he is almost always wearing it. She keeps the cap there as a reminder of him. The cottage is full of little reminders of her *papino*.

Lucia comes into the kitchen and begins to tidy up. She brushes up some of the papery thin skin of some garlic cloves. They are so light that they float in the small draught that she creates with the dustpan and brush. Today she is planning on baking some bread. A loaf of focaccio for starters. Lorenzo says that she makes the best bread that he has ever tasted.

Lucia sets about clearing the countertops to her right. There are two hessian shopping bags that contain some leftovers of the meal that they cooked for the English family up at the villa.

Opening up the bags, she grabs the tomatoes and takes them to the bowl where they will sit until used. She cannot understand some of the guests up at the villa who put their tomatoes in the fridge. They are idiots.

She returns to the bag and goes to grab the onions.

But there's a noise. Something metallic inside the bag.

She moves the onions and sees something.

It's a kitchen knife from the villa. It's in two pieces – the blade and the handle. And the blade is stained and bent out of shape.

THIRTY-SIX

ZOE

8.55 a.m.

Zoe can feel Harry's hand tight around her jaw. He's holding it so tightly that she's scared that her jaw bone is going to crack under the vice-like pressure. Harry is in her face. Shouting, screaming something. She can't seem to make out what he's saying. His mouth is foaming with fury. Her heart is thumping hard against her chest like someone is pounding it with a hammer.

Behind Harry, she can see the shimmering surface of Villa Lucia's infinity pool. Above that, the inky-black sky is dotted with silver stars. In any other circumstances, this would be perfect. But Harry is acting as if he wants to kill her. She's been on the receiving end of his temper tantrum before but she doesn't think she's ever seen him this angry before. It's as if he's completely out of control. Then Harry's open hand goes back, almost as if in slow motion, before swinging towards her face. She takes a step back to avoid the slap and Harry stumbles forward.

Zoe wakes with a start. Her pulse is racing, the carotid

artery thudding rhythmically in her eardrum. She takes a deep breath to try and calm herself and looks up at the high ceiling. It's not home. It's not the two-million-pound, six-bedroomed detached house in Dulwich Village. It's Villa Lucia.

And Harry is gone. He's dead.

The realisation hits her hard. The enormity of what's happened. And even though she's just dreamed that Harry was attacking her, her gut-wrenching loss brings tears to her eyes.

How has this happened? He was there in my dream only seconds ago. It felt so real. And now he's lying on some slab in a mortuary in Florence.

The thought of that image of Harry's naked body lying there makes her feel phyically sick.

Zoe sits up in bed and checks her phone. Messages of condolence from family and friends via text, Whatsapp and Facebook. Word has travelled like wildfire. She doesn't have the wherewithal to deal with it.

Beside her bed is a notebook that she has brought with her. Someone had recommended daily journaling as a way to emotional well-being.

The bloody irony, she thinks as she looks over at it. Instead, she spent the early hours writing a list of things she needs to do and other people she needs to contact about Harry's death.

I need coffee, she thinks. To say that she slept fitfully would be an understatement.

Dropping her legs over the side of the bed, she drags herself up and feels a little dizzy. She heads for the bathroom and goes to grab a toothbrush. Harry's dark red toothbrush is next to hers. His favourite colour to match the football kit of his beloved Arsenal. The sight of it brings the pain of her loss back in a horrible wave of grief.

'Oh, Harry,' she whispers as her eyes fill with tears.

Zoe wipes away her tears with a towel, trying to compose herself and avoid looking in the mirror. Often she despises the person looking back at her. She doesn't know if that's weird but she's been like that since she was a teenager.

She splashes her face with water. Once she's had coffee, she will come back and have a shower and get dressed properly. Maybe put on some make-up to make herself feel better. She knows that her eyes are puffy from crying.

She grabs her phone and the notebook and heads out.

Opening the bedroom door, Zoe pads along the cold stone floor down the hallway. Maybe she should go and check on Charlie? Or maybe it's best to let him sleep in. Like her, he's probably not slept very well.

The wooden door to the outside is open and sunlight is streaming through onto the tiled floor. Hearing voices from somewhere, Zoe goes out onto the patio and looks around.

Out of the corner of her eye, she notices something has been draped over the back of a wicker chair. It's the apricot-coloured maxi dress that she'd worn the evening before last.

That's where it is, she thinks, realising she hadn't seen it since then.

As she picks it up, Zoe sees that it's ripped at the shoulder. There are also a few dark splashes of what looks like red wine on it. She peers at the dress in confusion.

How the hell did that happen? she wonders. Did she actually get so drunk that she stripped off before going to bed? It's all such a blur.

Zoe's annoyed. It's an expensive dress and one of her favourites. Even Harry said she looked nice in it which was a miracle. The problem is that she doesn't remember going to bed that night so she has no idea how it got out here or how it got ripped. She decides to pop it back in her bedroom until she decides whether it can be salvaged.

Heading back down the hallway, Zoe arrives in the huge open-plan kitchen. She sees that Charlie is already sitting at the oak kitchen table nursing a coffee and staring into space.

'Hey,' she says and walks over to give him a hug. 'How did you sleep?'

'Not great,' he admits.

'No, neither did I,' she says as she looks at him with concern. 'I've had lots of messages from people. They're all asking how you're doing.'

Charlie nods but she's not sure that he's taken in what she's said. He's looking outside and lost in thought.

There is the echoing sound of footsteps and Cerys comes in from the hallway.

'Hi,' she says. She looks at them both with a concerned expression. 'How are you both holding up? Did you get any sleep?'

Zoe pulled a face. 'A bit. But it was fitful.'

Charlie doesn't answer.

'How about some fresh coffee?' Cerys suggests.

'Please,' Zoe says as she perches on one of the rustic wooden stools that are placed around the kitchen island. 'I'm just not sure what I'm meant to do with myself.'

'It's difficult, isn't it?' Cerys says, loading the coffee machine with a pod.

'I spent some of the night texting family and friends back. Everyone is in such shock but they're being so kind. A few of them have offered to fly out here to support us but I've told them there's no need.'

'Do you want me to get you the details of the British Consulate in Florence?' Cerys asks.

'I've got it already, thanks,' Zoe replies. 'I've written a list of things I need to do.'

Cerys nods as she brings over a coffee. 'Here you go... Keeping busy is probably a good idea.'

'Thanks,' Zoe says and then she closes her eyes as they fill with tears. It all feels too much.

Cerys gives her a hug. 'If there's anything you need, or anything you want me to do, please just ask.'

'Thank you,' Zoe whispers as she attempts to pull herself together.

She senses Charlie looking over at her. She meets his gaze and says very quietly as she shakes her head, 'I just saw your dad's toothbrush... I can't believe he's gone.'

'No,' Charlie mutters under his breath, but he seems detached.

'I'll be back in one second,' Cerys says and she walks out of the kitchen to the hallway.

Zoe notices a change in Charlie's manner. It's as if he's brooding on something.

'Are you okay?' she asks.

Charlie shrugs. 'I just think we need to get some kind of perspective here. Dad wasn't exactly a saint.'

For a second, Zoe can't quite believe what Charlie is saying.

'What are you talking about, Charlie?' Zoe protests. 'Someone murdered your father!'

'Most of the time, he wasn't a very nice person. You just seem to have forgotten all that,' Charlie says with a frustrated shrug.

'Whatever your father was,' Zoe says, feeling shocked by what Charlie is implying, 'he didn't deserve to be killed.'

'I just don't think you know what he was capable of,' Charlie snaps. 'He wasn't a good man. You don't know what he got up to when he wasn't at home.'

'Is there something you're not telling me?' Zoe asks. It seems as if Charlie knows more than he's letting on.

'No.' Charlie is speaking quickly, the anger rising in his voice. 'Dad treated you and me badly. He treated everyone like shit, Mum. And sometimes I really did wish him dead.'

'Charlie, that's enough,' Zoe whispers, her voice breaking as tears gather in her throat. 'I can't have this conversation.'

Charlie gets up from the table and looks at her. His anger seems to have changed to disappointment. 'Fine, Mum. Just bury your head in the sand, as always.'

She watches Charlie as he walks towards the glass doors to the outside, slides them open and leaves.

Zoe takes a moment to compose herself. She's hurt by Charlie's words.

Harry did have his good points, she tells herself. *He provided for his family.* Deep down he was a loving father to Charlie – he just struggled to show his love. And that was because he'd been damaged by his own parents. And now she knows he was trying to work on this.

I won't have it that what's happened to Harry is anything other than a horrible, terrible tragedy, she thinks angrily as she feels all the emotion overwhelming her.

Zoe takes a swig of her coffee and tries to calm herself down. Maybe caffeine isn't the thing but she can't survive without a morning coffee.

Cerys comes in with a perplexed look on her face.

'You okay?' Zoe asks.

'Stupid question,' Cerys says with a frown. 'But you haven't seen a MacBook lying around anywhere in the villa?'

Zoe shakes her head. 'Sorry, no. Why?'

'Just that it's missing from the drawer in the hallway,' Cerys explains. Then she goes directly to a drawer in the dresser and pulls it open. 'Shit!'

'What is it?' Zoe asks.

'I have a cash float in here,' Cerys explains. 'I use it to pay Lucia and Lorenzo but it's gone.'

'You're sure?' Zoe asks.

'Yes.' Cerys nods. She's baffled. Then she looks at Zoe. 'It's not much, about a hundred euros, but it's gone. Someone's taken it.'

'Oh gosh,' Zoe says. 'Maybe someone did come in here and

take stuff. And then Harry saw them trying to get away.' The
thought of Harry trying to stop someone who had robbed the
villa and getting killed as a result is suddenly so vivid in her
head it makes her shudder to think about it.

'I'm trying to think if there's anything else,' Cerys says,
thinking out loud. 'My spare car keys were in here. And they're
gone too.'

Silence.

They look at each other.

THIRTY-SEVEN

CERYS

9.33 a.m.

I come out of the front door of the villa and see a car pull up. Detective Saachi gets out. He's wearing designer sunglasses and smart jacket with a crisp, white polo shirt underneath it. He gives me a half wave as he retrieves a briefcase and folders from his boot. Everything about him is very cool, I think. And attractive. I know that's not appropriate but I'm only human. And to be honest, it's been a while and I'm a bit horny.

Oh God, Cerys, that is definitely NOT appropriate.

A few moments later, a windowless, dark navy van with *Forense* written on its side pulls up next to Saachi's car. I assume that this is a Forensics Team.

'*Buongiorno*,' Saachi says in his deep voice as he approaches.

I give him a nod. '*Buongiorno*.'

'Shall we go inside?' Saachi suggests as he points to the villa.

'Yes, of course.' I lead the way. I can feel my anxiety growing but I've promised myself that I'm not going to have a drink until the afternoon. Maybe even the evening. I felt slightly jittery when I first woke up which might have been a little bit of the withdrawals from my drinking. It's hard to tell with everything that's been going on.

As we go inside, the cool air-conditioning hits my face and makes me feel a little better.

We get to the hallway and I can't help but stop and look at him. 'I know you asked me if anything was missing. There is. A laptop, some money and car keys. Sorry, I should have looked a bit more thoroughly.'

There, I've said it. I think it's very important that he knows this as soon as possible.

'Okay.' Saachi's expression implies that this is significant. 'Maybe we can go and sit down. I would like to talk to Mrs Collard as well. There are a few things I need to run through with her this morning. But can you make a list of everything that you think has been taken so I can take that with me? And I need you to show me where the things were taken from so my forensics can examine them and look for prints and DNA.'

I lead him into the living area and we go and sit down where we had the previous day. We don't even discuss it.

'Do you think it's significant?' I ask. I can't help but wonder. It's so horrible to think that someone actually came into the villa to steal things. And that person then killed Harry.

'Possibly, yes,' Saachi replies.

I hear the sound of footsteps and Zoe comes in.

'Mrs Collard,' Saachi says, gesturing for her to sit down on the two-seater sofa.

'Hi there.' Zoe looks drawn and so tired. Poor woman. I can see that she's holding an iPhone in her hand.

'As I was saying, there are a few things that I need to go through with you this morning,' Saachi explains to Zoe. 'I am going to need you all to give a DNA sample and your finger-prints to my forensic team...'

'Really?' Zoe says, looking confused.

'It's completely routine,' Saachi says, trying to reassure her. 'We create what we call an elimination sample. If we really do think someone came here on Sunday night, we have to be able to look for any DNA and fingerprints that don't belong to anyone who was at the villa.'

'Yes,' I say in a confident tone that implies that this makes total sense. I'm trying to get on the right side of Saachi. I just hope that I don't come across as obsequious. I know that I can sometimes be like that and then I hate myself for being too eager to please.

Zoe gives a nod of understanding. She looks relieved by Saachi's explanation.

Saachi then asks, 'I understand that there was a row on Sunday night? Your husband left the table angry?'

Zoe frowns and glances over at me.

'Oh, that,' I say in a nonchalant tone. 'I wouldn't say it was a row. Just a debate. Semantics, that's all.'

Saachi pulls a face. 'Semantics?'

Why did I use the word semantics?

'The use of language,' I explain. 'It really was just a heated discussion. No more than that.'

He nods but it's hard to tell whether my explanation has satisfied him.

Zoe holds up the iPhone she found. 'I managed to find my husband's mobile phone yesterday afternoon.'

Saachi gives her a curious look. 'You found it? Where did you find it?'

Zoe turns and points towards the back of the villa. 'Charlie and I went for a walk down a hill. There's a little spot by a bench. Somehow I managed to see it on the ground between two trees.'

Saachi has a serious expression. He pulls a blue rubber glove from his jacket pocket and a clear evidence bag.

I'm getting the feeling that he's not impressed that Zoe has picked up Harry's iPhone and brought it back to the villa.

Standing up, Saachi takes the phone with his gloved hand and pops it carefully into the clear plastic bag.

'Oh God.' Zoe's face falls. 'Should I have left it where I saw it and not picked it up?' she asks.

Saachi nods. 'Yes, that would have been better. But you must take me to where you found it immediately.'

Zoe looks at me and pulls a face like a scolded schoolgirl. To be honest, I would have left the phone where it was. Maybe it's because I spend my life watching true crime boxsets on Netflix and reading police procedural novels.

Saachi gestures to the doors to the outside. 'Show me, please.'

Zoe and I get up.

THIRTY-EIGHT

LOWRI

9.33 a.m.

Taking a black Public Enemy 'Don't Believe the Hype' shirt from her wardrobe, Lowri pulls it over her black bikini top and stretches it down so it covers most of her denim shorts. She goes over to the end of her bed to retrieve her Hilfiger sliders and notices something on the floor. There's some dry earth and a few pine needles. Then she remembers that's where Charlie kicked off his trainers the previous evening.

'Bloody hell,' she mutters under her breath as she leaves her room and heads for the kitchen where she retrieves a pink plastic dustpan and brush. It's got a picture of Wham! on the handle –she and her mum had found it in a tacky shop in Florence. They'd both thought it was too kitsch not to buy. She returns and sweeps the dirt and needles up and takes them to her bin.

Her mobile phone pings with a notification. It's her dad. She ignores it.

She scrolls through various apps and messages on her

phone. Friends from home who've seen Harry's murder reported on the BBC news. Most of them have Written *WTF!?!* along with asking if she's okay. Then she sees her TikTok app. It strikes her that she hasn't been on it for a few days. In fact, since 'that night'. And then something awful strikes her that makes her stomach lurch.

Fuck. I was recording something in TikTok when Harry came in! I totally forgot about that. Shit.

Going onto her TikTok profile page, she can see that there is a video saved into drafts. It's run for the full ten minutes that the TikTok platform allows and then stopped.

Lowri's hand starts to shake as she wonders what's on the video.

She feels sick as she starts to play it.

There she is in front of the camera, holding her guitar, introducing the song that she plans to post. Then off camera, Harry's voice. As the video continues, Lowri watches herself nervously move across her bedroom. And then Harry comes and sits down on the bed.

Holding her breath, she watches in horror as Harry gets up and circles around as she backs away against the wall. And then he's against her.

Lowri's eyes are full of tears. She can't watch any more. For a moment, she thinks she's going to hyperventilate. As her fingers shake, she presses the button to delete the video and it's gone forever.

Jesus.

Her breathing is quick and shallow. She wipes the tears from her face.

'Are you okay?' asks a voice.

She jumps out of her skin.

Shit!

It's Charlie and he's standing in the doorway – just as his

father did two nights ago. But Charlie is the complete opposite of his father.

'You made me jump!' she says, startled.

'Sorry.' Charlie looks concerned. 'You've been crying,' he says as he sits down on the bed and gently rests his hand on her arm.

'Yeah.' She nods. There is a comfort in having him sit next to her. Then she gestures to her iPhone. 'The other night... I was recording one of my TikTok videos when your dad came here.'

Charlie frowns and then the penny drops. 'You've got a video of what happened?' His face falls.

'Not any more,' she reassures him. 'Don't worry, I've deleted it. I don't want anyone to ever see it.'

'No.' Charlie looks relieved.

'What are our mums up to?'

'They're walking around with that detective,' Charlie explains. 'And there are some sort of forensic people wandering around too.'

'You can stay in here if you like,' Lowri says with a smile as she moves closer to him so that she's nestled into him. She feels better having Charlie with her. 'As long as you haven't got dirty trainers.'

'What?' he says with a confused chortle.

'Doesn't matter.' She laughs. Some of the shock and distress that she felt from seeing the video has dissipated.

She looks at him and their eyes meet. She can feel the spark of attraction between them.

'You're so sweet,' Lowri tells him as she kisses him briefly on the mouth.

Charlie pulls an amused face. 'I'm not sure I want to be sweet.'

Her phone rings and she looks at it. It says *Dad*.

Lowri's mood changes. 'For fuck's sake,' she mutters under her breath.

Her dad keeps ringing her to check that she's okay. She's reassured him that she's all right. In fact, speaking to him on the phone makes her feel more anxious.

Charlie gives her a quizzical look.

'It's my dad,' Lowri explains and immediately feels awkward saying this after Charlie's loss.

'Oh right,' Charlie says but he's clearly none the wiser.

'I know he means well,' Lowri says. 'But there are a limited number of ways I can tell him that I'm all right.'

Charlie looks at her. 'Did you tell him what happened on Sunday night?'

'God, no.' Lowri shakes her head. 'He's overprotective enough already. One of the reasons I moved over here was to get away from having my life micro-managed. He'd catastrophise every time I left the house. Where are you going? Who are you meeting? How are you getting back?'

Charlie raises an eyebrow. 'Sounds suffocating.'

'It is,' Lowri admits as she takes Charlie's hand and they move onto the bed so that they are lying together, propped up on pillows.

For a moment, Charlie reaches over and delicately moves a strand of hair from her face.

'That is literally the opposite of what my dad was like,' he says. 'He had zero interest in anything I was doing.'

There is a poignant silence.

'I'm sorry,' Lowri says softly, reaching out her hand to his face.

'It's fine.' Charlie shrugs. Then he looks at her with a hardened expression. 'There's no point pretending that my dad wasn't a selfish, self-absorbed, predatory bastard.'

'No, of course not,' Lowri agrees quietly. She'd like to open up about her own father's similar behaviour when she was growing up. But she's never told anyone. And it feels too scary to say it.

'I'm not going to rewrite history just because of what's happened to him,' Charlie says in a cold tone.

THIRTY-NINE

ZOE

9.43 a.m.

Zoe, Cerys and Saachi have made their way across the villa gardens, circumventing the areas that have been cordoned off by police evidence tape. No one has said anything. Zoe isn't sure what to say. It's not the place for idle chit-chat and she's concerned that Saachi is annoyed that she didn't leave Harry's phone where she found it. And she certainly isn't about to tell him the real reason why she wanted to grab Harry's phone and look at it. That she suspected he was having an affair only to find out that he'd been messaging his therapist.

Why didn't Harry tell me he was seeing a therapist? The question has been playing over and over in her mind ever since she first read the message on Harry's phone.

As they begin to make their way down the dusty path that takes them down the hill at the back of the villa, Zoe remembers how she'd try to encourage Harry to see a counsellor or therapist on various occasions. He said that he wasn't going to pay someone to sit and listen to him talk. That was ridiculous. People who went to therapists were pathetic, self-absorbed navel-gazers. Zoe wonders what prompted his radical change of heart. Maybe Harry had been in so much pain that he felt desperate and willing to try the one thing he'd always ridiculed.

I just wish he'd told me that he'd started to see someone. It feels like a terrible tragedy that just as Harry had decided to deal with his demons, he'd been taken away. It doesn't seem fair.

The emotion floods up through her whole body and her eyes fill with tears. No, it just doesn't seem fair. Harry wasn't a saint. But he was damaged. And he'd finally found the courage to try and deal with the way he felt and possibly the way he behaved.

As they arrive at the bench, Zoe takes a deep breath to compose herself. The thought of Harry as being vulnerable and in pain has really got to her. It feels like actual physical pain somewhere inside her. She sniffs and wipes her face.

Cerys turns, looks at her and sees that she's been crying. She gives Zoe an empathetic look, comes over and gives her a quick hug.

'Thank you,' Zoe whispers.

That was the thing about grief, it came in waves. Zoe had been reading some stuff online about how to deal with loss. She was relieved to read that it was normal for grief to be compli-cated if the relationship with the deceased had involved both good and bad times. That definitely summed up her and Harry. One article described how the surviving partner could undergo a range of emotions such as sadness, relief, numbness and even gratitude. Zoe had felt comforted by the knowledge that her swings in emotions were quite normal.

Saachi looks at her. 'Can you show me, please?' he asks politely, breaking her train of thought.

'Yes, of course,' Zoe says as she composes herself and then wanders over towards the line of trees. She looks down at where she thinks she picked up the phone. The soil at the base of the tree isn't as dry as you'd imagine and it's dotted with pine needles from the trees above. Zoe eventually points. 'There, I think.'

Saachi crouches down to take a closer look at the ground where she has indicated.

'Here?' he asks.

'Yes, I think so,' Zoe says apologetically. She knows she should have left Harry's phone where she found it.

Cerys gives Zoe a reassuring look. *She's so lovely*, Zoe thinks to herself. Cerys has been so supportive.

Saachi sees something. He takes out a pair of blue forensics gloves and snaps them on. Then he pulls a pen from the inside pocket of his jacket.

Zoe gives Cerys a quizzical look.

'Have you found something?' Cerys asks.

'Possibly,' Saachi mumbles as he uses the pen to move some soil and pine needles.

Zoe takes a step forward to look. 'What is it?'

Saachi stands up, puts the pen back into his jacket and takes off the gloves. Then he looks at them. 'There are some foot-prints there.'

Zoe lowers her eyes to the ground. 'They're probably mine.'

'No, they're definitely not yours, Mrs Collard,' Saachi says, looking down at Zoe's feet. She takes a size four. 'These belong to a man and they are big. My guess is a UK size twelve, but that's just a guess.'

'It can't be Harry's.' Zoe says. 'He took a size nine.'

Saachi shrugs. 'I will let the forensics team take a cast of it and then we'll know.'

FORTY

CERYS

11.58 a.m.

The police have now all gone, thank goodness. They will be back again though so it's only a temporary respite from the anxiety. I'm cleaning the villa's kitchen from top to bottom. It makes me feel calmer and more in control. That along with a couple of slugs of vodka. Maybe I can get through the whole afternoon now without drinking anything else. I'm not going to promise myself that I can get to bed tonight with no alcohol. That feels too hard to think about. Let's just say 6 p.m. Yes, that feels like something I can manage.

I remove the steel rings from the cooker and scrub at the tiny brown stains. It's satisfying watching them disappear and the metallic colour now shines. I take pride in my work. I rub a damp cloth across the tiny green tiles of the work surfaces. I wish the surfaces were granite as the grout in between the jade-coloured squares tends to attract and hold crumbs and dirt.

'Hello, hello?' says a chirpy voice.

My stomach tightens and I immediately get a nauseous feeling in my gut.

I recognise the voice.

It's Nick.

He's wearing a navy baseball cap. Then again, he's always worn a baseball cap ever since I've known him. I know it's to hide the fact that he's bald. He's so vain. And he looks taller and lankier than I remember.

'Hi, I didn't know you were coming.' I say it in a nonchalant tone. It sounds as if it's almost a pleasant surprise – which it's not. But I don't want any confrontation. My body and mind are programmed to avoid confrontation with Nick at all costs.

Nick looks surprised. 'After all that's happened? As soon as Lowri told me you've been told not to leave here, I jumped on the first plane to Florence.'

He says it as if he wants a medal for Father of the Year.

There is an awkward silence.

'Where are you staying?' I ask, praying that he's not going to ask to stay at the villa or on the sofa at the annexe. That would be unbearable.

'Little Airbnb down the road,' Nick replies. 'A little rustic cottage with Tuscan decor. Looks like a film set.'

'Sounds nice,' I say, because I have to say something and I need everything to remain calm and pleasant.

God, I really do hate this man. He's more pretentious than ever and so incredibly uncomfortable in his own skin, I think as I hold my features in a half smile.

'Where is my little *principessa*?' Nick asks. He's referring to Lowri and it makes her squirm inside. He's always infantilised her and he's still doing it.

'I'm not sure,' I reply. 'Maybe out in the annexe.'

'Okay, I'll try out there then,' Nick says, gesturing outside.

I nod and then say, 'I'm making some lunch in a bit if you'd like some?'

We're like strangers that have just met. The conversation is so stilted and wooden. I kick myself for offering lunch. Why do

I feel the need to placate Nick so much? I know the reason. Every time I do or say something that mollifies him, my anxiety lessens and I feel relief. So that pattern of behaviour becomes an addictive, compulsive habit that feels impossible to break.

'Yes, that would be lovely,' Nick says with a smile.

Then I remember that I've had a drink. My fretfulness increases. Nick can spot my drinking from a mile away. Well, you know what I mean. I'm desperate for him not to know that I've been drinking. Not only because I fear his reaction. I want to prove to him that I'm not a mess now that we're divorced. That's what he predicted when he left the villa for the last time and flew back to London. That I wouldn't be able to cope on my own. That I was a pathetic excuse for a mother, wife and human being.

I take a breath to compose myself. 'Great. Lucia said she's going to give me a hand. Have you seen her? I know she'd love to say hello.'

I can't help myself. By the time Nick left, Lucia had made her feelings towards him pretty obvious. She loathes him. It wasn't anything that she said. Just the looks, expressions and body language.

'No, I haven't seen her,' Nick said, looking guarded. 'I saw Lorenzo by the pool. Looks like he's draining it.'

'The police have said we can use the pool again,' I explain. 'Although, I'm not sure that anyone is going to want to swim in it after everything that's happened.'

'No,' Nick agrees. 'I don't suppose they will. Have the police said anything?'

I frown as I'm not clear what he means. 'About what?'

'About what happened?' Nick says. His tone is patronising. 'It must have been someone trying to rob the villa. Is that what they think?'

'Yes. I think so,' I say. My anxiety is making my head muddled.

'You think so?' Nick snaps.

'I mean...' I'm feeling flustered. I feel like a stupid pupil being badgered by an irate teacher. 'There were a few things taken from the villa. I told the lead detective. When I asked if that meant they now thought Harry had been killed by someone who came to break into the villa, he said that was "one line of enquiry".'

Nick pulls a face. 'One line of enquiry? What does that mean?'

'I don't know, Nick,' I snap. I don't want him here. He makes me feel so uncomfortable and uneasy. 'You'll have to ask him.'

'There's no need to be rude, Cerys.' He gives me that searching look that I've seen so many times before. 'I was just asking.'

'It's been quite stressful and upsetting.' I sigh.

'Yes, of course.' Nick nods. 'I'm surprised you haven't been drinking with everything that's going on.'

Ah, and there it is, I think.

But I'm not going to rise to it. I have been drinking because it's the only way I know of coping. So fuck him and his judgement.

'Right, well, I'd better get on,' I say as I turn and search the kitchen for something to tidy or clean. I need him to leave.

'I'll go and find Lowri, then,' Nick says, sounding annoyed. He always sounds annnoyed.

I wait for about thirty seconds and then turn to check that he's gone.

He has.

I let out an audible sigh of relief.

Seeing Nick has brought back so many disturbing memories.

I need a drink. God, I need a drink.

Scuttling over to the bottles of spirits, I pull out the Smirnoff vodka.

My hands are trembling. My pulse is racing and breathing is shallow.

For fuck's sake, I think angrily.

I unscrew the top and then listen carefully to check that no one is around.

It's silent apart from a strong breeze blowing through the open door to the outside.

Tipping the bottle up to my mouth, I gulp. And then gulp again.

Jesus, the taste is so disgusting.

As the vodka hits my empty stomach, I feel it radiate warmth. But I also feel like I might vomit. Maybe I've overdone it. Swigging mouthfuls of neat vodka can't be good for your digestion.

I put the bottle back and then wait. And after a few minutes my nervous system starts to be anaesthetised and I can cope again.

I wander over to the bin and lift the lid. It smells stale and needs to be changed. Now the booze has kicked in, I feel like I don't have a care in the world. I take both sides of the black refuse sack, give it a pull and it slides quite easily out of the bin. It feels satisfying. I tie it up and put it to one side while I tear off a new bag and place it inside.

Grabbing the bag of rubbish, I head for the door in the far corner that leads out to a small yard at the back of the house. It's where our bins and recycling are kept until Lorenzo picks them up and drives them down to the municipal rubbish and recycling site about five kilometres away.

Sliding the bolts that secure the door, I then turn the key and head out into the sunshine. The yard is a bit scruffy. I keep telling myself to ask Lorenzo to give it a tidy and paint the brickwork.

Going over to the large plastic chest-shaped bin, I lift the lid and I'm instantly hit by the overwhelming stench of rotting food. I hold my breath as I hoist the bag inside.

Out of the corner of my eye, I spot something.

A screwed-up item of clothing. It's a sort of peachy apricot colour.

I reach over, grab it and pull it out. I let the dress unfold and drop down as I hold it with both hands.

It's an expensive-looking maxi dress. And it's the one that Zoe was wearing the night that Harry was killed.

I notice that there's a sizeable tear on the shoulder and neckline. It's as if someone has pulled and ripped it. It's not something that could be easily repaired but it's such a shame.

And then I see something else.

Several dark splashes and stains on the middle of the dress.

I peer at it intently. At first, I think it's red wine. But it's not the right colour.

And then I realise.

It's blood! What the...?

My head spins.

As I look at the dress and the bloodstain, I wonder how the police forensics team missed it. They must have searched my bins. It doesn't make sense.

Unless Zoe hid it and waited for them to finish their search.

What do I do with it? I don't want the police to find it. I don't want Zoe to face any awkward questions. She's been through enough already.

For a moment, I get a flash of memory from that night. Zoe and me dancing around, singing at the tops of our voices. It's all such a blur.

I know what I must do. I close the bin and put the dress down on the top.

Walking back into the kitchen, I listen carefully to make sure that no one is around. Then I open one of the drawers and retrieve a box of matches. I can't work out if what I'm about to do makes perfect sense or if in my slightly drunken state I'm doing something very stupid.

Frankly, I don't care. It makes sense to me.

Going back outside, I close the door firmly behind me. I walk over to the dress and lay it out. Then I strike a match and hold it to the bottom seam and watch as the material catches alight. The orange flame flickers a little in the breeze. Then it begins to take hold and soon flames engulf the whole dress and it drops from where I've put it and onto the ground.

Another thirty seconds and the dress is no more than black ashes which I kick until they float up into the breeze and dance away.

FORTY-ONE

LOWRI

12.11 p.m.

Lowri moves a tress of blonde hair and pushes it behind her ear. She sits at her bench, headphones perched around her neck, and guitar in hand. She didn't sleep well. There have been flashbacks and anxiety dreams about Harry attacking her or chasing her. Then she wakes in a sweat, gasping for breath. It's horrible. She's seen what male violence has done to her mother and fears the same is happening to her. It doesn't seem fair.

Trying to put those thoughts out of her head, she gazes out across the view of the vineyards, olive groves and rolling hills. Legend has it that it's the landscape that forms the backdrop to the world's most famous painting, the *Mona Lisa*. Leonardo Da Vinci was born in the village of Vinci which is less than twenty miles away. It blows her mind that the great Italian painter looked at this very view and was inspired to create that picture.

Lowri looks down at her guitar and pushes her fingers against the strings to form an A minor chord. She likes minor chords. They give a song a darker, sadder tone and, after everything that's happened, that's how she's feeling. She likes how

Stevie Wonder and George Michael took the major chord progressions and clichés of popular music and twisted the tone with minor ones.

'Thought I'd find you here,' says a voice.

Lowri recognises the voice and feels instantly nervy.

'Dad?' she says, sounding confused.

'Hello, sweetie,' her dad says, coming towards her with a beaming smile.

Putting down her guitar, she gets up hesitantly.

Before she can move, he has come over and wrapped his arms around her. She reciprocates but his appearance has unsetttled her.

'What are you doing here?' she asks, making sure that she sounds pleased that he's here.

'I came to see you, silly,' her dad says. 'I can't believe what's happened.' He steps back and looks at her. 'Are you okay?'

Why does he continue to talk to me like I'm still twelve?

'Yeah, I'm okay.' Lowri nods. 'It feels a bit surreal, if I'm honest. Are you staying here?'

'No.' He shakes his head. 'I didn't think that was a good idea with everything that's been going on. I flew in late last night and I've got a lovely little Airbnb down the road.'

Thank God, she thinks with relief.

Lowri takes a moment and then looks at him. 'Have you seen Mum?'

Her dad nods with a wry smile. 'Yes, I just saw her up at the villa. She didn't look well. She looks tired.'

Lowri shrugs. What did he expect? 'We're all in shock. I don't think any of us are sleeping very well.'

'Of course,' her dad says with an empathetic expression. 'It's so horrible. What have the police said? I mean, they must think that this... Harry?'

Lowri nods. 'Yes, Harry...'

'He interrupted or tried to stop someone who'd come up to

rob the villa? I mean it couldn't be anything else, could it?' her dad asks.

'I don't know,' Lowri replies. She doesn't really want to talk about it. She came here to write some music and try to forget all about it for a while. 'But no, I don't suppose there's any other explanation.'

'Of course not,' her dad says empathetically.

A moment of awkward silence passes between them.

'Why, have the police said anything else?'

Lowri gives him a quizzical look. *Why is he so keen to know the police lines of enquiry?* 'Dad, I really don't know what the police are thinking. They haven't told us anything,' she says but she's aware that she sounds a little irritated.

Her dad puts his hands up in an appeasing gesture. 'Okay, okay. I'm just worried about you. You and Mum are up here in this villa.'

'I don't think there's a maniac on the loose, Dad!'

'No, of course not,' Nick agrees.

FORTY-TWO

ZOE

1.58 p.m.

The wind picks up and swirls as though in annoyance. Zoe holds the pages of the book that she's trying to read. *The Power of Now* by Eckhart Tolle. She can't concentrate. It's impossible. The irony of reading a book that suggests the only way to live a happy, peaceful life is to be present in the moment – in the now. The mantra that reminds us that there are two days that we have no power or control over. Yesterday and tomorrow.

Zoe puts the book down. She can't concentrate as memories seem to be a continual loop. She remembers the time she rang Harry's hotel room in New York when he was on a business trip and his assistant, Lisa, answered. Despite Harry brushing it off and telling her that Lisa was there because they were running through his schedule, it had been 11 p.m. in New York. She knew it was bullshit and it made her feel sick. She wondered why she wasn't enough for him. Why couldn't she make him happy enough so that he didn't want to look elsewhere?

Some of the memories were darker. The times that Harry had lost his temper with her, thrown her across a room or into furniture, or gripped her in utter fury and smacked her across the face. The day Harry had thrown her to the floor of their bedroom and Charlie had walked in to ask if 'Mummy was all right'. Charlie had been about six or seven. Why hadn't she left Harry there and then?

Taking a deep breath, Zoe tells herself it wasn't as easy as to just leave Harry. She needs to be kind to herself. And as she and Charlie move on without him, she'll support her son every step of the way.

Sitting forward on the lounger, Zoe stretches out her right leg and looks at the bruises on her knee and her thigh. They're starting to darken to a plummy black. She has no idea how she got them. It must have been from the other night when she and Cerys got hammered. The night that everything changed. It was what she and her friends would call UPI in her twenties. An Unexplained Party Injury. She used to think that was hilarious and the sign of having had a great night out.

For a moment, she looks across and sees that Lorenzo is draining the swimming pool. She hasn't been to the pool since she sat next to Harry's dead body the other morning. She's not sure if she's strong enough to go down there. She finds herself transfixed by Lorenzo. His white T-shirt is tight around his torso. He's got lovely biceps and arms and a muscular chest and back. But it's not this that's the most attractive thing about him. It's the casual confidence and stillness that he seems to exude with everything he does. A loose-limbed cool as if he doesn't have a care in the world. She bets that he's an incredible lover. Strong, passionate but attentive. Harry was none of those things. He seemed to think the goal of their sex life was for him to achieve an orgasm and then he would sleep.

Zoe sees something out of the corner of her eye. Two cars are driving up the track in the distance. The second vehicle is a blue police car with a white stripe. It looks very filmic as they throw up a fine cloud of dust in their wake as they go. There is something about their speed or urgency that unsettles Zoe. She tells herself not to be silly. The police will be coming and going to the villa for days.

Sensing someone heading her way, Zoe turns and notices Cerys. She's wearing a plain T-shirt and long shorts. It's unusual to see her looking a bit dowdy. The arrival of her ex-husband and Lowri's father, Nick, seems to have totally thrown her. Zoe knows from their mainly drunken, confessional chats that Cerys and Nick had a pretty unpleasant split. Even though Cerys hasn't gone into great detail, it sounds as if Nick is a bit of a prick. In fact, some of the things she's told her about him seem to directly mirror Harry's personality.

'Hey,' Cerys says. She's trying to sound breezy but Zoe can see how distracted and uncomfortable she is.

Zoe gestures over to the two approaching cars which are now closer and have turned up the steep final approach to the villa.

'As they say in all the best films, looks like we've got company,' Zoe says and then wonders if making such a light-hearted comment is appropriate. She wonders that every time she opens her mouth at the moment. But Cerys has assured her that humour is sometimes the only way to get through something as dark and tragic as what's happened in recent days.

'I'd better go and see what they want,' Cerys says wearily.

Zoe gets up from the lounger and puts her feet into her sandals. 'I'll come with you.'

She feels guilty that it was her husband who was killed in Cerys's villa and turned her and Lowri's lives upside down.

They both wander together across the grass and towards the top of the track where the car parking area is for the villa.

Zoe recognises the first car. It belongs to Detective Saachi.

Saachi gets out. He gives them a nod hello as he goes to the back seat where he retrieves his linen jacket and briefcase.

'*Buongiorno*,' Saachi says but there is something very serious in his manner that Zoe finds unsettling.

'*Buongiorno*,' Zoe and Cerys say in unison.

Saachi points to Nick's rental car. 'There is someone else here?' he asks.

'My ex-husband,' Cerys explains. 'He was concerned about our daughter after everything that's happened.'

'Your daughter must stay here. She cannot leave the country yet,' Saachi says sternly. 'You do understand that?'

'Yes,' Cerys replies but she looks disconcerted by Saachi's words and tone.

Saachi looks at her. 'And when did your ex-husband arrive in Italy?'

'Last night,' Cerys says.

'I will need to talk to him.' Saachi gestures to the villa. 'There is something I must show you this morning. But I need everyone. Your son and your daughter.'

Zoe feels the sudden tension in the pit of her stomach. *What is he talking about?*

FORTY-THREE

CERYS

1.58 p.m.

We've all been asked to come to the living room by Saachi. Despite the cold of the air-conditioning, I can't seem to get my breath. My head is a little fuzzy as I sit down on the sofa next to Cerys. We look at each other anxiously.

There is a tense silence as everyone finds a place. Lowri sits in the big, brown leather armchair and Charlie is on a footstool beside her. I think there is something going on between Lowri and Charlie. I can see it.

But my focus is on why Saachi has asked us all to be together. I'm watching him like a hawk. Is he going to produce some piece of evidence that will unlock the key to finding Harry's killer? It has to be something significant. The tension is horrible.

Saachi opens his briefcase, takes out a small laptop and opens it. He puts it on the coffee table. 'I'm going to show you something. You don't need to say anything until we have watched it but I must warn you that it will be difficult for you to see.'

Watched what? What is he going to show us?

I can feel Zoe move uncomfortably next to me and sit forward.

'I'd like to sit in on this, if that's okay?' says a familiar voice.

It's Nick.

I turn around to look at him. The very sight of him unsettles me.

Saachi raises an eyebrow. 'And you are?'

'Nick,' he says in that haughty voice that I hate so much. 'I'm Lowri's father. I think I should be here for her.'

'No,' Saachi replies firmly. 'I only want those who were here at the villa the night that Harry Collard was murdered.'

There is a moment when Nick looks like he's going to argue.

Then, 'Fair enough,' he says. 'I guess that makes sense.'

God, he just can't stand being told what to do, I think to myself. And then a nasty thought pops into my head – I wish it had been him and not Harry that we'd found floating in the pool.

Lowri reaches out her hand and Charlie takes it.

Nick turns and leaves but I can see how much it bothers him that Saachi has effectively told him to go away.

What the hell is it with male pride and ego? Jesus!

'Please, I'd like you to watch this,' Saachi says quietly as he presses the space bar on the laptop.

A TikTok video of Lowri appears. She's standing in her bedroom in the annexe with her guitar.

What the hell is going on?

I look over and see that Lowri's eyes have widened in utter panic. I have no idea why Saachi is showing us this.

'Where did you get this?' Lowri snaps in horror.

I know that Lowri used to find it uncomfortable showing strangers her music but her reaction seems extreme.

Saachi looks at her. 'We have your phone number, Lowri, and we requested access to your iCloud.'

'No.' Lowri is visibly shaking. 'I don't want you to look at this.'

Charlie stands up angrily. 'This isn't right. It's a violation of Lowri's privacy.'

'What is it?' I demand but no one answers me.

Saachi fixes them with a stare and says very sternly, 'Please sit down, Charlie.'

Charlie gives Lowri a supportive look. Whatever it is, it seems that both Charlie and Lowri know. I feel panic rising in my chest.

On the screen, I watch as Lowri wanders across the bedroom, plays some music and then takes off her top. She has clearly forgotten to stop the phone recording the TikTok video.

'Will someone please tell me what's going on?' I ask, feeling agitated.

'What is this?' Zoe asks.

But then I hear a voice.

'Knock, knock.'

It's Harry's voice. And I feel an icy chill run down my back.

On the video, Lowri looks over at Harry. She seems uncomfortable and she's standing just in her bra. She looks young and vulnerable.

Harry comes into shot and says something else inaudible and then I can hear him saying, 'I just came over to apologise for what I said earlier.'

Zoe leans forward and peers at the screen.

'Okay. Don't worry about it,' Lowri says.

I can see from Lowri's body language that she wants him to go.

Harry comes over and sits on her bed.

'Charlie tells me you're a talented singer-songwriter,' Harry says looking at her.

'I wouldn't say that,' Lowri replies. 'Look, I'm really tired so if you...'

As I glance over at Zoe, I can see her staring in horror at the laptop screen as Harry tells Lowri about his job and that he wants to hear her music.

My pulse quickens. I can't believe that I'm watching my own daughter in a sickening situation. A situation I'm all too familiar with.

I can feel my anger and fear growing as Harry asks for a massage. It's as if he's read Weinstein's or Epstein's guide to seducing young women.

I look over at Lowri and her eyes are full of tears but she won't catch my gaze. Charlie has clasped her hand in his to comfort her.

'A massage?' Harry asks as if this is a completely normal request. 'I'm sure you've given someone a massage before.'

'No, I haven't,' Lowri replies. She takes a deep breath. 'Actually, I'd like you to leave, please.'

Harry gets up from the bed.

'I can pay you, if it's a problem,' Harry says with a smile. 'Shall we say £200? That's pretty good for a fifteen-minute massage.'

My stomach twists as I see Harry move towards Lowri. I feel sick with dread about what is going to unfold before my eyes.

'I'm not going to give you a massage,' Lowri says, sounding scared. 'And if you don't leave, I'm going to shout at the top of my voice.'

'What the hell are we watching?' I gasp under my breath to no one in particular. My heart is racing.

Harry is getting angry as he moves towards her. 'Come on. You're not going to do that. Do you know how useful I could be to you getting a record deal?' He clicks his fingers. 'I can get you signed like that. And all I want is an innocent massage. I don't think that's too much to ask, is it?'

'Get out,' Lowri hisses.

Harry is still moving towards her and she's forced to back away from him.

'Why are you being like this?' Harry asks, shaking his head. 'You want people to hear your music, don't you? I know some of the best producers in the world. And I can do that for you. I think you're actually being a bit ungrateful, Lowri.'

'I want you to get out right now,' Lowri shouts.

Harry reaches out and tries to touch her face but Lowri ducks her head away.

'Just fuck off!' she yells.

'Oh my God,' I gasp. I can hardly bear to watch this.

Harry grabs her by the wrist. 'What the fuck is the matter with you? You need to do what I've asked you to do, do you understand me? Don't make me angry.'

I get a sudden flash of when I was attacked in London.

Suddenly, Harry pushes himself against her forcing her back into the wall. He's pulling at her skirt. His hands are all over her legs and crotch.

Lowri screams, 'GET OFF ME!'

My eyes fill with tears. It's agonising. I want to look away.

'No, no, no. Get the fuck off of me!'

I stand up. It's unbearable to see. My pulse has gone through the roof. I'm suffocating.

'Turning me down is a big mistake, Lowri.'

'GET OFF ME!'

And then I see a figure come in from screen left.

It's Charlie.

Charlie grabs Harry and yells, 'Get the fuck off her!'

Charlie and Harry are fighting.

'I fucking hate you,' Charlie snaps.

Harry punches Charlie in the face and he crumples to the floor, holding his nose.

Lowri attacks Harry. 'You bastard! You sick, fucked-up bastard!'

Harry smiles. 'Don't be so bloody naive, Lowri.'

Harry leaves and Lowri crouches down to see if Charlie is okay.

Charlie looks across the bedroom in the direction that Harry left. 'I'm going to fucking kill him.'

'Come on,' Lowri says, helping Charlie back onto his feet. 'Let's get you cleaned up. And you need to get some ice on that.'

They walk past the camera and out of shot.

The empty bedroom is left on the screen.

Saachi reaches over and presses pause to stop the video.

My face is streaked with tears. I race over to Lowri and take her protectively in my arms. I hug her tightly. She's shaking like a leaf. 'I'm so, so sorry that happened to you.' Then I look at her and put my hand to her tear-streaked face. 'Why didn't you tell me what he did?'

'I was too scared,' Lowri sobs.

'It's okay,' I cry. 'I've got you. You're safe now.'

Charlie has been crying too. He looks up at them. 'We didn't want to get into trouble.'

'Oh, darling,' Zoe says as she goes to comfort Charlie. 'Why didn't you come and tell us immediately?'

'You were both too drunk,' Charlie says, with no judgement implied. 'Then the next morning, we found Dad in the pool... It's my fault. I told Lowri if we told you what Dad had done the night before, it might look really bad for us.'

Zoe frowns and pushes a strand of hair from Charlie's face. 'I know you'd never harm your father like that, darling. You're not like that.'

Saachi gets up and gives them all a meaningful look. 'I am afraid this video is very significant as evidence.'

'Don't be ridiculous! You can't possibly think that Lowri or Charlie are involved in what happened to Harry,' I protest anxiously. But I can see that it doesn't look good.

'Come on!' Zoe thunders. 'Charlie wouldn't do that to his father.'

Saachi raises an eyebrow. 'Your husband sexually assaulted Lowri. And the video clearly shows Charlie saying that he is "going to kill" his father. When I questioned them, they both lied about the last time that they saw Harry.'

'Of course they did. They were frightened,' Zoe insisted.

'I have to take them both to Florence with me,' Saachi explains calmly. 'I have to question them there formally now that I've seen this video. And because they gave me false statements.'

Lowri's face is full of terror. 'Mum!'

'You can't do that!' I shout. 'They're both British citizens.'

Saachi shrugs. 'They're subject to Italian law while they're here. Just like anyone else.'

'I'm going to ring the British Consulate,' Zoe says, her voice full of panic.

I glare at Saachi. 'What about all the things that have been stolen from the villa?' I point out to him.

'Please. They are not under arrest,' Saachi says with an empathetic expression. 'Let me talk to them both. I can hear their side of the story. And then we can take it from there.'

'I'm coming with my son,' Zoe snaps.

Saachi shakes his head. 'No. I made an allowance the first time that I spoke to Charlie. But he is over eighteen. And I want to hear their stories separately.'

Charlie looks to Lowri and then Zoe. 'We have to go with him,' he says in a whisper. 'It's going to be okay.'

Lowri nods but she's in floods of tears.

A female uniformed officer appears and Saachi signals for

her to lead Lowri and Charlie out of the villa and towards the cars.

'Mum!' Lowri sobs.

'It's okay, darling,' I say, trying to steady my voice as I reassure her. 'I'm going to ring the British Consulate right now. You're going to be fine. Just tell them the truth.'

FORTY-FOUR

ZOE

7.27 p.m.

The light is beginning to wane over Villa Lucia. Zoe sits on the patio lost in thought. It's hard to get the images she saw on the video out of her head. Close-ups of Harry pinning Lowri to the wall, his hands groping her. She's so ashamed. It's her husband doing that to Lowri. Zoe feels utterly humiliated by Harry's actions. This is the man she chose to spend her life with. He's the father of their son. It makes her shudder.

I was responsible for bringing him here. I booked the holiday. It's partly my fault that Harry attacked Lowri, isn't it?

And then Zoe's thoughts turn to Charlie. Dragging his own father off a poor defenceless girl. And then Charlie telling Lowri that he's going to kill Harry.

What if Charlie confronted Harry and it got out of hand? Charlie was so angry. She doesn't blame him. Harry's actions are unforgiveable.

I can't think like that. Charlie isn't capable of—

'How are you getting on?' a voice interrupts her dark thoughts.

Zoe blinks as she's jolted into the present.

Cerys comes and sits down on a wicker chair to her right.

'Hi,' Zoe says quietly. She's spent the last few hours calling anyone and everyone she can think of to see what they can do for Charlie and Lowri. The British Consulate in Florence were understanding but told her that until any formal charges were made, they couldn't officially get involved. However, the very kind man called David told her that he would be putting in a call to Commissariato San Giovanni, the main police station in Florence, where they were taken.

'Did you find out anything?' Cerys asks. She's clearly agitated.

'The man at the consulate told me not to worry,' Zoe explains. 'He said that as far as he could see, Charlie and Lowri had been taken in for voluntary questioning. They haven't been arrested or charged with anything.'

'Yet,' Cerys says and then pulls a face. 'Sorry... I can't help but worry.'

'No, of course not.' Zoe nods. 'I'm the same.'

'Maybe we should drive up there,' Cerys suggests. 'I feel so useless just sitting here.'

'They did ask us to stay here,' Zoe reminds her. 'I don't think there's anything we can do sitting in a police station. I also managed to speak to a friend of mine's husband, Rupert. He's a barrister. He told me the same as the consulate. Because they lied on their statements, they've been taken in. But at this stage, it will just be to get their version of events on Sunday night.'

Cerys nods but she looks totally lost in thought. 'I can't get that video out of my head.'

'I'm so, so sorry.' Zoe leans forward and looks at her. 'I just don't know what to say to you.'

'You're not responsible for Harry's actions, Zoe,' Cerys tells her firmly. 'From what you've told me, his behaviour has been atrocious for a long time.'

'Yes, it had been,' Zoe admits quietly. 'But I feel so responsible.'

'You're not,' Cerys reassures her. 'You can't think like that.'

Zoe shakes her head fretfully. 'I can't believe that they didn't tell us.'

'They were scared.' Cerys takes a deep breath. 'I can see why they didn't.'

There is a tense silence.

Zoe knows they are both overwhelmed by the shock of their children being carted away and the dread of what is going to happen to them. And there is something that neither of them have mentioned. Neither she, Cerys nor Nick have openly questioned whether or not Charlie or Lowri attacked Harry by the pool. She can't bring herself to think that Charlie did that to Harry. But there's a little voice in her head that says that she's seen Charlie explode at Harry's behaviour at home. They've had physical fights before. And then what she saw on the video. Harry punching Charlie to the floor and Charlie telling Lowri that he was going to kill him. She feels physically sick at the thought of it.

Nick comes out through the patio doors holding a bottle of beer. Zoe can't work him out. On the surface, he seems considerate and friendly enough. But she knows from what Cerys has told her, he has a much darker side. Zoe has seen glimpses of his temper and his arrogance already. Since Harry's death the private villa has become more of a communal space, Nick swans around like he owns the place. And much of the way he acts and what he says just seems disingenuous. It all feels somehow rehearsed.

'I just spoke to a journalist friend of mine who knows about this type of thing,' Nick explains. He then sits on the arm of the chair rather than sitting in it properly. It feels false and mannered. 'He confirms what we thought. They'll be interviewed separately so they can give their side of what happened.

Once they've done that, they should be free to go unless there are discrepancies in what they've told the police.'

Nick has a strange expression on his face as if he wants to say something more but he's holding back.

Cerys gives him a challenging look. 'What?'

Nick frowns as if he has no idea what Cerys is referring to.

'If you've got something else to say, Nick, then just say it,' Cerys snaps. 'Our daughter is sitting frightened in an Italian police station so just spit it out.'

Nick looks uncomfortable. 'It's just... You're sure that stuff went missing from the villa that night?'

'Pretty certain,' Cerys replies. 'Why?'

'No, I just...' Nick then stops and swigs from the bottle of beer.

He really is a strange man. What on earth did Cerys ever see in him? Then Zoe reminds herself that she married Harry. The dark irony.

'That would point to someone coming here to rob from the villa,' Nick continued. 'And that Harry interrupted them or confronted them and that's why...' He doesn't finish the sentence.

'Yes. What's your point, Nick?' Cerys sounds frustrated.

'If I'd found my father sexually assaulting a young girl,' Nick explained, 'and then he punched me to the floor... well, I might be very tempted to go and attack him.'

Zoe feels a surge of anger at what Nick has said. She's lost for words.

'For fuck's sake, Nick!' Cerys's eyes widen in anger. 'Charlie had nothing to do with what happened to Harry.'

'You don't know that.' Nick shrugs and looks at Zoe. 'No offence but we don't know Charlie, do we? He's been here a couple of days. And now our daughter is stuck in a police station.'

'He's not capable of doing that,' Zoe snaps. She wants to go and slap Nick for what he's implying.

'Jesus, Nick! You're such a prick!' Cerys sneers as she shakes her head.

'Yeah, well, it's better than being a drunk.' Nick snorts as he turns and goes back into the villa. 'I'm just looking out for our daughter.'

There is an awkward silence.

Zoe's eyes well up. It's all too much. She feels completely overwhelmed. What's happened to Harry? And now Charlie.

'Hey.' Cerys goes to her. 'Ignore him. He's such a wanker. I'm embarrassed.'

Zoe blows out her cheeks and tries to compose herself. 'It's not your fault.'

Cerys looks at her intensely. 'Charlie and Lowri had nothing to do with what happened to Harry. We both know that.'

Zoe doesn't say anything but there's part of her that's not so sure.

FORTY-FIVE

CERYS

Three Years Before – Wednesday, 12 August 2020

I'm sprawled on the sofa, still in my pyjamas from the morning.
There's nothing to get dressed for. I'm in a foggy alcoholic haze.
On the rug beside me are three empty bottles of cheap white
wine. It's the only thing that's passed my lips since I woke to the
sound of Lowri leaving for school at 8.10 a.m. Actually, I didn't
wake. I came to. It would be hard to classify it as waking from
sleep in anyone's book.

Last night Nick and I had another monumental row. I said
some very unkind things, but then again, so did he. Then it's all
a blur. An alcohol-induced blackout until I came to this morning. I hadn't wet myself which was a definite bonus, I guess.

Reaching down, I take my fourth and last bottle of white
wine and unscrew the top.

I don't care. I'm past caring. I lift the bottle to my dry lips
and glug like I'm drinking Ribena. I've long stopped using a
glass. What's the point in pretending that I'm having a glass of
wine? I've drunk nearly a third of the bottle by the time I stop.
That should do the trick. I'm now classified as alcohol depen-

dent, which means that I have physical withdrawal symptoms when I stop drinking alcohol for any long period of time. I sweat and shake. The other day I dry-retched in the morning and couldn't get my breath. I thought I was going to die. Then I wondered if that was such a bad thing.

Lowri came back from school over two hours ago. I know that she hates seeing me like this. And I know that she is hanging out with friends or going to their houses after school to avoid coming home. Today she came into the lounge, looked at me with utter disgust. She said 'Jesus Christ' and then went upstairs.

It's been eight months since I was attacked. Well, raped, to be precise. Since that man pretended to take me to a bedroom and then forced himself upon me. It was very dark but I can still see his face. And of course, I reported it to the police the next day but by then I'd washed all the forensic evidence away. I had to shower. I felt so horrible and disgusting when I got home. I scrubbed at my skin. Where he touched me.

My counsellor says that I'm suffering from PTSD. I have flashbacks, panic attacks and depression. And the only thing that stops all that is alcohol, so I'm hardly going to stop drinking. I actually think that if I was stopped from drinking, the emotional pain, fear and self-loathing would drive me to suicide. So, my guess is that death by white wine is going to take longer and so essentially I'm actually prolonging my life by drinking this much.

Nick's reaction to the attack has been anything but compassionate. I know that he can't think of me being with another man. It doesn't seem to matter that I was raped. I can see it in his face. Another man was inside me and it's eating him up. And of course, he's blamed me on several occasions. He doesn't believe that I was spiked. He tells me that I drank too much and that somehow I asked to be attacked. The joke is I know he's continuing to have an affair with the woman I saw leaving here in a Mini last summer. He denies it on a regular basis and says that the attack has made me paranoid. His aggressive control-ling behaviour has reached new peaks. But I accept it. I have to. I can't work and I have no money. I can't leave because I have nowhere to go. I'm not about to go and make myself homeless. So, I just sit, drink and pass out on a loop.

Suddenly the front door opens and then shuts. I can feel my pulse quicken a little. Even though I'm drunk, I still feel anxious at the thought of him coming through the door.

I hold my breath and the door to the lounge opens.

Nick looks at me. His face is full of thunder. It always is. Then he points to the mess that I'm surrounded by. 'I like what you've done with the place,' he says caustically. 'And nice of you to clear up the kitchen too.'

I've only staggered to the kitchen to retrieve my wine from the fridge. I can't cope with how dirty and untidy it's become. I like my wine cold because it masks the flavour of the cheap taste. Nick has tried taking money and bank cards from me so I can't buy any more alcohol. But I always find a way. Order a new bank card. Get booze delivered online. Where there's an alcoholic will, there is always a way.

I can see Nick's nostrils flare in anger.

'I'm sorry,' I whisper.

'You're sorry?' he snaps. 'I don't think that's going to cut it. You're ruining my and Lowri's life. You're a fucking disgrace!'

'I don't know what to say,' I say in a whimper.

'Did you ring that woman from AA to see if she can take you to a meeting?' Nick asks through gritted teeth.

'No. They're just a bunch of religious weirdos,' I lie. I've been to AA meetings. The people are lovely and very support-ive. I've met alcoholics from all walks of life – architects, teach-ers, nurses, plumbers, a CEO of a charity. And the religious aspect of AA is vague and optional. It's more about being spiri-tual. In fact, I sense deep down that the only place I'm ever going to get sober is in AA. But there's a huge problem. They stipulate total abstinence. And at this precise moment, I don't want to stop drinking. In fact, it's not about 'want'. It's that I'm terrified of stopping and having to live without the comfort of drink. I can't see how that is possible.

Nick throws his keys onto the table angrily and then comes towards me.

I flinch. I know what's coming.

Grabbing me by my hair, he pulls me and looks into my face. 'Look at the state of you. You're a fucking mess.'

'No, Nick. Please.' I'm shaking and scared.

Nick slaps me hard so that I can feel the side of my face burn. 'You asked for that. You've ruined my fucking life.'

'Sorry,' I whisper as he lets my hair go and I fall back onto the sofa.

'I'm surprised anyone would want to rape you,' he sneers as he turns and leaves the room.

I reach for the bottle of wine and put it to my lips again.

FORTY-SIX

LOWRI

Tuesday
7.58 p.m.

Lowri glances down at her nails for a few seconds. She's been biting at her cuticles because she's so anxious. The room that Detective Saachi put her and Charlie in about ten minutes ago at the Commissariato San Giovanni is very plain and stuffy. There are two old-fashioned fluorescent strip lights parallel to each other on the ceiling. The floor is black and a little dusty. Over in the far corner are several metal filing cabinets and white cardboard boxes stacked on top of each other with dates written in marker pen. Lowri assumes that they are boxes of evidence like the ones she's seen on television police dramas.

Charlie is leaning forward on his wooden chair and looking at the floor. Then he glances up at her. 'This is all my fault.'

Lowri shakes her head. 'No, it's not.'

'It is.' Charlie looks despondent. He says quietly, 'I'm the one who told you to lie about what happened with my dad.'

'Yeah. And I said that I didn't want to do it,' Lowri replies under her breath. 'But then I changed my mind. I decided to lie to them.'

Charlie sits up and looks at her. 'Yeah, but you never would have done it if I hadn't put that thought in your head in the first place.'

Lowri puts her finger to her lips to tell him to keep his voice down. 'You don't know that. I might have done.'

'No.' Charlie shakes his head. Then he reaches over and takes her hand. 'I'm really sorry we're in this mess.'

'You haven't got anything to apologise for,' Lowri reassures him. 'Seriously. We haven't done anything wrong except tell a lie because we were scared. We haven't got anything to hide, have we?'

'No,' Charlie says but he looks perturbed.

'Charlie?'

Charlie takes a second and then whispers, 'What about when I had a row with my dad by the pool? Should I tell them that?'

Lowri's eyes widen in disbelief. 'Jesus, Charlie! Of course you tell them. You didn't have anything to do with what happened to your dad so you've got nothing to hide. Don't lie about anything.'

Charlie nods. 'Yeah, you're right.'

For a moment, they sit in silence.

Lowri remembers the look on her mum's and Zoe's faces when they watched the video. They were both so upset. Watching the video with them reminded her what a terrible thing Harry did to her. Lowri doesn't know if she's somehow blanked it out of her mind but she feels numb when she thinks about the attack. It's like it didn't happen or was a dream.

'I don't know why we're here anyway,' Charlie says.

Lowri gives him a puzzled look. 'What do you mean?'

'All those things that went missing from the villa,' Charlie explained. 'Well, they were clearly taken by the person or people who came to rob stuff.'

'Yeah.' Lowri nods.

'And that's what happened to Dad, isn't it?' Charlie says. 'He saw them and something happened. He tried to stop them.' He sounds like he's trying to convince himself.

'That makes sense,' Lowri agrees. 'I can't see what else could explain it.'

Charlie narrows his eyes. 'So, why are we here?'

'Because that detective saw the video,' Lowri says. 'He wants to know why we lied to him.'

'But he must know.' Charlie looks frightened and leans forward on his chair again. 'He's not stupid. It's obvious that we were just scared about telling him. And he knows that stuff has been stolen from the villa. So, why isn't he out there looking for whoever came to the villa? Why are we here?'

Lowri can see that Charlie is getting frantic.

'I don't know,' Lowri admits.

'What if they've got something else?' Charlie asks. His foot is jigging nervously.

'What do you mean?' she asks.

Charlie's eyes are roaming nervously around the room. 'What if they've got something else they want to talk to us about?'

'What are you talking about, Charlie?'

'Maybe they've got other evidence,' Charlie says. 'Something that makes them think that one of us was involved in what happened to Dad.'

Lowri can see how agitated Charlie is but she doesn't really know what he's talking about. 'Like what?'

'I don't know,' Charlie snaps at her. 'Something.'

'Charlie?' Lowri says softly. 'Look at me.'

Charlie takes a few seconds and then he glances at her.

She's not sure but it seems that Charlie is bursting to tell her something. It's making her feel very uneasy.

'Is there something that you haven't told me?' Lowri asks gently. 'Something that the police might ask us about?'

'No...' Charlie looks on the verge of tears. 'I don't know.'

He then buries his head in his hands.

'Charlie? What is it?' Lowri asks him urgently. 'You can tell me, whatever it is. I promise.'

After a few seconds, Charlie takes his head out of his hands and looks like he's about to say something terrible. He looks so lost and frightened.

'What is it?' Lowri asks as she reaches out to touch the back of his hand.

The door to the room opens which startles them both.

Saachi takes two steps inside and looks over.

'Lowri,' he says and gestures. 'If you could follow me, please?'

FORTY-SEVEN

CERYS

8.11 p.m.

I take a long gulp of vodka as I sit on the patio. I haven't seen Nick since he stormed off. His car is still here so he hasn't left yet. And Zoe is talking to a friend on her phone upstairs. I'm still angry at Nick for what he said about Charlie. He's such a prick.

Then I hear footsteps in the distance going along the path at the front of the villa and towards the cars. I wonder if Zoe is going out but I know she's had a few drinks and she didn't mention it.

Getting up, I realise that I'm a little unsteady on my feet. I've definitely had a few too many drinks. However, I don't care. Someone's been murdered in my villa and my daughter has been sexually assaulted. Then she's been taken away by the Italian police for questioning. If anyone has a fucking right to have a few drinks, it's me!

I squint a little at the fading light above. Then I walk around the side of the villa towards the shaded car parking area. I see a figure opening a car door.

It's Nick.

'You going?' I ask. I realise that my tone is confrontational but that's just how I'm feeling towards him.

Nick turns and looks me up and down. 'Yes.'

I frown. 'You've been drinking.'

'No,' he says with that supercilious expression. 'I've had two bottles of beer. I can control my drink, remember?'

Oh, fuck off.

Before I can reply, Nick says, 'I'm driving up to Florence.'

'Are you? Why?' I ask.

'Why do you think?' Nick says with a sneer. 'I can't sit around getting drunk while Lowri is in a police station on her own.'

'We were told not to go and to stay here,' I point out.

Nick gives a conceited shrug. 'I don't care. Lowri must be terrified so I'm going.'

I raise an eyebrow. 'But she's not on her own.'

'Oh, you mean Charlie?' Nick snorts derisively.

'You don't know Charlie,' I say. 'What's your problem with him?'

'Problem?' Nick snaps. 'I've seen the video. His scumbag of a father tried to rape our daughter. They have a fight and Charlie *promises* that he's going to kill him. The next morning, the scumbag is found stabbed in that pool. You work it out, Cerys! Because he's dragged our daughter into all this when she's the real victim.'

'You're way off, Nick,' I say, shaking my head.

He glares at her. 'Am I?'

'You seem very convinced about all this,' I say. I know I'm drunk and therefore argumentative but I'm feeling brave. And I enjoy winding Nick up. I don't think he'd dare come over and hit me with Zoe around.

Nick shrugs. 'I'm just going on what I've seen. It's obvious.'

He goes to get into his car.

'Try not to have a crash on the way and die, eh?' I say caustically.

Nick just stares at me, shakes his head, gets into the car and starts the engine.

FORTY-EIGHT

LOWRI

8.19 p.m.

Lowri looks around the interview room. Her anxiety is now overwhelming. In fact, she doesn't think she's ever been this scared before. She's in an Italian police station talking about her sexual assault and a murder. This stuff just doesn't happen to people like her. Her stomach is tight with nerves.

The room is brightly lit, with stark white walls and very simple wooden furniture. There are a couple of posters on the wall beside her. They're in Italian but they look like public awareness campaigns. The air is warm and, even though Detective Saachi isn't smoking, it smells of cigarette smoke and stale coffee.

Saachi is sitting on the other side of the table from her looking through some papers. His laptop is to one side.

Lowri's mouth is dry. She picks up the small white plastic cup of water that Saachi brought her ten minutes ago. Her hand is so shaky that she needs both to hold it steady as she puts it to her lips. She takes a tiny sip as she fears that gulping the water might make her sick.

Eventually Saachi looks over at her and gives her a reassuring look. The lower half of his face has taken on a slight shadow as he hasn't shaved and it's getting late.

'Lowri, I am just going to ask you a few questions. And all I want you to do is answer them truthfully. Do you understand?'

'Yes,' Lowri replies but the word gets caught in her throat and she has to cough to clear it. 'Yes.'

'Okay.' Saachi points at some recording equipment. 'And I am going to record this interview in case anything you do tell me needs to be used as evidence at a later date. But you know that you are not under arrest?'

Lowri nods. 'Yes.'

Saachi reaches over to press the red recording button on the machine. Lowri spots a tattoo of something like an eagle on the top of his right arm, underneath his shirtsleeve.

There is a long electronic beep which seems to last an eternity.

'Interview held with Lowri Williams, 8.20 p.m. Interview room one, Commissariato San Giovanni. Present are Detective Franco Saachi and Lowri Williams,' Saachi says clearly and then he looks over at her. 'Lowri, can you tell me in your own words what happened last Sunday night when Harry Collard came to your bedroom.'

Lowri takes a deep breath to compose herself. 'I was going to record a TikTok video in my bedroom but I wasn't in the mood. I put some music on and started to get undressed. Harry came to the door of my room and started to talk to me. Then he came in and sat down on my bed.'

'Did you think that was strange?' Saachi asks.

Lowri nods. 'Yes. I hadn't asked him to. And I don't really know... I didn't really know him so it made me feel uncomfortable.'

'Yes.' Saachi nods and then gives her a look for her to continue.

'And then he started to tell me about how he was a very powerful record A&R director. And that he might be able to help me with my career.'

'Did that make you feel happy? That he wanted to help you?' Saachi asks.

'Not really.' Lowri shakes her head. 'I thought he was being creepy. And I already thought that him sitting on my bed telling me this was a ploy of some kind.'

Saachi raises an eyebrow. 'Ploy? Sorry, I...?'

'I didn't think he was sitting there because he genuinely wanted to help me,' Lowri explains.

Saachi nods. 'So, like a trick? Because he was promising this because he wanted to have sex with you?'

His comment jars with Lowri for a second.

'Yes,' she says quietly. 'That's what I thought he was doing.'

'Please, continue.'

'Then he suddenly stood up and walked towards me,' Lowri says. 'I was trapped against the wall. He tried to kiss me. And his hands were all over me. He was trying to pull off my skirt...' She can feel her pulse is racing just talking about it. She takes a breath.

Saachi gives her an empathetic look. 'It's fine. Just take your time.'

'I was trying to fight him off but I couldn't,' Lowri says. 'And then Charlie came in and pulled him off me. Harry punched Charlie in the face and he fell to the floor. And Harry left.'

'Right,' Saachi says with a thoughtful expression. 'And that was when Charlie said "I'm going to fucking kill him"?'

Lowri nods. 'Yes. But he was just angry.'

'And then what happened?' Saachi asks.

'Charlie had some blood on his nose so we went to the bathroom and cleaned it up. Then I got some ice from the kitchen, put it in a tea towel and gave it to Charlie. Then Charlie said he wanted to go back to the villa and he left.'

'And you didn't see Harry again?' Saachi says.

Lowri shakes her head. 'No.'

'What about Charlie?'

'No,' Lowri replies. 'Not until the next day when they found Harry.'

'Did Charlie see his father after he left you?'

Tell the truth. Just tell the truth.

'I'm not sure,' Lowri says unconvincingly.

God, why did you say that! she thinks.

Saachi narrows his eyes. 'You're not sure?' He sounds unconvinced.

Taking a breath, Lowri nods. 'Charlie told me that he saw Harry by the pool after that and they had a row. But he swore that he had nothing to do with what happened.'

Saachi takes a few seconds to process what she's told him. She assumes that Saachi didn't know this and it's a significant development. But Lowri knows she has to tell the truth about everything now.

Lowri can feel the growing sense of guilt. What if Charlie is arrested? What if they convict him on what she's told them?

'Lowri,' Saachi says, breaking her train of thought. 'I'm going to show you something on the video that we found on your phone.' He reaches over to his laptop, opens it and then starts to tap on buttons.

Lowri nods but she has no idea what he's going to show her. 'Okay,' she says as she reaches for the cup of water. Her hands are still shaking. She just wants the interview to be over. But then she's going to have to face Charlie. She hopes she'll have the opportunity to tell him that he needs to be honest about his row with Harry by the pool.

'Here,' Saachi says as he turns the laptop screen to show her the video. The volume has been muted. He fast forwards through to the point at which Charlie arrives and is then punched to the floor. Then he pauses the image.

Why is he showing me this? Lowri wonders.

Saachi takes his index finger and then points to the window on the far side of Lowri's bedroom. The blinds are still up.

Lowri squints. As far as she can see the window is just dark glass.

'I'm not sure what I'm looking at.' Lowri shrugs. 'Sorry.'

'Let me zoom in a bit for you,' Saachi says.

The image gets bigger so that it's now just the bedroom window on the far wall.

And then she can see it.

She does a double take and looks again.

There's a figure standing outside the annexe looking in through the window!

What the fuck!

It's impossible to see the face but there's definitely someone there.

Lowri feels a chill run up her spine.

FORTY-NINE
LUCIA

8.25 p.m.

Lucia looks over at the clock on the mantelpiece, reaches over to the remote control and switches the television over to the Rai 3 channel. Her favourite soap opera *A Place in the Sun – Un posto al sole* – is going to start in ten minutes. It's been going since the mid-nineties and is set in an apartment block on the seafront in Posillipo in Naples. Lorenzo didn't used to like to watch it as he used to say that it was stupid and totally unrealistic. And he was Neopolitan, so he should know. But in recent years, Lucia has managed to persuade Lorenzo to watch it with her. And now he's hooked. Sometimes she teases him, reminding him that he used to scoff at her for watching the soap religously. Sometimes she suspects that he likes it more than she does.

Their evening ritual is to put the kettle on, make a coffee and then settle down on the sofa together with a packet of *amaretti di Saronno*, their favourite almond cookies.

Lucia hasn't seen Lorenzo for nearly an hour so she goes into the kitchen, pops the kettle onto the hob and lights the gas.

Then she wanders outside. The evening is warm. Earlier she saw Nick driving past, heading for the main road. She knew it was him because he was wearing his trademark baseball cap. Lucia and Lorenzo used to joke that he probably slept in that cap! Lucia was glad when Nick left the villa a year ago as he made her feel very uncomfortable when she was up there. He was always angry – mainly at Cerys. A horrible big man. A *ragazzo prepotente*. A bully boy.

The light is on in Lorenzo's workshop. She can hear the terrible Italian pop music that he plays while he's in there. Sometimes she wonders if he goes in there to get away from her. She doesn't mind if he wants some space or time to himself. As long as they sit down every night to watch the television, cuddle on the sofa and drink coffee with almond cookies.

Knocking at the door, she looks into the workshop. Lorenzo is hard at work repairing a couple of sunloungers from a villa about a mile away. He's using a welding iron and wearing protective goggles. She thinks he looks very manly. Masculine. *Maschio*. She feels lucky that they still find each other so attractive.

'Enzo?' she calls, using the shortened version of his name that he prefers. He tells her that only his mother ever called him Lorenzo after the age of ten.

He doesn't hear her.

'Enzo?' she calls again.

He hears her, turns off the welding iron and then pulls up his goggles. He gives her an enquiring look.

'Are you coming?' she asks him.

He smiles as he pulls off the goggles and removes his black protective gloves. 'Yes, of course.'

Then she thinks of something.

'What happened to the broken knife that we brought down from Villa Lucia the other night?' she asks.

'I have it here. I'm going to fix it,' he tells her.

She knows that the blade had come out of the handle.

'No. Don't bother.' Lucia shakes her head. 'Throw it away.'

'Really?' Lorenzo frowns. 'I've straightened the blade and I think I can repair it.'

'I don't want you to repair it,' she snaps. 'Throw it away.'

Lorenzo shrugs. 'If you're sure?'

'Yes. Put it in the municipal bin when you next drive over to Montespertoli,' she says.

'Okay.' Lorenzo nods, giving her a look.

'Sorry,' she says and gives him a kiss on the cheek. She's being crabby. 'Come inside now.'

She takes his hand as they go in and Lucia heads for the kettle, which is now boiling, and makes two cups of coffee.

FIFTY

LOWRI

9.27 p.m.

Lowri is looking at the surface of the wooden table in the room where she is waiting in the Commissariato San Giovanni. It's been nearly an hour since she was led back to this room and Charlie was taken away to be interviewed. And there was no time to tell him what she had told Saachi about his row with Harry later on Sunday night.

She can't get the image from the video out of her head. The idea that there was someone outside her window looking in. It makes her shudder just thinking about it. The only explanation is that it was the intruder who had come up to rob the villa. And presumably the person who had killed Harry. Part of her is freaked out by the idea of this stranger at her window. However, part of her is also relieved. It means that any suspicions she had about Charlie have virtually gone.

Lowri looks up at the clock on the wall. It's nearly 9.30 p.m. The waiting is unbearable. She traces her finger over some water marks on the wood on the table. Moving her forefinger in a circular pattern. Then she taps her nails. It feels impossible to sit still.

What's taking so long? Then Lowri panics. What if Charlie has now been arrested? Their phones were taken from them when they arrived, so she can't call anyone. She wants to speak to her mum or her dad. Either will do. Just a friendly, reassuring voice.

Suddenly the door opens and Lowri flinches nervously.

A uniformed police officer shows Charlie in.

He looks a little shell-shocked.

As she gets up, she's trying desperately to read from his expression and body language what's happened in the interview.

'Hey,' she says and gives him a hug.

'Hey,' Charlie whispers and he holds her for a few seconds. It's just what they both need in that moment. Physical touch and support.

Lowri moves back and searches his face. 'How did it go?'

'I told him everything,' Charlie explains but she can see that he's still shaky. 'I told him about rowing with my dad by the pool.'

'Good, that's good.' Lowri sighs in relief. 'So did I.'

'Yeah, that's what we agreed. Just tell the truth about every-thing,' Charlie says as he goes and sits down. 'He asked me what size my feet were.' He looks confused.

'Really?'

Charlie shrugs. 'Maybe they've found footprints somewhere.'

'Maybe...'

Lowri raises an eyebrow. 'Why, how big are your feet?'

'Only little,' Charlie admits. 'Size eight.'

Lowri gives him a knowing look. 'Oh, so it's not true what they say about men with small feet?'

Charlie smirks.

'Sorry.' Lowri shakes her head with a wry smile. 'I just don't know if I'm coming or going.'

'It's fine. Humour is good,' Charlie reassures her in a soft voice.

'Yeah, otherwise I think I'm actually going to go mad.'

Silence.

'Did he show you the video?' Lowri asks nervously.

Charlie nods.

Before they can talk about it any more, the door opens again and Saachi comes in. He has a clear evidence bag with both their mobile phones inside.

Walking over to the other seat, he sits down.

Lowri can feel her heart thudding away in her chest. *What? What's happening to us? Are you holding us? Say something, please.*

She can hardly get her breath as she wills Saachi to speak.

'Thank you for coming in and telling me what happened,' Saachi says in a calm voice. 'There are a few things that I need to clear up with you and then you will be free to go.' He looks at Lowri. 'Your father is here to take you back.'

Oh, thank God. Lowri is consumed for a few seconds with utter relief. There was part of her that thought she'd never get out.

'In your statements, you said that both of your mothers were in bed when Harry came to your bedroom?' Saachi asks. 'Is that correct?'

Lowri nods. 'Yes. They were both a bit tipsy so...'

'Tipsy?' Saachi asks with an almost amused look.

'Sorry. A bit drunk,' Lowri explains. 'So me and Charlie made sure they got to bed okay. They were both asleep by the time we left them.'

Saachi nods as if taking this in. 'And Lucia and Lorenzo? Did you see them?'

Lowri shakes her head. 'No. They must have left around 10 p.m.' She looks to Charlie for confirmation.

'I didn't see them after we ate,' Charlie says. 'I saw Lorenzo packing up some stuff in the kitchen and Lucia stacking the dishwasher. But I didn't see them again so they must have left.'

Lowri could see what Saachi was doing. By a process of deduction, everyone in the villa that night was accounted for. She, Charlie and Harry were in the video. Her mum and Zoe were asleep in bed. Lucia and Lorenzo had gone back to their cottage.

Saachi furrowed his brow and looked over at Lowri. 'And your father is here in Italy, isn't he?'

'Yes,' Lowri said.

'I'm sure I have it written down but when did he arrive?'

'He flew in last night,' she explained.

'Right,' Saachi says deep in thought. Then he takes their mobile phones out of the evidence bag and hands them back. 'Here you are.'

'Thanks,' Lowri says, still worrying that there's going to be some catch and they won't be able to leave.

'Thank you,' Charlie mumbles as he gets up to take his phone.

Saachi gives them a half smile and points to the door. 'You are free to leave. And your father is waiting for you in reception.'

FIFTY-ONE

CERYS

Two Years Before – Friday, 12 March 2021

Eddie walks over and gives me a hug. I'm overwhelmed by emotion. I'm scared about going back out there. Into the real world. 'Handsome Eddie', as I call him, has been my counsellor at the rehab where I've been for the past eight weeks. We're in the middle of the Hampshire countryside, close to the New Forest. It's a safe bubble. As it's a twelve-step programme rehab, I've been taken to AA, NA and CA meetings on a regular basis. I've found a real connection and hope in the meetings. The people are lovely, friendly and non-judgemental. After all, as they tell me, they've all been where I've been at one time or another. The beginning of my journey to sobriety. Some of their stories are very dark and harrowing. They make mine sound like a teddy bear's picnic. One night I sat next to Ciara. In her thirties, she had been sexually abused by her stepfather as a child. Eventually she had ended up street homeless in Dover. She got into a rehab, got sober seven years ago, and is now a trained nurse in an A&E department. She told me of her incredible gratitude to AA and that she was a walking miracle.

Because of the anonymity, everyone in the AA meetings has a nickname. Some are obvious – Plumber Dave, Teacher Tom or Irish Jim. But then there is Chris Shorts, who wears shorts whatever the weather. Lady Jane who has a very posh accent. And Pam the Jam, who used to bring her home-made jam to meetings.

This morning, I sit and look out at my rehab group. There's eight out of the initial intake of twelve left. Part of me is scared. And part of me is excited and relieved that I've got this far. Some just 'walked' because they didn't really want to stop drinking. Others were asked politely to leave when a secret stash of booze was found in their room or they failed the regular, mandatory breathalyser tests. Handsome Eddie is a recovering alcoholic himself. All the counsellors are. It makes sense. It's hard to talk and counsel someone going through the hell of addiction unless you've been there yourself. And that's how places like AA work. It's just one alcoholic talking to another.

I have a bit of a crush on Handsome Eddie. Sometimes he doesn't mince his words with us though. He reminds us that alcoholism and addiction are killer illnesses. He tells us that the government statistics about annual deaths from alcoholism are far lower than the reality. If an alcoholic is drink-driving and crashes into a tree and dies, their death is recorded as an accident. If an alcoholic falls down the stairs and breaks their neck – another accident. If they develop alcoholic dementia, it's that which is recorded. If they have a heart attack due to the terrible stress alcohol places on the body, it's just a heart attack. And suicide while under the influence of alcohol is still just suicide.

Some of our sessions here have been hilarious. The funny stories about the things we did to hide our drink from others. Keith, a gay salesman from Kent, who hid two huge bottles of vodka in his oven while in blackout. His partner, Stephen, put a chicken on to roast on a Sunday afternoon. After half an hour, the oven exploded, shooting the oven door and chicken across the kitchen. Or Maggie who used to fill a large rubber duck in the bathroom full of vodka when her husband was out at work. He would run her a bath, frisk her before she went into the bathroom and was then baffled how she managed to get hammered every time.

However, there is also a serious message here. Last week, Eddie looked at the group just after we had gathered for the morning session. We had done a group meditation and a reading from one of the daily readings books. Eddie looked slowly around the room. There were ten of us there. And then he told us the stark facts of our future. In five years' time, only two of us would have solid long-term recovery. Two of us would still be drinking, relapsing and then drinking again. And six of us would be dead! That really brought me up sharp. I felt my whole body react in that moment. I couldn't believe it. I've grown to love the people I'm in rehab with. We eat together, have coffee together and then pour out our hearts to one another. In the evenings, we travel to meetings together in the rehab minibus or sit and watch movies, play pool or go for a walk. I've held daily yoga sessions with some of the women. We're all so close. And six of us aren't going to make it.

That evening I told Nick on the phone how determined I was that I was going to be one of those two people. He told me that he believed me. Since going into rehab, our relationship has changed so much. He says that he can see how much I've changed and that I'm the woman he fell in love with all those years ago. Nick and Lowri have come to visit from London nearly every weekend. Being away from Lowri is killing me. At first, she was very quiet and standoffish when she came with Nick to visit. I think she was still angry at me for what I'd put her through in the past couple of years. However, I've tried to explain to both of them that alcoholism is a disease. It's not something I've chosen to suffer from. It's not a lifestyle choice. That doesn't mean that I'm not responsible for what I've done in the past. It doesn't absolve me from any of that. But I keep telling them how determined I am to keep working my twelve-step programme and remain sober. And now I can see that Lowri is glad to see me well, happy and healthy.

I've been looking at going back to teaching yoga when I leave and return to London. I know how much holding the classes in rehab has done for my mental well-being in the past two months. Nick is being incredibly supportive of that too. I don't blame him for the way he treated me towards the end. I don't blame him for losing his patience and lashing out. He'd had enough of my behaviour. I understand that and I've shared that with the group on many occasions.

I take a breath and look at the group with a smile. I'm going home. Wow, the thought of that gives me such a thrill. They all smile back at me. Such a range of people sitting there. Our youngest is only thirty and our oldest is sixty-three. A doctor, an architect, a car salesman, a CEO of a marketing company and a professional golfer.

I explain in detail everything I'm going to do once I step outside the rehab to keep me sober. Regular AA meetings, a sponsor, meditation and readings. Everyone claps and whoops. They all give me a hug and I wonder if I'll ever see any of them again. There have been lots of promises that we'll visit and stay in touch. I hope we do. I've made such good friends.

Eddie gives me a hug, leads me out of the building and towards the car park where I'm due to meet Nick to take me back to London. Eddie gives me some parting advice and leaves me.

I see Nick get out of the car and my heart leaps. I feel so different. I feel like I've been given a new life and a new way of seeing things. I'm so bloody lucky, I tell myself.

'Hey, stranger,' I say as Nick comes over and takes me in his arms.

'You look so well.' He beams as he takes my suitcase and we head for the car.

At that moment, the sun comes out from behind cloud and shines down on us. It feels like a sign or something. I know I'm being silly but I have such a sense of positivity and peace.

Getting into the car, I look over at Nick and smile. 'Thank you. I don't know what I'd do without you.'

'I just want the old you back,' Nick says as he leans over and kisses me.

'Well, this is the new me.' I laugh. 'A much better version of the old me.'

Nick looks at me. He's got something to tell me.

'What is it?' I ask with a quizzical look. I'm not sure I want any surprises.

'Sorry,' he says with a smile. 'I wasn't going to tell you before we get home. But I can't wait.' He grabs his phone, taps the screen and then after a few seconds he shows me.

A beautiful white holiday villa with a pool and blue sky.

'Wow,' I say. 'Are we going on holiday?'

'Villa Lucia,' Nick announces in a slightly odd way.

'Okay.' I frown. 'What's going on?'

Nick is beside himself with excitement. 'Hear me out before you say anything. This villa is in Tuscany. It's for sale. I've done the sums. I've had our house valued and I've spoken to my parents who are willing to give us most of the rest. Plus I've got my book advance.' He flicks the screen to show me another photo. 'So, there's this two-bedroomed annexe here. That's where we'd live. We run the villa as an Airbnb. You do yoga classes in the morning. We can provide breakfast. There's a couple who live five minutes away who will do all the washing, cleaning, gardening and the pool for the current owners.'

'Jesus, Nick,' I say. I'm feeling overwhelmed.

'I can write my book,' Nick says with a boyish grin. 'It's a new start for me and you. And we get to live in this beautiful place. And we can afford to do it.'

'What about Lowri?' I ask.

'My parents say she can stay with them while she finishes off her A levels this year. Then she comes out to Tuscany for the summer and then she's off to university,' Nick says excitedly.

'If she goes to university,' I say. Then I look at Nick's excited face. It's hard not to get swept up in his enthusiasm. 'It sounds amazing.'

'It's just what we need,' he says as he reaches over and squeezes my hand. 'It's just what *you* need. A completely new start.'

However, my anxiety is starting to rocket. We've been told to keep things very simple when we leave rehab. No trips, no holidays, avoid parties and pubs. Get to lots of meetings in the local area. What Nick is suggesting goes against everything I've been told to do.

'What?' he says with a frown. His tone has changed and he sounds disappointed.

'It's nothing.' I want to please him. I don't want to let him down or make him angry. 'It's just...'

Nick looks at me. His disappointment is turning to anger. I can see it. I know the tell-tale signs. 'I thought you'd be pleased?'

'I am. I think it's an incredible idea,' I say with a reassuring smile. 'Just not now. My counsellor told us to keep things simple when we leave here. Go to meetings. No holidays. Nice and peaceful. Nothing stressful.'

Nick narrows his eyes in disbelief. 'Stressful. I'm suggesting that you teach open-air yoga in the Tuscan countryside at a beautiful, luxury villa. Does that sound stressful?'

My pulse is racing. His anger is scaring me. 'No, it doesn't. Of course it doesn't.'

'Well, what's the bloody problem, Cerys?' he snaps.

'My meetings,' I mumble apologetically.

'They have meetings online, don't they?' Nick says, shaking his head. 'You told me you can go on Zoom AA meetings all around the world.'

'Yes, but I...' I don't want to tell him that it's just not the same. There's nothing as powerful as physically sitting in a room with other alcoholics and sharing how you feel. Getting to know them over the weeks and then months.

'But what?' Nick bangs his hand angrily against the steering wheel. 'I'm doing this for you. I thought you'd be fucking happy! What the fuck is the matter with you?'

There is a tense silence.

I'll do anything to placate Nick now. I can't stand my overwhelming anxiety when he gets this angry.

'I'm really sorry,' I tell him softly. 'It's a brilliant idea. We should go and do it. It'll be exciting. And the online meetings are really good.'

Nick nods thoughtfully as he calms down. 'Sorry. I didn't mean to shout. I've just been so excited about this.'

'No, I'm sorry,' I tell him as I put my hand on his. 'It's going to be the best thing we ever do. I know it is.'

Nick nods, smiles at me and starts the engine.

FIFTY-TWO
LOWRI

Tuesday
9.56 p.m.

It is forty kilometres from Florence back to Villa Lucia. Lowri's dad said that it shouldn't take more than forty-five minutes at this time of night. Having made sure that they were both all right, her dad drove them away from the police station in virtual silence.

Lowri's emotionally drained. Exhausted and bone tired. Her nerves feel frayed and brittle. The image of the person at the window in the video haunts her. She shifts uncomfortably in the passenger seat of the small Peugeot rental. Charlie is in the back.

Her dad is tall – six foot four, she thinks. He looks silly driving such a small car, but he's a cheapskate so it was probably the cheapest hire car he could get. It feels uncomfortable to be in such a confined space with him just sitting in silence. Some-times he seems so angry. An uncontrollable rage that scares her. He rages against the world and the hand that he's been dealt. It's as if he is still waiting for his big break as a political writer or journalist. But he's in his early fifties and Lowri suspects that's never going to happen.

She gazes out at the streets of Florence. They are buzzing and busy, full of lights, people, scooters and cars. Couples walking hand in hand. Lowri assumes that they are tourists on holiday either going out to dinner or having just finished. They drive past the Piazza del Duomo. The distinctive dome of the Florence Cathedral, built in the thirteenth century and a masterpiece of Renaissance architecture, looms above them. As she looks out, all Lowri wants is for her life to go back to some kind of normality. She wants to walk the streets of Florence, get a gelato or a coffee and do what everyone else seems to be doing. Instead she feels like she's trapped in a never-ending nightmare. A few minutes later and they are in the suburbs before they join the main road heading south. She spots a sign for Montespertoli which is now thirty-five kilometres. Lowri knows that's close to the villa. She just wants to get back, see her mum, shower, eat, smoke a spliff and drink beer.

'What did they ask you?' her dad asks, eventually breaking the silence.

Lowri has already explained to her dad what was in the video, that Harry had attacked her and Charlie had effectively come to the rescue. But her dad hasn't actually seen it. She'd begged him not to watch it.

Lowri shrugs. 'They just asked me to tell them exactly what happened on Sunday when Harry came to my room.'

'And you told them everything?' her dad asks.

'Yes,' Lowri says, suddenly unsure of herself. She realises that she's been so relieved to get out of the police station and head home, she hasn't told him about the figure they'd been shown in the video looking in at the window.

'They showed us that someone was watching what happened from outside,' Charlie says from the back of the car.

Her dad frowns.

'On the video from my phone,' she explains.

'What?' he asks coolly.

'You can see someone looking in,' Lowri says.

'Are you sure it's not a trick of the light?' her dad asks. He seems agitated. It's not surprising after everything that's happened.

'No.' Charlie shakes his head. 'There's definitely someone there. That detective showed us.'

'Can you see who it is?' her dad asks.

'No,' Lowri responds. 'I'm not sure if they've got that image-enhancing software. Maybe they'll be able to clean up the image and get a clearer idea.'

Her dad looks over at her. 'They told you they were going to do that?'

'No,' Lowri says. 'I just thought they might.'

Lowri glances back and sees that Charlie is looking out of the window, lost in thought. She can't imagine how he's feeling after the events of recent days.

'Are you okay?' she asks in a gentle voice.

Charlie looks at her and gives her a reassuring nod. 'Yeah, you know.'

'Maybe it was Lucia or Lorenzo?' her dad suggests.

'They'd left by then,' Lowri explains. 'It could well be the person who came up to rob the villa checking the place over.'

Her dad frowns. 'We don't actually know that Lucia or Lorenzo had left, do we?'

Lowri glances over at him. 'What does that mean?' She doesn't like what he's trying to imply.

'I'm just stating facts,' he replies with a haughty raise of his eyebrows.

Lowri looks out of the window again. She doesn't want to get drawn into her dad's theories. The dark Tuscan countryside is rushing past. The thick trees that cover the hillside seem impenetrable. As they get closer to the villa, the terrain becomes mountainous. Steep swathes of rock loom above them as they weave around the precarious roads. The sky above is covered by a thick blanket of cloud. There is no moon and no stars. All Lowri can see is an unsettling inky-black void.

FIFTY-THREE

CERYS

One Year Earlier – Saturday, 11 June 2022

It's been two hours since the guests left and Nick is roaming around the villa like a bear with a sore head. We have until tomorrow to clean and prepare Villa Lucia for the next guests to arrive. Lucia has already stripped the beds and taken the sheets away to wash. Lorenzo has cleaned the pool and checked that the pH and chemicals are in balance.

I don't think Lucia likes me. In fact, I know that she doesn't. I can sense it. Not in anything she says. She's very polite, accommodating and helpful. But she resents us being here. I understand that it was her father and uncle who built the original villa. And of course, it's named after her. But that was decades ago. Sometimes I wonder why she seems so unhappy. Lorenzo is a man who most women would not kick out of bed for dropping crumbs, including me. Their cottage is idyllic. They don't seem to struggle for money, with all the work they have for the local villas in the area. Maybe it's something else. And it's not for me to judge, is it? Who knows what goes on behind closed doors.

Sitting down at the table on the decking, I look out at the view. The colours are just so vivid in the sunlight. Like an impressionist painting. I remember going to the Musée d'Orsay in Paris in my twenties and spending hours just sitting and looking at the enormous canvases. I was mesmerised by a painting of a poppy field by Monet – *Coquelicots*. The representation of sunlight on the French countryside just took my breath away.

'Haven't you got anything to do?' snapped an irritable voice.

It's Nick.

He's got that expression on his face that he seems to have been wearing increasingly in recent weeks. Irritable and discontented. While drunk the other night, Nick admitted to me that he's regretting taking on Villa Lucia. It's more work than he imagined. I think that's a joke. The only thing Nick has to deal with are the bookings, taking and returning deposits, and any queries that guests might have before a visit. All of the hard work is done by Lucia, Lorenzo and myself. But Nick seems to resent having to do anything. He's struggling to write his political history of Britain book for which he's been paid a decent advance. He says he can't concentrate.

Now that we've been here for eight months, I also realise that being isolated here means that Nick's controlling behaviour is becoming increasingly suffocating. He quizzes me every time I drive over to Montespertoli to visit the supermarket or stop and have a coffee. He's suspicious. I know that he thinks that I'm meeting someone. He's always been like that. Insanely jealous, which is a joke when I know that it's Nick who's had affairs in the past. It's got to the point where he will now stop his writing and insist that he comes with me wherever I go. He makes a feeble excuse that he needs something from Montespertoli – paper, printer ink or some other kind of stationery. When I offer to get it, he makes more excuses of why he needs to accompany me.

Nick also seems to have an opinion on everything I wear when I'm going out or even meeting new guests. Dresses are 'too revealing', shorts are 'too tight', and the remotest sign of cleavage when I'm wearing a top provokes a disapproving tut and look. Jesus, it's exhausting.

And this control and jealousy has severely impacted my recovery. When we first arrived, I was attending two or three Zoom AA meetings online a week. I found a lovely meeting in Putney and a wonderful woman called Pam to be my sponsor. However, Nick's attitude to my meetings has become increasingly hostile. 'That's it. Off you go to your little fucking AA mates and leave me on my own all night,' he tells me. He suspects that Pam is actually a man that I'm having an affair with. So, I've cut down my meetings. Once a week and now rarely. Pam texts me to see how I'm doing but I don't reply. Instead I reassure Nick that my sobriety is just fine and I don't really need to go.

But I do. I knew that I would. I was warned eight months ago that my sobriety had to be my number one priority or else I'd lose it. I'd become one of those six people in that room that Eddie had predicted would die. Recovery is now way down my list. I convinced myself I didn't need a programme of recovery. I'd come this far without drinking, how hard could it be? I could do it on my own, no problem.

But I started drinking again three days ago.

And not the odd secret glass of wine here and there. Full-blown alcoholic drinking.

That's what they told me in rehab. Your drinking will go straight back to being as bad as when you stopped. And often it's even worse.

It is worse. The compulsion to keep drinking is driving me insane.

So far, Nick hasn't noticed. But that's not going to last.

I'm drunk on vodka and it's not even lunchtime. I take the

glass that's in front of me. The liquid is clear and there's ice. But it's not water. I take a mouthful. I don't care.

'Don't ignore me,' Nick growls.

I give him a nonchalant shrug and say nothing. I don't care.

But he recognises something in the shrug or the look I've given him.

In a flash, he's reached over and snatched the glass from under my nose. Then he lifts it and sniffs.

Oh shit, here we go, I think. The tone of my voice inside my head sounds weary but also amused. This was inevitable.

'Are you fucking joking?' he screams at me.

I don't reply. What am I going to say?

Suddenly, he slaps me hard around the side of the head. The force of it knocks me off my chair and onto the decking.

'You stupid fucking bitch!' he yells. 'How could you do this to me?'

I look up at him and smirk. I hate him so much in this moment, I wish him dead. I know me smirking at him is going to drive him insane with fury. I used to do it to him in our house in London.

'Don't you...' Nick is seething.

I let out a drunken cackle. I want him to hurt me more. I think that's what I deserve. *Come on, Nick. Show me what you've really fucking got. Show me that you're a real man!*

I want him to kick me to death so I can be out of this pain that's inside my head.

Nick tries to kick me but I put my hands up to stop him and my little finger snaps back.

'I fucking hate you,' Nick says and he spits on the floor beside me as if to demonstrate this.

I force myself to laugh more as he storms away back to the annexe.

FIFTY-FOUR

ZOE

Wednesday
12.12 p.m.

Taking a mug, Zoe goes over to the coffee machine where she stands for a moment deep in thought. Nick has come inside and is wandering around erratically. He's been acting strangely all morning.

Zoe slept in late. Actually, when she woke she just watched Charlie sleeping next to her. He slept there all night. The ordeal in Florence had really taken it out of him and he had dozed off almost as soon as his head hit the pillow. It reminded her of the times he'd slept in the bed with her when he was younger. Every time Harry went on a work trip abroad – usually the US. It was just their routine that Charlie slept with her when Harry was away.

'Excuse I,' Nick says as he brushes past her and grabs a bottle of Smirnoff, goes to the fridge where he lifts out a bottle of tomato juice.

Zoe ignores him but she can smell the booze on his breath. She yawns and then stretches. It had taken her a very long time to get to sleep last night. She could have done with a sleeping pill or something. She just couldn't get the images from the video of Harry attacking Lowri out of her head.

I was married to that monster, she thinks to herself. *What the hell does that say about me?*

Affairs or one-night stands behind her back were one thing. And she never had enough proof – just gut-churning suspicion. But this was a sexual assault on a young woman. A girl. What the hell was wrong with him?

And then, as she watched Charlie's chest rise and fall, his face peaceful as he slept beside her, Zoe felt her heart breaking. Her precious child, now damaged for life after witnessing his father sexually assaulting a girl and then to see him dead in the pool the following morning. How on earth was he going to deal with all that?

Maybe if she'd been braver and left Harry when his behaviour had become truly toxic, she could have protected Charlie. But no, she'd clung to Harry pathetically. What kind of mother did that make her?

The sound of ice dropping into a glass shakes Zoe out of these thoughts. She sees Nick over at the dining table creating another jug of Bloody Mary. He seems pretty drunk already and it's only just gone twelve.

Nick must have realised that she's watching him, because he turns to meet her gaze. There's something deeply unpleasant about this man.

'After all that yesterday,' Nick says with a smug grin, 'I thought a few Bloody Marys with brunch might be just the thing.'

'Why not?' Zoe replies, forcing a smile. She has no desire to drink all day so she presses the button on the coffee machine and watches as the stream of fresh espresso fills her cup.

How is all this going to end? she wonders. What she would give now to be walking carefree through Dulwich park, or ambling around the Dulwich Picture Gallery. A pub lunch with friends. The heat, tension and isolation of the villa are starting to really get to her. She feels suffocated.

Then she realises that at some point she's going to have to organise getting Harry home, and a funeral. She can't even begin to think about that.

'Hi, Mum,' Charlie says as he wanders in.

'Hey, sleepyhead,' Zoe says but Charlie seems distracted and even agitated. 'Do you want a coffee, darling?'

Charlie shakes his head. 'I'm all right.'

'There are Bloody Marys on the go if that's more your poison,' Nick says as he stirs the jug with a wooden spoon and then pours himself another glass.

'I'm fine,' Charlie says, with a frown, looking at Nick.

'Well, cheers,' Nick says merrily as he takes a sip from the glass and then wanders outside to the decking where he's been sitting reading and drinking all morning.

Zoe watches Nick go. His behaviour is even more bizarre this morning than yesterday. A sort of forced chirpiness that seems at odds to what's been happening at the villa in recent days and the general mood.

'Have you seen Lowri?' Charlie asks very quietly as he comes over, and Zoe spots that her son is also studying Nick with an almost suspicious expression.

'Everything all right, Charlie?' Zoe asks with a frown.

'I need to see Lowri,' Charlie says urgently.

Zoe gestures. 'I think she's over in the annexe. What's going on, love?'

Charlie gives her a dark look. 'She texted me. She says she thinks she knows who was up here at the villa on Sunday night snooping around.'

FIFTY-FIVE

LUCIA

12.24 p.m.

Lucia is outside pegging out towels and bedding from Villa Lucia. One of the fitted sheets from one of the bedrooms had been put into the laundry basket. As Lucia put it in the washing machine, she saw that there was a blood stain about the size of a fist in the middle of the sheet. She assumed that it was due to a woman having *le mestruazioni*. However, she noticed as she hung the sheet out, the blood stain hadn't quite gone. She sighs as she will have to wash the sheet again at a higher temperature.

She spots something out of the corner of her eye. A car is turning into their driveway. Her heart is in her mouth as it always is when someone arrives unannounced at their home. There are Lorenzo's past problems that he left behind in Naples for starters.

A figure gets out of the car. It is Detective Saachi. Even though there is no real reason to feel anxious, Lucia can't help but get butterflies at the sight of his car. She imagines the worst. Maybe Saachi looked into Lorenzo's background and saw that he was wanted for questioning over the murder of Paulo Piri-ante of the Bassilino family.

'*Buongiorno,*' Saachio says giving her a half wave hello.

'*Buongiorno,*' she replies in a friendly tone but she's still on tenterhooks as to what he wants.

'Is your husband around?' Saachi asks as he looks over at the workshed.

Why is he asking that? Lucia wonders anxiously.

'Erm, yes,' she says cautiously.

'It's okay,' Saachi reassures her. 'I need to speak to the both of you. It won't take more than a minute or two.'

'Oh, I see.' Lucia is relieved by what he's told her. 'I'll just get him. Would you like to come in?' she asks, gesturing to the door that's open.

Saachi stretches and looks up to the sky. 'Actually, it's a beautiful morning. There's no need.'

'Of course.' Lucia wanders away towards Lorenzo's shed. She pokes her head inside and sees that he's sitting with his feet up on the workbench reading a magazine. She gives him a look.

'What is it?' he asks her in a whisper.

'It's okay,' she says. 'It's that Detective Saachi. He wants to ask us a couple of questions. I'm sure it's nothing.'

'Okay,' Lorenzo replies as he puts the magazine down and follows her outside.

Saachi is waiting for them, holding his notepad and pen. 'I'm sorry to disturb you both again. I just need to clarify a few things.'

'No problem,' Lorenzo says with a shrug.

'On Sunday night,' Saachi says as he flicks the pages of his notebook, 'you left the villa at around 10 p.m. Is that correct?'

'Yes,' Lucia replies.

Saachi looks over at them. 'Both of you together?'

Lorenzo nods. 'Yes, that's right.'

'And you didn't go back to the villa again? You didn't forget something and have to go back?'

'No, nothing like that,' Lucia replies, wondering why they are going over the same details again.

'And you didn't see anyone hanging around that you didn't know or recognise?' Saachi asked.

'No,' Lorenzo says, shaking his head.

Saachi then points up to the front of their cottage where their security camera is mounted. 'Does that work?'

'Yes.' Lorenzo sounds almost proud.

Saachi looks deep in thought. 'Do you record everything?'

'Yes,' Lorenzo replies. 'I wipe the files every month to make more space.'

'So, you would have been recording on Sunday night?' Saachi asks.

'Yes.'

Saachi frowns, turns and then points to the track. 'Does it cover that track too?'

Lorenzo nods. 'Yes.'

Lucia can't understand what use it would be to see their security camera footage from Sunday night. That man was murdered up at the villa. What use is seeing what's on there?

'Can you show me?' Saachi asks.

'Of course.' Lorenzo gestures to the cottage. 'Please. Come in.'

Lucia follows them inside where it is dark and cool compared to outside.

'Would you like a coffee? Or a glass of water, perhaps?' she asks Saachi as Lorenzo goes over to the laptop on the living room table and turns it on.

Saachi gives her a kind smile. 'Thank you, but I'm fine.'

'Here we go,' Lorenzo says as the laptop screen bursts into life. 'What would you like to see?'

'Can you show me what your camera picked up from 11.30

p.m. onwards?' Saachi says quietly, perching on the low window sill to watch.

'Yes, no problem,' Lorenzo says as he clicks on various files, finds the right one and then begins to play the footage forward at high speed. When the timecode at the bottom of the screen shows 2330 he stops it. 'From here?'

'Can you play it forward but slowly?' Saachi asks.

Lorenzo nods. He presses play and adjusts the speed.

Lucia watches from a distance but she can't believe that there's anything on there. If someone did come to rob the villa at that time, they wouldn't just drive up there and park, would they?

Suddenly, there is an image of a car driving up the track.

'There,' Saachi says pointing.

Lorenzo pauses the video and plays the footage back. The timecode reads 2346.

He plays it again.

This time he stops it as the car passes the end of their drive.

Lucia takes a step forward and sees that it's a small car.

And the number plate is visible.

Lorenzo squints. 'I think I can read the number plate.'

Saachi takes a moment as he looks at the screen. 'It is okay. I know that car and who it belongs to.'

FIFTY-SIX

LUCIA

Two Years Before – Tuesday, 11 May 2021

Lucia puts the red onions and garlic into her shopping bag and hands the stallholder two euros. The market in Montespertoli is every Wednesday and she loves it. The colours and smells. Everything about it. And of course, she's been coming here since she was a child.

Montespertoli is a lovely little medieval town south of Florence. *Città del vino* – it's one of Tuscany's most famous wine capitals. Its main street – Via Roma – has butchers, bakers and the wonderful Gelateria Fiorentina. Lucia treats herself to one of their *bacio di noce* gelatos – chocolate and local walnuts. She rarely changes her choice. *Bacio di noce* was her gelato of choice when she visited Montespertoli with her father and uncle.

Lorenzo has gone to meet some friends at a bar in the town's main square, Piazza del Machiavelli, named after the family that owned the area in the fourteenth century. She likes the fact that Lorenzo has a few beers and chats to the other men. She can see that it's good for him.

As Lucia moves along the various stalls, she picks out local produce as she goes. Cheeses, cured meats, vegetables, fruit. The stalls are mainly set up under white or green awnings that shield the owners and their produce from the blistering sun. The square itself is cobbled and flanked by two-storey buildings that are painted in lovely biscuity browns and creams. Many of the stall owners have been coming to Montespertoli for decades and Lucia catches up with them, gossiping about local news and politics.

With her bags now full of produce, Lucia begins to make her way over towards the town's sixteenth-century Baroque church – Chiesa di Sant Andrea. It suffered damage in the Second World War but that has now been repaired. Going inside the cool, dark interior, Lucia crosses herself and bows her head. She moves slowly over to a triptych of the Madonna with saints and kneels down to pray. She prays for the souls of her dear departed mother, father and uncle. And she prays for Lorenzo and asks God to keep them safe from the troubles that he left behind in Naples. She tells God that Lorenzo is now a good man. He's gentle, kind and caring.

And then her prayers turn to Cerys, the woman that owns Villa Lucia with her husband, Nick. Lucia knows that she must pray for Cerys even though she does find it difficult to feel sorry for her. Lucia has resented Cerys ever since she and Nick bought her villa. She can't help but feel jealous that they get to live up there when that should have been her and Lorenzo. It just doesn't feel fair.

But Lucia has started to notice Cerys's terrible unhappiness. She drinks too much. Like Lucia's father, Cerys drinks to stop herself from feeling so sad. Her husband, Nick, is a vile pig of a man. She has heard him shout at her and call her dreadful names. He tells her that she is worthless. And she has seen bruises too. What kind of man does that to a woman? He must be a despicable coward. Sometimes she wants to tell Lorenzo to go and give Nick a taste of his own medicine. Let's see how brave Nick is then.

And so, despite the jealousy and bitterness, Lucia knows that she must pray for Cerys. She must ask that Cerys finds some kind of happiness and peace in her life, as God. *Luke 2:13–14 Peace to all men and women on earth...*

FIFTY-SEVEN

LOWRI

Wednesday
12.25 p.m.

Lowri sits against the pillows on her bed and looks in shock at the screen of her laptop. Maybe she was just seeing things. She has just messaged Charlie to come and have a look to make sure it wasn't her imagination. If she's correct in her thinking, then the repercussions are going to be horrific. It's unthinkable. That's why her breathing is shallow and her stomach's in knots.

Charlie appears in her doorway and looks at her. 'What is it?'

'I need to show you something.' Lowri points at her laptop praying that Charlie can't see what she can and that she's got it all wrong.

Please, God, let me be wrong!

'Erm... Okay.' Charlie looks baffled as he comes over and she moves across the bed so he can sit next to her.

Lowri takes a deep breath to compose herself before launching into what she's about to run past Charlie.

'What am I looking at exactly?' Charlie asks as he peers at

her laptop screen. At the moment, there is just a very dark blurred image on it.

But that's not what she's found.

'Okay.' Lowri blows out her cheeks and looks at him. 'I logged into my iCloud and I downloaded that TikTok video from Sunday night.'

Charlie narrows his eyes. 'Why?' he asks. 'Why would you want to watch that again?'

'I didn't want to watch it again,' she reassures him. 'I just wanted to look at whoever is looking through my window.'

'Okay.' Charlie shrugs. 'But you can't see anything really. We saw all that last night at the police station.'

'Yes, that's true.' Lowri takes a moment. 'A while ago, Mum gave me some old photos of her and my grandparents. They were taken in the sixties or seventies, I think. Some of them were a bit blurred, out of focus or the colour was bleached. But I found this online app that allows you to upload those photos. Then the app uses AI to fill in the gaps, clear up the image and the colours.'

Charlie pauses, frowns and then the penny drops. 'You took a screenshot of that person at the window from the video and uploaded it to that app.'

Lowri nods but she begins to feel teary and upset. 'Sorry... I...' Then she shakes her head.

'What is it?' Charlie asks gently, putting a hand on hers.

'I'll show you,' Lowri whispers as she wipes the tears from her face and then loads the AI-enhanced image.

The frame loads and then Lowri zooms in on the window.

Although the image of the person at the window isn't crystal clear... it's clear enough.

Charlie's eyes widen and then he looks at her. 'That's your dad,' he says under his breath.

She nods slowly.

Her dad's baseball cap is visible and the lower part of his

face – chin and mouth. It's enough for them both to know who it is.

'Jesus,' Charlie mutters. 'He said he didn't fly until Monday night.'

Lowri nods. She knows this. She's already processed all this. Her dad lied about when he arrived in Tuscany.

'And if he saw Harry attacking me...' Lowri can't finish the sentence because it's too distressing for her to say out loud.

Charlie nods. She can see he knows exactly what she's implying. He takes her in his arms.

'Hey,' he says gently. He's about to lean in and kiss her when they're interrupted by a voice at the door.

'Everything all right?'

It's her mum.

Lowri looks at her. For a moment, she thinks about snapping her laptop shut and hiding all this from her. But she's sick to death of keeping secrets. And she can't keep this from her.

'Mum, I...' Lowri hesitates.

'Lowri? What is it?' Her mum can sense the anxiety in Lowri's voice.

'I need to show you something,' Lowri says, aware that she's about to turn everyone's world upside down again.

'What is it?' her mum repeats. 'You're scaring me...'

'I managed to take the image from the video and get it enhanced,' Lowri explains as she turns the laptop to show her. 'We think we know who was looking in at my window.'

Her mum stoops down and peers at the screen. Then her face falls when she recognises who it is.

FIFTY-EIGHT

CERYS

12.27 p.m.

I'm striding out of the annexe and heading for the villa. Fury doesn't begin to describe how I'm feeling in this moment. For some reason, I haven't had a drink this morning so my head is clear and my thinking rational. My heart is thumping as the adrenaline courses through my veins. After everything that man has put me through.

Marching down the path that leads to the empty pool, I need to know what Nick was doing here, what happened and why on earth he's been lying to all of us.

Nick turns and sees me heading for the decking where he's sitting peeling an orange and reading some thick political tome.

'Fancy a drink?' he asks with a smug grin.

And as I stride across the decking towards where he's sitting with a bemused look on his face, I have no fear. For whatever reason, I'm not afraid of him. In fact, I see him for everything he is. I hate him. With every step I take, I remember the psychological and physical abuse. The shame. Somehow I'm shedding the fear and anxiety as I march defiantly towards him. If I had a weapon I would gladly kill him in that instant.

'What the fuck were you doing here on Sunday night, Nick?' I bellow. I know that maybe there should be more control to my confrontation but there's not. My rage is murderous.

Nick pulls an amused face and lifts his sunglasses. 'What are you talking about? Are you drunk again, Cerys?'

You utter prick! I want to punch him.

His eyes are bloodshot and I can see that it's Nick who is in fact drunk. In fact, he looks hammered, which is unusual.

'I've seen the video, Nick,' I snarl as I lock eyes with him.

Lucia, who is returning some washed bedding to the villa, appears from the side of the villa carrying striped washing bags. She stops when she hears me shouting.

'What video?' Nick snorts with derision as he gets to his feet. He towers above me but I don't care.

'Our daughter found it,' I snap at him. 'The person looking through the window on Sunday night. Watching her nearly getting raped. That was you, Nick. We can see it's you.'

The colour drains from his face. 'No, don't be so utterly ridiculous.' He splutters scornfully.

'We can see your face,' I say and then point to his head. 'And that stupid bloody cap. What the hell were you doing up here?'

Nick's a little unsteady on his feet. 'I wasn't here,' he sneers. 'So, it can't be me.'

'Stop lying, Nick!'

'Everything okay?' Zoe asks as she comes out of the villa to see what all the shouting is about.

'No, it's not!' I point at Nick and look at Zoe. 'He was here on Sunday night.'

'I wasn't,' Nick protests, shaking his head.

Even though I'm shaky, I'm also focused and alert.

'What?' Zoe asks in disbelief.

'It's his face at the window in the video,' I tell her and I gesture to Nick's deck shoes. 'I should have thought about it. The size twelve footprints where Harry's phone was found. I only know one person with size twelve feet.'

Nick's eyes are now moving nervously. *I've got him.* I can see he's scared and I love it. He's finally getting a taste of his own medicine.

Zoe looks perplexed and starts to walk down from the villa. 'But you told us you flew in on Monday night. Why did you lie to us?'

Nick is lost for words.

'You saw Harry attack our daughter,' I say angrily. 'Then you disappeared. Why the fuck didn't you do something, Nick? What's wrong with you?'

'Nothing happened,' Nick mutters anxiously as he takes a step backwards. 'I swear to you.'

You lying bastard!

Lucia has moved closer and she looks at Nick with disgust. 'You are a very stupid, nasty man.'

Nick turns to look at her with utter contempt. 'What?'

Lucia gives Nick a withering look and points down to her cottage. 'We have a camera on our house. You drove up here on Sunday just before twelve. The detective saw your number plate. You were up here.'

'I... I can explain,' Nick stammers as he looks back at me, holding out his hands. 'Okay, I was up here. I admit that. But I... I didn't see him attack Lowri. I just saw Charlie and Harry having a fight and Harry storming out. I had no idea what had happened.'

'What?' Zoe exclaims.

'And you expect us to believe that?' I snort angrily.

'I don't care what you believe.' Nick looks terrified. 'That's the truth... I didn't... I didn't kill him.'

Out of the corner of my eye, I spot two dusty trails coming up the track from the road.

It's Saachi's car followed by a dark blue marked police car.

Bingo. Here comes the cavalry!

I point to them. 'That's all right, Nick. You can explain all that to Detective Saachi in a couple of minutes.'

Lucia scowls at Nick. 'Looks like you're going to prison.'

Nick's eyes roam around, wild with panic. 'No. This is all wrong.'

You nasty, pathetic bully. You're going to get what you deserve, I think triumphantly.

I love watching Nick squirm. It's the moment I've been waiting for for so long.

'What did you do to my husband?' Zoe asks in disbelief.

Suddenly, Nick grabs the knife that he'd been using to peel the orange.

Shit!

In a swift move, he grabs me, swings me around and puts his arm around my neck. Then he puts the knife to my throat.

It happens so quickly that I'm completely caught off guard.

'Jesus Christ, Nick!' I yelp.

'I'm not going anywhere,' he shouts to everyone as he backs away off the decking.

'Nick!' Zoe says in desperation. 'Don't be so bloody stupid!'

I'm struggling but Nick has me in a vicelike grip as he keeps moving backwards.

'What the hell are you doing?' I croak. His forearm is hard against my windpipe.

'Just shut up!' he bellows into my ear.

We're moving backwards quickly but Zoe and Lucia are both following.

'Stay back!' Nick yells at them. 'I'm warning you.'

Zoe and Lucia look shocked but stop in their tracks.

'The police are going to be here in about two minutes, Nick!' I yell in desperation. I have no idea what he thinks he's doing. And I'm pretty sure neither does he.

'Come on,' Nick growls as he pulls me roughly.

He's going to break my neck if he squeezes any harder.

'You're making this a hundred times worse,' I gasp.

'I told you to shut up,' he hisses at me.

Lucia locks eyes with me, gives me a meaningful look and turns and hurries away. It's as if she's trying to tell me something.

I can feel the hairs of Nick's forearm against my chin and smell the booze on his breath.

'Nick!' I croak as I try to breathe. My head is spinning as I suck in air.

Then Nick moves around to my side, still brandishing the knife and arm around my neck. But now we're moving at speed uphill.

I try to shrug him off but he's too strong for me. I can also see he's desperate and if I run, he might stab me.

I'm terrified. My mouth is dry and my pulse is thundering.

The wooded area is to our left.

The wind picks up and I get a welcome breeze across my sweaty face. I breathe in deeply through my nostrils. The familiar fragrance of pine and eucalyptus.

'Where are we going?' I demand as I stumble on. The ground feels hard and uneven through the thin soles of my canvas shoes.

'Shut up!' Nick snaps and then gives me an almighty shove. I stagger forward and nearly lose my footing. 'Stop talking. You never know when to stop talking!'

Where the hell are we going?

'Just let me go. What are you doing? Just look at yourself,' I say, trying to make Nick see sense. 'What about Lowri?'

'Shut up, Cerys!' he screams.

He's drunk and completely out of control.

'Stop this right now, Nick! Please,' I say, trying to placate him.

The azure sky is enormous and wide above us. A short-toed eagle glides and bobs on the air currents in the distance. It's as if it's watching us.

'Be quiet! I'm trying to think,' he thunders loudly at me as he drags me on again.

'I'm not going anywhere,' I pant and stop walking. My chest is heaving as I try to get my breath.

'Come on!' Nick grabs at my hair and shows me the knife. I get a flashback of when we lived in London. It was one of his trademark moves. Yank my hair, get in my face and slap me.

Looking ahead, I finally realise where we're going.

He's taking me up to the plateau where I take my yoga classes.

The plateau that overlooks the Bajarra marble quarry.

I frown as I try to keep my footing. 'Why are we going up here, Nick?' I wheeze but I'm starting to panic.

'Because I like it up here,' Nick pants. He looks back to see if anyone is following.

There's no one.

Not yet, anyway.

'And then what?' I ask, trying to get my breath as he drags me along the hard ground which is getting steeper.

Maybe I should try to escape? But I know that if I run, he'll probably catch me and then what?

The plateau is less than two minutes.

What does he think he's going to do when we get up there?

I get a dark, sinking feeling as I begin to think about the plateau and the huge drop into the ravine below.

'Jesus, Nick. You're pathetic,' I say, trying a different tack and mocking him. I want to lash out and get him to react like the old days.

'Shut up or I will cut you.' Nick pulls my hair hard again and I stumble on.

'No you won't,' I scoff.

'Try me,' he replies but it's unconvincing.

And then there it is up ahead.

The flat plateau of ground with tall, dark trees either side looms into view.

It would be spectacular if I wasn't so frightened.

And beyond the plateau, the deep rugged valley of brilliant white marble that gleams in the midday sun and stretches out as far as the eye can see.

I have to squint just to look at it. The eagle is still floating high above, watching our every move. It tilts its wings to circle us in a long, smooth arc.

The landscape looks ethereal in this light. Like a science fiction film set on a different planet or world. The white of the jagged marble is luminous and stark against the rich blue of the Tuscan sky.

'What are we doing here?' I'm gasping. We've been marching uphill in the baking sun for over ten minutes.

Nick pushes me backwards and I stumble and fall to the ground.

'What are we doing here?' I ask again, scowling up at him as I sit up. He has his back to the vibrant blue sky and the dazzling ridges of marble.

'You know, when I used to live here, I'd come here on my own,' Nick recalls, his chest heaving still. 'I'd look out and think this must be the perfect place to die.'

'Okay,' I say, wiping the sweat from my brow and top lip. I don't like the sound of that one bit.

I look out at the valley below us. It's so deep that it gives me a slight sense of vertigo.

Nick takes a step forward and brandishes the knife. 'Get up!'

Now I'm fearing that Nick is going to do something really stupid. He's lost all hope and has nothing to lose. As I look at the precipice which is ten yards away, I'm terrified that I'm somehow part of Nick's wretched plan to leave this earth.

'No.' I shake my head. If he thinks I'm going to let him take me with him over that two-hundred-foot drop in some warped double-suicide pact, then that's not going to happen without a fight.

'Get up,' Nick snarls at me.

I shake my head. 'We have a daughter, Nick.'

'I don't care,' Nick hisses. 'She's better off without us in her life.'

'You don't mean that,' I say. I'm desperate to make him see some kind of sense. 'She'll be devastated if anything happens to us.'

Nick shakes his head. 'You think I'm going to spend my life in an Italian prison?' He snorts angrily.

'I don't care what you do,' I snap at him, still sitting on the ground. 'But I'm not moving from here.'

Moving aggressively, he goes to grab my hair again. 'We'll see about that.'

As he pulls, it feels like it's tearing my scalp.

'Get off me,' I scream, grabbing at his arm and digging my nails into his skin until I feel the moisture of blood on the tips of my fingers.

I'm now fighting for my life.

'Jesus,' Nick recoils.

I hook my leg behind him and he trips and falls to the ground.

Then I scramble to my feet.

Nick's doing the same.

I can see the knife gripped firmly in his right hand.

I start to stumble into a sprint.

Come on, Cerys. Run!

My legs feel heavy.

If he catches up with me, I know he's going to stab me. He just doesn't care anymore.

Nick tackles me to the ground.

We're wrestling, grabbing each other.

I see the flash of metal.

I roll away just in time to avoid Nick's slash.

And then I'm up on my feet.

He's going to kill me.

Nick gets to his feet.

'Get away from her!' screams a voice.

For a second, I think I'm hearing things.

I turn to my right and I see Lucia.

She's holding a double-barrelled shotgun and pointing it at Nick.

'Get away from her!' Lucia cries again at the top of her voice.

Nick freezes. He's brandishing the knife.

'No chance,' Nick snorts shaking his head.

Lucia moves forward and aims the gun at Nick's chest.

He begins to back away with a manic amused look on his face.

'You are a bad man,' Lucia tells him with a dark look.

Nick takes another step backwards. He's trying to work out if she really will fire the gun.

'Lucia,' I say. I don't want her to shoot him. I don't want Lucia to be the one to go to prison.

Glancing back, Nick sees that he's running out of ground between him and the edge of the precipice.

He stops and looks at me. 'Don't worry.' He snorts with his wild eyes fixed on mine. 'She's not going to shoot me.'

Lucia raises an eyebrow. 'You don't think so?'

'No.' Nick shakes his head, wields the knife and makes as if he's coming towards me.

Oh my God!

Lucia points the gun above his head and fires a warning shot.

CRACK!

The noise is thunderous and seems to split the air in two.

Nick stumbles back in surprise.

Lucia waves the gun at him. 'I'm taking Cerys with me. And you can stay here until the police arrive.'

But Nick has lost his footing.

The heel of his deck shoe slips as the earth on the very edge disappears.

And he's falling backwards.

Nick looks directly into my eyes in terror and reaches out to me.

I take a step forward as if I'm going to run to save him.

I can't let him fall to his death, can I?

Even after everything, my instinct is to help him.

But then I stop myself.

Our eyes meet. He can see I've made my decision.

No. Not anymore. I need to be free of you.

Then he's floundering, arms flailing.

Nick falls backwards and disappears.

There's no scream. No noise.

Just an eerie silence.

After a few seconds, Lucia and I move gingerly and look down into the valley.

Nick's twisted body is lying face up across a rock about halfway down the slope.

He's dead.

For a few seconds, I stare at Nick's body.

'He was a bad man,' Lucia mutters as though his death is justified.

Maybe it is.

'Yes, he was,' I say and I turn.

I'm overwhelmed by sadness as I look down at him.

But there is also relief.

Coming up the slope are Detective Saachi and three uniformed police officers.

FIFTY-NINE

CERYS

4.47 p.m.

It's late afternoon and I'm sitting in an interview room at Commissariato San Giovanni police station in Florence. Detective Saachi is sitting opposite me and although he's recording the interview, he's stressed at various points that I'm not under arrest, nor am I a suspect in Nick's death. Lucia has also been brought in for questioning but it was made clear to me that she is just there to describe the events leading up to Nick's tragic death.

The air in this room is thick and musty. I can smell cigarettte smoke from somewhere – maybe outside on the street.

Saachi runs his hands through his hair as he sweeps it back off his chiselled face. He looks tired. The bags under his eyes are darker and more pronounced.

So far, I've detailed everything that happened today. I stress that Nick intended to take both me and him off the ledge for some warped reason. The fact that he fell instead is immaterial. I don't feel any guilt over his death. He was going to kill me. But

I am still haunted by the final look he gave me when he realised that I wasn't going to rush to save him.

I look at Saachi. 'Lucia saved my life by firing a warning shot. I don't want her to be in trouble.'

Saachi shakes his head. 'In Italy we have "reasonable force". Nick had a weapon. Lucia De Nardi feared for her life and for yours. Firing a shot to scare him is not an offence in such a situation. And if he fell because of that, then Lucia De Nardi is covered by our self-defence laws. She will face no charges.'

I breathe a sigh of relief. 'Thank you.'

Saachi leans forward. 'Just a couple more things for me to tie up here and then you can go,' he reassures me. I love Saachi's strong, calm manner. He is a man completely comfortable in his own skin. There is no hint of ego or show with him. His inner confidence means there's no need for it. And that is incredibly attractive. It strikes me that he is the complete opposite of men like Nick and Harry.

'Of course,' I reply.

'Now that it's been a few hours since your ex-husband fell into the quarry,' Saachi says, 'are you sure he didn't say anything before that? No confession to Mr Collard's murder, nothing like that?'

I take a moment to think. 'Actually, he did say that he didn't want to spend the rest of his life in an Italian prison. I don't know if that's a confession. I guess it is in a way.'

Saachi nods in a noncommital way as he scribbles this down. 'Yes. Maybe.'

I search my feelings again and notice that I still don't really feel anything about Nick's death. I'm just numb. And I realise that it could have been me lying down there in that canyon with him.

I look over at Saachi and catch his eye. I know there's something I have to ask him. 'Are you convinced that it was my ex-husband who murdered Harry Collard?'

Saachi doesn't react for a few seconds. He's choosing his words carefully. 'Obviously, I cannot discuss the details of this case with you. But I can also tell you that we will not be looking for anyone else in connection with Mr Collard's murder either.'

Right. That's a relief in a way.

There is relief that we are no longer stuck in some terrible limbo at the villa anymore. And there will be some relief for poor Zoe and Charlie that the person who killed Harry has been discovered. There might even be a sense of justice that Nick is now dead too.

Saachi then looks over at me with a meaningful expression and gestures. 'You may go. And thank you for your help today. It has been a very troubling time for you and your daughter. And for Mrs Collard and her son.'

I get up and give him a nod of thanks. 'It has been very difficult. But I hope that in time, we can all make a new start and move on.'

'Goodbye,' Saachi says but before I can reply, he's reached to turn off the recording equipment.

I go to the door and open it. Then I walk down the narrow corridor and past two male detectives who are wearing their gold badges around their necks like lanyards. I wonder why Saachi doesn't do the same with his.

As I turn into the reception area of the police station, I see Lowri waiting. My heart skips a beat. She's staring into space with a bereft look on her face. I wonder what all this is going to do to her.

Then she sees me and gives me a half smile.

Getting up, she walks over.

'Is everything okay?' she asks me. Her face is puffy and red from where she's been crying.

I nod. 'Yes, darling. Everything is fine. I'm free to go now.'

We turn and make our way towards the exit.

SIXTY

LOWRI

Forty-Eight Hours Later – Friday, 14 July 2023
11.47 p.m.

It's nearly midnight and Lowri is lying on her bed. The death of her father weighs heavily on her mind. Everything feels so surreal. Like a deep, dark hole of blackness. As if she's wading through the blurred reality of a dream.

My dad murdered a man that attacked me before falling to his death? I just can't comprehend it. This can't be happening, can it?

Things had felt dark and strange in the villa after Harry was killed. But now, everything has taken on a whole new level of weird.

Lowri frowns as she contemplates the events of recent days. Then she lets out an audible sigh and shakes her head. She feels like her head is about to explode.

There's a protective part of her brain that steers her away from dwelling on reality. As if that part of her conscience is telling her that it's too much for her and she needs to give herself time to process it all very slowly.

Lowri looks at her phone to try and distract herself. She clicks on a James Taylor playlist on Spotify. One of her dad's favourites. The track 'Fire and Rain' plays and she stares up at the ceiling. The lyrics are poignant as James Taylor asks for Jesus to look down and see him through another day.

It must be such a relief to have a strong faith, she thinks. *A hope or certainty that death isn't an end.*

The thought of that finality hits her deep inside. Her dad is gone forever. She will never see him again. A wave of grief brings tears to her eyes. Her lips are trembling as she blinks and she wipes her face with the palm of her hand.

There is a gentle knock on her door.

It's Charlie.

'Hey,' he says with his usual lopsided smile.

'You packed?' she asks him as she sniffs and wipes away the tears.

Charlie nods but he stays by the door.

Lowri gestures for him to come over to the bed.

He seems awkward, even shy, as he approaches and then sits down. 'How are you doing?' he asks, looking at her with genuine concern.

'Erm... "I don't know" is the honest answer,' she admits. The range of emotions have been way beyond anything she's ever experienced in her life. She hopes she never has to go through any of this again.

Charlie gives her a nod of recognition. Of course, he knows more than anyone how she's feeling.

'I like this,' Charlie says of the music. 'Don McLean?'

'James Taylor,' she corrects him as she leans over to her bedside table and takes a spliff.

'Yeah. My dad loved James Taylor,' Charlie says thoughtfully. 'He said it was real music.'

'So did mine.' Lowri looks at him, putting the spliff in her mouth and lighting it. 'I'm playing it to remember him, but it keeps upsetting me.'

'Maybe it's cathartic,' Charlie suggests as Lowri passes him the spliff.

'Yeah, I think it probably is.'

They fall into a comfortable silence while they listen to the song.

'I can't get used to the idea that I'll never see him again,' Lowri admits quietly.

'I know.' Charlie nods sadly. 'My dad was fucked up. I know that. But he was still my dad. And a few weeks ago, we sat at home watching some old comedy film he wanted to show me from the eighties. He was in hysterics. I can picture his face. His eyes all creased, Cry laughing...' Charlie's voice cracks. 'And that has gone forever. I'm never going to do that again with him. Ever.'

Lowri gives him a look of recognition. 'It's never black and white, or good or bad, is it? My dad was a prick and a bully. But he loved me. And yeah, there were moments when we'd have a real laugh. Or he'd tell some terrible dad joke and I'd groan.'

The music plays, filling the silence that has settled in the room. The weight of their shared experience seems to hang in the air like an invisible thread, connecting them.

'Beer?' Lowri asks after a while, pointing to the little cool box.

Charlie raises his eyebrow with a smirk. 'Do you always have beers and weed in your bedroom?'

'Pretty much.' She smiles back at him. 'Weed, cold beer and great music. It's the Holy Trinity for me.'

Opening the cool box, she takes two cold, dark green bottles of Peroni and passes him one. He twists off the top and takes a swig.

'I see what you mean,' Charlie says as he clinks his bottle against Lowri's.

'What do you think you'll do when you go home?' Lowri asks.

Charlie shrugs. 'There's the funeral. I need to make sure Mum's okay too. I just don't know. I'm taking each day as it comes at the moment.'

Lowri nods as she blows smoke up into the air. 'Me too.'

'I don't suppose you know if you'll even stay here,' Charlie asks.

'No.' Lowri shrugs. 'But all of Mum's money is tied up in the villa so we're stuck here for now. And maybe she'll want to stay here anyway.'

Silence.

Charlie sips from his beer again. 'I know this might sound stupid, but I wish...' Then he stops himself from saying whatever was next.

Lowri looks at him. 'You wish what?' she asks gently.

'I wish me and you could have spent more time together... without all this...' Charlie shakes his head.

She knows what he's trying to say.

'So do I,' she says.

Then they just look at each other for a second.

They both give a quizzical smile.

Charlie leans towards her and points at her eye. 'You've got something on your eyes,' he says under his breath. 'It's make-up, I think. Just close your eyes for a second and I'll get it for you.'

Lowri assumes it's from when she was crying.

She closes her eye and for a second nothing happens.

What's he doing?

Then she feels Charlie's soft lips on hers as he kisses her.

Nice trick, she thinks as she kisses him back.

Their kiss becomes more passionate as he strokes her face tenderly and then moves her hair away from her neck.

Slowly they move back onto the bed as their limbs intertwine.

SIXTY-ONE

CERYS

11.49 p.m.

'I can't believe how warm it is still,' Zoe says, glancing at the time on her phone.

We've both been sitting outside for about twenty minutes. Zoe has been packing their suitcases as they have an early flight to Heathrow in the morning. She's also had the hideous task of packing up all Harry's belongings too – they're being couriered back to their home in Dulwich. She can't bear to take them on the plane with them.

Zoe sips from her wine and then looks at me. 'You're sure you won't join me in a drink? Last night and everything.'

I shake my head. Since I watched Nick fall from that ledge, something has shifted inside. For whatever reason, I've finally admitted that I can't drink alcohol safely. I'm an alcoholic. As soon as I start, I cannot stop. I want to stop drinking more than I want to drink. And if I continue, I'm going to lose Lowri. And I'll lose Villa Lucia.

'I'm fine, thanks,' I say with a polite smile.

There is silence as we both gaze out at the view. The moon

seems bigger than usual and it's throwing down a lovely vanilla-coloured light on the shadowy hills and vineyards in the distance. Lights from other villas, cottages and farmhouses are dotted across the vista and twinkle like distant stars.

'The day we arrived seems like a lifetime ago,' Zoe says quietly.

'Yes.'

Then Zoe turns to look at me. 'I don't think I'm ever going to properly grieve for Harry after what I saw in that video,' she admits. It feels like she's trying to reassure me that she is utterly ashamed of what Harry put Lowri through.

'You're not responsible for what he did,' I remind her gently.

Silence.

'And I'm going to find it very difficult to do that for Nick. I'm struggling to remember if he had any redeeming features.' Then I see Zoe looking directly at me. 'Isn't that so terribly sad?'

'Yes... it really is.' Zoe gives me a nod of true recognition as her shoulders sag. 'I can't help but wonder what people are going to say about Harry at his funeral. There will be the usual platitudes. But everyone knows what he was like. Pompous, rude, sleazy, predatory. They might not say it on the day, but that's how he'll be remembered. What a terrible summation of a life. What a waste.'

I take all this in and wonder what Nick's funeral is going to be like. His brother, Ben, has messaged to say that he will be organising it. I don't like Ben. He owns a bookshop somewhere in the Lake District. I've only met him and his wife, Fiona, a handful of times, but he has the same arrogant disdain for nearly everything as Nick.

'I'm trying to put all that to one side,' I say. 'My priority is Lowri. She doesn't know what her dad was really like. I tried so hard to keep it from her.'

'She's lucky in that way,' Zoe says. 'Charlie was more than

aware of what Harry was like. Especially since...' She doesn't finish her sentence but we both know what she's talking about.

There is a reflective silence. Neither of our lives are going to be the same again.

There is something I need to ask her.

'At the risk of changing the subject...' I begin, my voice tentative, almost apologetic.

'Please do.' Zoe sighs with a mixture of relief and exhaustion. 'I need to talk and think about something else for a bit.'

'It's just that I noticed that you threw away that beautiful apricot maxi dress,' I say, watching closely for her reaction. I think of the ripped neckline and the blood stain which has been turning over in my mind. I'm pretty sure that there's a logical explanation but I destroyed it in an act of sisterhood, and I need to find out.

'Yes, I did,' Zoe confirms, her eyes still fixed on the twinkling lights in the distance and her voice flat.

'Shame,' I murmur, the word hanging in the air between us.

'It couldn't be repaired,' she explains. 'And it was vintage anyway, so no great loss.' She drains the last of her wine and stands, the movement decisive. 'Right, I'd better get to bed.'

I rise too and she pulls me into a hug, her arms tight around me. 'Thank you doesn't really do it. But you've been amazing, Cerys. I really don't know what I would have done without you here.'

As we step back, I search her face. 'You take care of yourself,' I say softly. 'And we must stay in touch.'

Zoe reaches out and takes my hand for a moment, squeezing it gently. 'Yes, I'd really like that.'

I watch her walk away, and it dawns on me that she hasn't really explained what happened to the dress at all, or the blood stain.

SIXTY-TWO

CERYS

Four Weeks Later – Friday, 11th August 2023
10.49 a.m.

I look up at the sky over the South London Crematorium which is within the grounds of Streatham Park Cemetery. Even though it's August and warm, the sky is full of grey clouds which mask the sun.

Little groups of mourners talk in hushed voices. Although I've messaged Zoe a few times to see how she's doing, I haven't seen her. We have said that we'll go for lunch while I'm in London. I've had no contact from the Italian police in recent weeks. And even though the British press and media did report on Harry's murder for a day or two when it happened, there has been nothing since then. All I know is that Nick's friends and family have been told that he died in a tragic accident while in the Tuscan hills.

Jesus, if only they knew!

I watch Lowri chatting to cousins, uncles and aunts. She looks so grown-up in her black jacket and skirt. I've exchanged the odd few words with Nick's brother, Ben, and Fiona, but it's no more than pleasantries.

And of course, I've had the odd disparaging look. I'm the alcoholic ex-wife who drove Nick from Italy back to London with her terrible behaviour. Part of me was surprised that I wasn't asked not to attend today. But I want to be here for Lowri.

The hearse arrives and drives very slowly towards the doors of the crematorium as we all stand back. Then we are ushered inside and handed an order of service. Lowri stays outside with Ben and the cousins as they are going to walk Nick's coffin inside to the strains of 'Anywhere Like Heaven' by James Taylor. There won't be a dry eye in the place!

I sit at the back, out of harm's way, and look at the photograph of Nick on the front of the order of service. It was taken in our back garden nearly ten years ago. He's smiling and for once it's not the smug, knowing smile that he wore so often. He looks genuinely happy. And for a few seconds I do actually feel a sense of sadness and grief. We did really love each other when we first got together. In fact, we were both off our faces on ecstasy when we first kissed at a club in South London. And for a while, Nick hid his dark, controlling side from me. It came out very slowly in little temper tantrums, continuous phone calls when I was out and the questioning when I came back in. He was always so suspicious of where I'd been and who I'd been with. It became suffocating. Yet for some reason I never felt it was bad enough to leave him. And after these outbursts, Nick had been apologetic and promised to change. We got married and had Lowri. We had our perfect little family and I thought he'd change after that but it seemed to have the opposite effect. I became more and more isolated from my friends. Nick made sure of that.

The music starts and I watch Lowri walking beside the coffin as it's wheeled in on a trolley. She sits at the front next to her cousins. She's going to say a few words after Ben's eulogy. I love her so much it hurts. I just want to protect her from everything but I can't.

For the next half hour, I listen to the prayers, pretend to sing the hymns and watch a video that Ben's made from old family photos. Ben talks about Nick in glowing terms. He was 'kind, caring and generous. A family man. A brilliant political journalist and writer with a talent for cutting through the bullshit of modern politics and asking the difficult questions.'

I sit quietly on my own, wanting to shout out, *No, no, no. This is a fucking whitewash. You're all rewriting history here and it's shameful. Maybe he was all those things that you've talked about. But let's get some balance too. He was also an abusive, selfish, controlling narcissist who made my life hell for many years.*

But I'm not going to say anything. There's no point. I have acknowledged it in my heart; and I know what the truth is. And that's all that matters.

The wake is in a function room at a swanky pub close to Battersea Bridge. I know that I must show my face and go for Lowri's sake. The obligatory tray of flutes of Champagne are taken around but I decline politely. I'm back in touch with my old AA sponsor Pam who I'm meeting for coffee in Putney tomorrow. I drink a sparkling mineral water.

Knowing that Nick is no more than a pile of ashes is a strange feeling. I have a sense of closure and relief.

Lowri and I stay for as long as is bearable before we jump into an Uber and head back to our hotel.

And part of me says to Nick in my head, *Good riddance.*

SIXTY-THREE

ZOE

Monday, 14th August 2023
1.43 p.m.

Zoe stands by the bar of the basement in Shoreditch House. She's hired it out for Harry's wake. It seemed appropriate as he spent so much time here. And it was where she and Harry first met on the night of the Millenium. She's feeling numb and uncomfortable. The whole thing is a total sham. If one more record executive comes up and tells her that Harry was 'a great bloke', she thinks she's going to scream.

Harry's funeral seemed to go past in a blur. He's buried at Norwood Cemetery. Or at least, she watched his coffin being lowered into the grave with mounds of earth either side. And she, Charlie and other relatives and friends threw a flower onto his coffin and then left. Zoe doesn't know how she's managed to get through the week.

A very chic-looking woman in her late twenties heads her way. She looks like a model.

'Hi, I'm Lisa,' the woman says as she shakes Zoe's hand.

She gives her a quizzical look. Lisa seems quite drunk and she's got some tell-tale crumbs of cocaine on her left nostril.

It's 1 p.m. and people are doing coke at Harry's wake, Zoe thinks. *I guess that says it all.*

'I'm Harry's assistant at Kismet.' Lisa has a public school accent. 'Oh God, I *was* Harry's assistant,' she corrects herself and looks mortified. 'Sorry. I didn't mean to...'

'It's fine, don't worry,' Zoe reassures her and touches her arm.

'I just wanted to come and say hi,' Lisa explains. 'I can't imagine how you're feeling at the moment.'

Yeah, I'm struggling to get my head around that too, Zoe thinks.

'It's gonna be so strange without him at Kismet,' Lisa says with a frown. She looks genuinely upset.

Zoe knows she slept with Harry in New York.

'Well, it's good to know that he was kind as a boss,' Zoe says but she doesn't believe what she's saying. In fact, she hasn't believed 90 per cent of what she's said all day.

'Oh yeah. He insisted I went with him to Berlin for that dance-music conference in April,' Lisa explains. 'That's what he was like.'

'I didn't know he'd been to Berlin,' Zoe says, raising an eyebrow. In fact, she's certain that he didn't mention it because Harry had told her not long ago that he hadn't been to Berlin for years.

Jesus, Harry, Zoe thinks. *Did you ever tell me the truth about anything?*

'Oh God, sorry,' Lisa says, pulling a face.

'Hey, it's fine,' Zoe reassures her and then points to Lisa's nose. 'You've got a bit of...'

'Oh right, thanks.' Lisa wipes the cocaine away. She's not even embarrassed. 'Anyway, I just wanted to come and say how sorry I was.'

Zoe forces a smile. 'Thank you.'

Lisa turns away, spots someone she recognises and heads over to them.

Charlie looks over and they lock eyes.

They're both thinking the same thing.

Charlie puts down his drink and walks towards her, his head bent forward, avoiding eye-contact with anyone else but her.

'Ready to go?' Zoe asks him.

Charlie nods without hesitation. They've both had enough of all the bullshit. 'Definitely.'

'Come on, then,' Zoe says as she offers her arm.

Charlie takes it, and they head upstairs and then for the exit.

SIXTY-FOUR
[CH]LOWRI

Thursday, 14 September 2023
12.24 p.m.

It's a month since her dad's funeral and Lowri is packing up her stuff. It's time to move on from Villa Lucia. She needs to make a new start. It's hard not to keep remembering her father's death and Harry's attack and then murder while she's there. Her father left her his small flat in Crystal Palace in his will, so she's going to move there while she works out what she's going to do long term. If she has to take bar work to pay the bills and buy food, that's fine by her. And she might earn some money playing gigs.

Her phone beeps with a message. It's from Charlie.

> Hey. How r u? Ok? What time is ur flight? Xx

Charlie and Lowri have kept in touch since he and Zoe left. They've continually FaceTimed and messaged. Charlie wants to meet Lowri at the airport even though she insists that it's not necessary.

She grabs her phone and messages back.

> Flight lands at Heathrow @ 9.25am xx

Her phone beeps instantaneously.

> Cool. C u there xx

Lowri gets a little tingle inside when she thinks of Charlie meeting her off the plane. It's so romantic.

Grabbing her suitcase from under her bed, she then begins to take her clothes off the hangers and fold them neatly. She takes her phone, goes to Spotify, selects 'Vertigo' by Griff so that it plays on her Bluetooth speaker.

Then she takes a chair as she had stored a few things on top of her wardrobe – trainers, a rucksack, two bags and some other assorted items.

As she goes to take the trainers, she instead nudges them and one of them falls down the back of the wardrobe.

'Bloody hell.' She sighs under her breath.

Standing down from the chair, she grabs the wardrobe and uses all her strength to pull it out from the wall so she can get behind it and retrieve the trainer.

Suddenly, there's a metallic clang as if something has dropped to the floor.

Taking a step behind the wardrobe, she spots that a small metal grille has fallen on the floor. Up on the wall is a square cavity. It's about one foot square and looks like it might be where a small, old-fashioned air-conditioning unit was before it was all upgraded.

Reaching down, Lowri bends down, picks up the grille and goes to replace it over the cavity on the wall.

Inside she spots a plastic bag.

That's weird. What's that?

Taking hold of the plastic, she pulls it out. It's heavier than it looks.

Opening it, she does a double take at what she sees inside.

What the...?

A laptop, some car keys and cash.

Oh my God!

A cold shiver runs up her spine.

It's the stuff that her mum told the police had been taken from the villa when they thought they'd been robbed.

What the fuck is it doing in a bag in there?

Lowri's pulse starts to quicken. She's trying to work out what the hell is going on.

There's only one person who could have taken the laptop, car keys and money and hidden them.

Mum.

Then Lowri realises. The only reason for her mum to have taken these things was to make it look as if someone had burgled the villa.

It hits her like a ton of bricks.

Mum wanted the police to believe that there had been a robbery because...

God, no.

Lowri feels sick and dizzy.

She manages to make her way out of the annexe and spots her mum sitting out on the decking reading a book.

'Do you need a hand packing up your stuff?' her mum calls over as she looks up from her book.

'No,' Lowri snaps as she walks towards her.

'Everything all right?'

'No.' Lowri sits down and tries to get her breath. Then she looks directly at her mother. 'I moved the wardrobe.'

Her mum shrugs. 'Okay.'

Silence.

'I found the bag hidden in that alcove.'

Her mum doesn't react for a few seconds. Then she puts down her book.

'I see,' she says, her face expressionless as she pushes her glasses up so they rest on her hair.

'I see! Are you fucking kidding me?' Lowri cries with anger and frustration. 'Please, Mum.' Her voice drops to a whisper as she tries to steady her breathing. 'I need to know what happened.'

SIXTY-FIVE

CERYS

Monday, 10 July 2023
12.47 a.m.

I roll over and my mouth is dry. My head is thick and I'm still incredibly drunk. Looking up at the ceiling, I'm trying to piece together what happened. I can't remember anything.

Glancing at the bedside table, I see a large glass of water which I assume Lowri has left. My heart sinks. We had a deal that I wouldn't drink if she came to stay with me. Now I've ruined it. And it will only add ammunition to Nick's assertion that I'm a terrible, selfish human being.

I sit up because I now think that I'm going to be sick. My stomach is gurgling, and I've got that warning sign in my chest and throat. It's about thirty seconds before I vomit. Racing to the toilet, I make it just in time. I then wash my mouth out and look at myself in the mirror.

Jesus, Cerys, you really have done it again.

As I turn off the light, I get a waft of cigar smoke from somewhere. I react instantly because the man that attacked me in

London in December 2019 stank of cigars. I now have a Pavlovian-type response every time I smell them.

I know that Harry must be out there. Going to the door, I look over at the villa and see a figure standing by the swimming pool smoking a cigar.

Harry.

For a second, I tell myself to go back to bed.

But there's another voice inside my head that tells me that I have to go over there. It's time for me to have the conversation. To confront him with my growing suspicions. Logic tells me I've got it wrong, but my instincts are telling me the opposite.

I put on my flat sandals and walk unsteadily towards the pool. Even though I'm still very drunk, my heart is starting to thump against my chest. It would be so easy to turn and scurry back to the annexe but I'm willing myself forward.

Keep going, Cerys. Just keep going. You have to do this.

I come down the steps and Harry looks over at me.

'Couldn't sleep?' he asks with a smug look. He holds up a brandy. 'I'm having a nightcap if you'd like to join me?'

'No thanks,' I say. I sound unfriendly but I really don't care.

Harry shrugs with a smile. My impoliteness seems to have amused him. 'Okay, fair enough.' Then he frowns and points. 'Isn't that Zoe's?'

I look down. Somehow, I'm wearing Zoe's apricot-coloured maxi dress. Then I remember. In our drunkenness, Zoe insisted on me putting on her dress that I told her I loved so much. And she put on mine. We thought it was hilarious.

'Yes,' I reply but I don't want to talk about that. 'We decided to swap dresses, that's all.'

Harry pulls a disappointed face. 'Shame I missed that,' he says in a sleazy tone.

I don't say anything. I'm searching his face, his features, to see if it really is him.

'Any news on that wine tasting?' Harry asks before sucking on his cigar.

I take a step towards him and fix him with a confident stare even though I'm barely holding it together inside. 'You don't remember me, do you?'

Harry frowns. 'Sorry, I don't.' He cocks his head to the side. 'But I did think you looked familiar. Remind me.'

Is it really you?

'We met at a party in Barkstone Mews, Kensington,' I explain, feeling the anger well up inside. 'I had shorter, dark hair.'

I hold my breath.

In the next second, Harry either reveals he has no idea what I'm talking about, or I know for certain that this man standing in front of me is my rapist from four years ago. The man that ruined my life.

'Jasper's house?' Harry nods and then laughs. 'He throws bloody great parties, doesn't he?'

Jesus! My stomach lurches.

I realise that my gut instinct is spot on.

It *is* him.

My body trembles with the realisation.

I take a breath and glare at him. 'I didn't think so.'

Harry senses my enraged tone and raises an eyebrow. 'You didn't think so?'

'No, I really didn't,' I reply. I'm trying to stop myself from shaking but it's difficult.

'Really? Why not?' Harry asks as if what I'm saying is completely ridiculous.

'Because as soon as I walked in the door, you gave me a glass of Champagne,' I say, trying to get my breath. 'And you put something in it. In fact, you spiked it. And then when I was completely out of it, you took me upstairs for a lie-down. Except you... you...' I'm struggling to get the words out. 'You raped me.'

My head is spinning. I can't believe I'm actually standing here in front of this man.

Harry's face falls and he gives her a perplexed look. 'No. Sorry. You've got the wrong person.'

'I haven't,' I assure him. 'I asked around. It took a few months but eventually someone told me your name. It's you. I remember you.'

Harry frowns and takes a few seconds to think about what I've accused him of.

'Listen, I'm really sorry that happened to you. It's awful,' he says, shaking his head. He's definitely rattled. 'But that wasn't me.'

'Don't fucking lie to me,' I snap. 'You know what you did. I can see it in your face.'

There's an awkward silence.

Harry's expression changes from fear to utter contempt. Now that he's had time to process all this, he's decided to change direction and go on the attack.

'Look, I don't know what your problem is, but I don't need to go around raping women.' Then he takes a puff on his cigar. 'But let me assure you that if I did, I wouldn't choose you. You're not my type.'

I explode. 'Are you fucking kidding me?'

'No.' Harry gives me a conceited shrug. 'No offence, but I tend to go for the pretty young ones.'

My whole body is consumed with fury. I feel like I'm going to erupt with rage.

I turn on my heels and head into the villa. I need to have a drink, do something. I can't believe that I confronted him, and he said that. It doesn't feel real.

Marching across the kitchen, I go and grab the bottle of Smirnoff, twist the top off, put it to my lips and take two big mouthfuls.

I'm so angry I just don't know what to do with myself.

Getting drunk isn't going to do it. I need him to admit what he did. And I want to make him apologise. How fucking dare he talk to me like that!

I look at the knife block.

Right, I'll make him bloody confess. And I'll make him grovel. Arrogant prick.

Grabbing the handle of a kitchen knife, I pull it out.

I'll fucking show you!

I feel possessed.

I want to hurt him. I *need* to hurt him.

I storm out of the villa, the knife in my hand by my side.

Going down the steps, I can see that Harry is sitting on the low wall that runs along the back of the pool.

He sees me coming and rolls his eyes.

'Here we go,' he scoffs as he stubs out his cigar on the top of the wall.

He stands up and takes a few steps towards me. 'I think you just need to calm down. It was a long time ago.'

I can't believe it but suddenly I'm brandishing the knife like a mad woman.

'Calm down? You raped me!' I hiss at him.

Harry sees the knife and puts up a hand. 'Whoa, what are you doing?' he asks. He seems faintly amused, like I'm some silly woman who has got all this out of proportion.

'Just admit it. Admit that you drugged and raped me,' I hiss.

'Okay,' Harry says and pulls a face. 'I just don't remember it like that. In fact, I'm pretty sure you enjoyed it.'

'What!'

My eyes widen as I grip the knife tighter.

Harry takes a couple of steps towards me and puts out his hand. 'Just put that thing down, eh? Before someone gets hurt.'

Before I know it, I've lunged forward and plunged the knife into his stomach.

Oh God...

Harry looks at me in shock. He can't believe that I've done it.

Neither can I.

'You fucking bitch.' He groans as he comes towards me, grabs the dress and rips the shoulder.

Oh my God, he's going to kill me if he gets hold of me.

I slash the knife and cut his forearm.

'Jesus,' he yelps.

I'm terrified. But I've got to stop him.

He comes again, throwing his arms like a madman.

And I lunge again and the knife goes into him and hits one of his ribs.

It judders against the bone.

For a second, our eyes meet.

As I pull the knife out, it breaks.

The blade and handle fall noisily to the ground.

My hand has got blood on it.

Harry looks completely bewildered and then he looks down at his shirt.

Suddenly, his legs give way and crumple.

I watch as he falls face first into the pool, almost as if in slow motion.

For a second, he flounders. His arms and legs move as if he's trying to turn himself over.

But then he stops moving.

He's dead.

I turn and run. And I forget.

SIXTY-SIX

LUCIA

12th September 2023
5.26 p.m.

Lucia hands over a five-euro note to the market trader with a smile before putting the bags of grapes, oranges and tomatoes into her shopping bag. It's late afternoon and the sunshine is starting to fade. The air is filled with the smells of the market. Fresh herbs – coriander, basil and rosemary.

As always, Lucia has left Lorenzo chatting to his friends outside a bar on the main piazza. She doesn't mind. It gives her time to visit her favourite church, Chiesa di Sant Andrea. Lorenzo isn't as religious as she is. It allows her to sit quietly and think of those she has lost. Her mother who became so sick. And her father who was so incredibly sad. She hopes that they have now found some peace. And she thinks of Cerys. A couple of years ago, Lucia used to say a prayer for Cerys when her husband, Nick, lived with her at the villa. He was a nasty man but now he is dead. She wonders if he is in hell. She knows that's a terrible thought because Jesus taught us to pray and forgive sinners, in the same way as we ask for forgiveness from our own sins. But she still can't help but wonder if a man like Nick can be forgiven by God. And then she thinks of that man Harry. She wonders if either of them have found some kind of peace now that they are somewhere else.

Lucia puts a euro onto the collection plate, takes two small tealight candles, lights them and then places them with the others. She kneels, closes her eyes and prays for the souls of the two men she has just thought of. It's the right thing to do. Then she crosses herself, picks up her heavy shopping bags and makes her way out of the church. The air outside is lovely and warm compared to the cold chill of the church. And Lucia feels a great sense of peace.

For a few minutes, she walks towards the piazza with a feeling of lightness.

She passes a small wine shop – Il Fiaschetto – which is painted a rich cream colour with dark red writing. Two large wine barrels stand outside with large dark green umbrellas attached so that customers can sample the wine outside.

Arriving at the piazza, she sees it is busy with tourists and locals alike. A man is sitting playing the accordian, and the traditional Chianti folk music mixes with the sound of chatter and laughter.

As Lucia approaches, Lorenzo gets up and grins. He gives her a big kiss, grabbing a chair for her. He's drunk too much *vino nuovo*.

'You look beautiful,' he tells her under his breath and he pours her a glass of wine. Then he hands her the bowl of roasted chestnuts which are the traditional accompaniment of *vino nuovo*, especially when it is first made. She takes one.

'*Grazie*,' Lucia says as she sips her wine.

Lorenzo reaches over and takes the two heavy shopping bags and puts them by his feet. He will carry them to the car. He always does because he's a *gentiluomo*. A true gentleman.

For the next ten minutes, Lucia chats and laughs with

Lorenzo and his friends. Then his friends leave to go to a football game and Lorenzo and Lucia sit and finish their wine.

Lucia leans over and takes a small plastic bag from one of the shopping bags. Inside is fresh seafood – squid, mussels, clams and langoustines.

'I got this for us,' she tells him with a smile. 'Fresh in from Livorno.'

'*Fantastico*,' Lorenzo says. 'Then I will make us *cacciucco*.'

Lucia can't wait. Lorenzo makes an incredible fisherman's stew and serves it with toasted ciabatta rubbed with olive oil and garlic.

They get up to go.

'I forgot to show you,' Lorenzo says as he leans over to the table and grabs an English tabloid newspaper.

'What is it?' Lucia asks.

Lorenzo opens the paper. Inside is a story – *Stars turn out for murdered music mogul's funeral*. Harry's funeral. There is a photograph of a famous singer in a black coat and sunglasses.

Lucia shrugs, closes the paper and gives him a knowing look.

Lorenzo stops and examines her face. 'I know you went back up to the villa that night,' he says in an almost amused tone.

'I know you do,' she replies casually.

It's not something they've talked about – but they haven't needed to yet.

'In fact, it must have been about one when you went back,' he continues.

'Yes, I suppose it was.' She shrugs, playing along.

'But somehow you didn't see anything,' Lorenzo says with a dry, quizzical frown.

Lucia gives him a look as if to say that she saw everything. But they're playing a little game so she's not going to give him the obvious answer.

'I went into the kitchen. I'd forgotten to bring my bag of vegetables and leftovers back here,' Lucia explains casually. 'Then I just took a look around outside and down by the pool. I noticed that Cerys had forgotten to pick something up, so I made sure that I took it for her. That's all.'

'I bet Cerys is very grateful to you,' Lorenzo says.

'I'm not sure she even knows. But sometimes helping someone is enough in itself,' Lucia replies. 'Come on, I'm hungry.' She takes his hand and they head back to their car.

SIXTY-SEVEN

CERYS

Five Months Later – Sunday, 25 February 2024
1.53 p.m.

It's nearly 2 p.m. and I've made my way over to the annexe. I'm now sitting in the living room in front of my laptop, logging onto a Zoom AA meeting hosted in Putney. It's the meeting that I used to go to online when I first moved to Villa Lucia before Nick made it too difficult for me to attend. The meeting is run by Pam, my sponsor.

Two weeks ago, I attended the English-speaking AA meeting in Florence. It's on a Tuesday lunchtime and is run by two ex-pats called Bob and Richard who are well into their seventies. They seemed so excited to welcome me. I went again last week and did the main reading from *The Big Book*.

Last Tuesday, Richard and I went for a coffee in Florence after the meeting. And Richard said a few things that really struck home. He told me that he drank because he couldn't deal with his emotions or his head. And the only way he knew how to cope was to drink alcohol. So essentially, the first bit of AA is putting the drink down – and leaving it there. However, that's when the hard work starts. Because, as Richard explained, it was then that an alcoholic had to deal with life, their emotions, their dark past, without the anaesthetising effect of alcohol. And that was very scary. But with hard work, honesty and support, it can be achieved. Richard told me that he now had a peaceful life that he could never have ever imagined when he was drinking.

I thanked Richard for his time and advice. And whatever has shifted in the last two months, I'm incredibly grateful that it has. I realised last week that I haven't thought about having a drink for several weeks. And that is a miracle.

I look down now and a series of boxes with faces appear on the screen for the Zoom AA meeting.

Pam is a woman in her fifties with over twenty years sobriety.

'Evening, everyone,' Pam says gently. 'My name's Pam, and I'm an alcoholic. And welcome to this Zoom AA meeting from Putney. If we could just have a moment of silence for us to think about the still suffering alcoholic both inside and outside of the rooms of AA.'

Silence.

'Thank you,' Pam says. 'And I've asked Cerys if she will read the Preamble for us.'

'Hi, my name's Cerys, and I'm an alcoholic,' I say.

SIXTY-EIGHT

LOWRI

10.47 p.m.

Lowri squints up at the lights as she finishes the final song of her set at EartH – Evolutionary Arts Hackney. It's a great venue for new acts and the place is packed. For a moment she thinks that no one is going to applaud. But to her relief they do. Wildly. Whistling, clapping and shouts. She tries not to look embarrassed as she gives a wave and a little bow and leaves the stage.

Jesus, they actually really liked my stuff, she thinks, still in a bit of a daze.

A figure looms over her.

Charlie.

'You fucking nailed it!' he says with a big grin.

'Did I?' she asks, shaking her head and taking her guitar off.

'There's someone I need you to meet,' Charlie says excitedly. He's now working for a small, independent record label based in Brixton. Everyone there is young, energetic and positive.

'Okay,' Lowri says. She doesn't know what Charlie is talking about.

A young mixed-race woman in her mid twenties comes over. She has very short, dyed blonde-pink hair, eyebrow- and nose-piercings. She's wearing a baggy hoodie, baggy jeans and trainers.

'That was great,' the young woman says enthusiastically to Lowri.

'Oh wow, thanks,' Lowri replies.

'This is Gisele,' Charlie explains. 'Part of our A&R department.'

'Right,' Lowri says with interest.

Gisele raises an eyebrow. 'You're not signed, are you?'

Lowri shakes her head. 'No, I'm not.' She's starting to get excited as she wonders why Gisele asked this.

'Fancy making a demo for us?' Gisele asks.

'What? Really?' Lowri tries not to get too overexcited.

'Yeah, I loved what I heard tonight,' Gisele reassures her. 'You're definitely going to get some interest from some major labels.'

Lowri frowns. 'Am I?'

'Definitely. And they're going to offer you the world,' Gisele tells her. 'Release your music, albums. Do a tour. And then before you know it, nothing has happened and you're writing songs for Little Mix or someone. And they'll keep promising to release your stuff.' Gisele looks at her. 'We ain't like that. We believe in the integrity of an artist. Serious. Not like those dinosaurs. Their days are over.' Gisele looks to Charlie and smiles. 'Charlie-boy will set it all up. Nice to meet you.'

Gisele walks away and Lowri's eyes widen. 'Did she just say what I think she said?'

'Yes, she did.' Charlie laughed.

'Thank you,' Lowri says as she hugs Charlie.

'Nothing to do with me,' Charlie assures her. 'She loved your music.'

Lowri takes Charlie by the hand. 'Come on. We need to go out and celebrate.'

As they walk out onto the street, Lowri thinks about her mum. Everything they've been through and everything she told her. She doesn't blame her for any of it.

Grabbing her camera, Lowri turns to take a photo of her and Charlie.

'Come on,' she says as they pose with silly faces. 'I'm sending this to Mum.'

Giggling, Lowri writes a caption:

I smashed it, Mum! Wish you'd been here. Call u tomorrow. Love u xx

SIXTY-NINE

CERYS

Monday, 26 February 2024
9.00 a.m.

I'm sitting in my new favourite spot at my villa. The view is slightly different. It's been a week since the work has finished on my new pool. I've filled the old pool, resurfaced it and now there's a badminton court there. It looks totally different. It had to go if I was to stay here after what happened there. So, the brand new, super-duper infinity pool is now over to the left of the villa.

It's perfect.

I sit forward on the wicker sofa with soft plum-coloured cushions. The sofa has that little creak as I shift my weight. The tightly wound bamboo readjusting.

It's 9 a.m., yet the late-winter Tuscan sunshine is just about taking the edge off the early morning chill. It's eight degrees although it'll warm up to around sixteen by lunchtime.

My view still looks the same but also somehow different. The crest of the hill. The expansive vineyard and then beyond that, sprawling fields, a wood and low rolling hills for as far as the eye can see. A spectrum of colour. A landscape speckled by a handful of caramel-brown terracotta roofs of distant villas and farmhouses. Over to my right, an olive grove, golden fields and rows of umbrella-shaped trees.

But I feel different. I've already taken my sunrise yoga class at 6.30 a.m. But not up at the disused quarry. Just a flat piece of grass over to the right of the villa. Nothing fancy. But with this view, it doesn't have to be. I have guests for the week. Ellie and Lola. They're in their early thirties, married, and live somewhere on the south coast close to Brighton. And they're lovely. They told me they work in 'tech' but I'm not entirely sure what that means.

I've also got a special guest arriving today.

I finish my coffee, get up and as I head for the villa, I can hear laughter.

Inside the kitchen, Lucia is teaching Ellie and Lola to make bread. I've gone into business with Lucia and Lorenzo. We offer courses in traditional Tuscan cooking and bread-making workshops. All local produce and additive-free. And the bookings are through the roof.

'You look like you're having fun?' I smile at Ellie.

The whole place smells incredible, of dough, baking bread and fresh herbs.

'Making olive and rosemary focaccia in this villa in Tuscany,' she exclaims. 'Living the dream.'

Lola grins and gestures to me. 'Hey, it's Cerys who is living the dream. She bloody lives here.'

I give her my best humble smile. 'I'm very lucky.'

Then I catch Lucia's eye. She smiles at me. I can see the difference it's made since she and Lorenzo have started to come here every day to run their workshops. We're a team now. And the more I've got to know her better, the more she's told me about her childhood and growing up here.

As I glance out of the doors, across the patio, I can see a trail of dust coming up the track.

Great, that must be her, I think excitedly.

With a spring in my step, I walk out of the kitchen, down the hallway, out of the front door and head towards the villa's parking area.

A moment later, I see a white Audi turn the corner and a friendly face waving at me.

I grin as I wander over.

The driver's door opens and Zoe steps out. She looks so incredibly well.

'Hey,' I say.

'Hello,' she replies.

We hug and I say, 'It's so good to see you.'

'Yes,' Zoe says as we look at each other. Then she looks around. 'I really never thought that I'd be back here.'

'I'm so glad you decided to come,' I tell her.

Zoe points to the car. 'I'd better get my stuff.'

'Leave it for a bit,' I say. 'I'll make you a coffee. And then I can tell you all my plans.'

Zoe has agreed to come and live at Villa Lucia and help me run things. It took a while to persuade her. I told her it would be a new start for both of us. At first, she said she couldn't leave Charlie alone in London. But in recent months, Charlie has found a new zest for life. A job in an independent record company, a flat share in Hackney and his ongoing relationship with Lowri. I'm so pleased for the both of them, especially after everything they've been through. Zoe eventually admitted that she rarely saw Charlie as he was so busy with his new life. And he'd told her that moving to Tuscany was a brilliant idea. In fact, he told her he'd be annoyed if Zoe didn't make the move. And so that sealed it.

Now that Villa Lucia is offering courses, there seems to be so much more to do and I'm swamped.

I look at Zoe. 'And thank you for saying yes.'

Zoe points at the view. 'It's not a bad place to work and call home, is it? It definitely beats the South Circular on a rainy November night.'

'Definitely.' I take Zoe by the hand. 'I've redecorated Lowri's old room for you.'

We walk down the path, our arms linked through each other's, and step into the villa.

SEVENTY

CERYS

6.24 p.m.

Taking a damp cloth, I finish wiping down the surfaces of the villa's kitchen. I can hear Ellie and Lola splashing around in the pool outside. They told me earlier that this was the best holiday they'd ever been on. They've already told all their friends to book with us. 'Blue Chair' by Morcheeba is playing on the Bluetooth speaker. It sounds like the perfect soundtrack to the end of the day.

'I've finished unpacking,' says a voice.

It's Zoe.

She's now wearing a beautiful burned orange maxi dress and her hair is pulled off her face. She looks radiant and happy.

'Great,' I say with a smile. Then I gesture to the terrace. 'Go and sit down and I'll bring you a glass of rosé.'

Zoe gives me a quizzical look.

'Don't worry. Coke Zero is the strongest thing I drink these days,' I reassure her.

'Sure?' she asks and gestures to the kitchen. 'I don't mind helping clearing up. It's what I'm here for.'

I shake my head. 'I'm nearly done. And it's your first night. Go on. I'll be out in a few minutes.'

Zoe looks directly at me. 'This is going to be great, isn't it?' she says as if looking for a little reassurance. Moving here is a big step for her.

'Of course,' I say encouragingly. 'We're going to have a lovely life here.'

Zoe's face breaks into a beaming smile. 'Thank you.'

She turns and heads outside.

Out of the corner of my eye, I see someone approaching from the hallway.

It's Lucia.

'Hi. Busy day?' I ask her.

'Busy, yes.' Lucia nods and then nods in the direction of the decking and the pool. 'Those girls are very funny but they are, how you say, a little bonkers?'

I let out a laugh. 'Bonkers. Yes. But then again I think we're all a bit bonkers, aren't we? It's the only way to survive.'

Lucia gives me a knowing look. 'Yes.'

I notice that she's holding a small wooden box. I give her a questioning look.

'It is a present for you,' Lucia explains. 'It is nothing much.'

'Thank you.'

She hands me the box and I'm intrigued to see what is inside.

I open it up and see that inside is a brand new, stainless-steel kitchen knife. It's about eight inches long.

And it's virtually identical to the one that I grabbed and used to stab Harry.

For a moment, I feel a little uneasy.

Lucia spots this and puts a comforting hand on my arm. She points to the knife block on the far side of the kitchen. 'I know that there is a knife missing. I just thought I'd get you a new one.'

'Thank you,' I say as I begin to wonder the significance of the gift.

It's the one thing about that night that has never been resolved. What happened to the knife?

Lucia looks at me. 'I know the last one got broken by accident. So I took it and I threw it away. It was no good.'

My eyes widen in realisation.

I feel the tears well in my eyes at the thought of what Lucia did for me by her actions. I'm overwhelmed.

'Thank you,' I say, but my voice trembles with emotion.

I put the knife down, take a step forward and embrace Lucia.

'Thank you,' I whisper.

'*Non c'e problema,*' Lucia whispers back as she hugs me. 'It was the right thing to do.'

A LETTER FROM THE AUTHOR

Dear Reader,

Thank you so much for reading *Last Night at Villa Lucia*. I really hoped you were hooked by Cerys's story.

If you'd like to join other readers and keep in touch, there are two options. To stay in the loop with my new releases with Storm:

www.stormpublishing.co/simon-mccleave

And if you'd like to receive two FREE novellas, along with occasional newsletters and updates about my new books:

www.simonmccleave.com/vip-email-club

If you enjoyed this book and could spare a few moments to leave a review, that would be hugely appreciated. Even a short review can make all the difference in encouraging a reader to discover my books for the first time. Thank you so much!

Although this book is in many ways a classic whodunnit, my true motivation for writing this story was for me to explore much darker themes of toxic masculinity, alcoholism and abusive relationships. I have my own experience of all three. Domestic abuse thrives under the cover of a silence that is motivated by fear, a warped sense of loyalty and a culture of denial. More than half of children growing up in this kind of environment will develop PTSD and they will also be twelve times more likely to suffer from addiction. As an alcoholic now seven years into recovery, I wanted to explore the nature of active addiction. I think it's important to remember that alcoholism is a psychological disease and not a lifestyle choice. Hopefully, through this book I've managed to explore these subjects with honesty, sensitivity and compassion.

Thank you for coming on this powerful journey with me.

www.simonmccleave.com

facebook.com/simonmccleaveauthor

x.com/simon_mccleave

instagram.com/simonmccleaveauthor

tiktok.com/@simon.mccleaveauthor

ACKNOWLEDGMENTS

I will always be indebted to the people who have made this novel possible.

Firstly, to my incredible editor, Claire Bord. From the moment Claire and I started to discuss the idea for this book, I could see that she shared my excitement for the story. Working with Claire on this has been a joy. We share the same sensibilities, and she has supported my vision for the book with patience, enthusiasm and some incredible notes throughout. Thank you for pushing me to deliver the best book I can.

To Oliver Rhodes and the rest of the Storm team – Alexandra Holmes, Naomi Knox, Chris Lucraft, Elke Desanghere and Anna McKerrow.

To my superb agent, Millie Hoskins. Thanks for all your hard work and for championing me and my books at every opportunity.

To my stronger half, Nicola, whose initial reaction, ideas and notes on my work I trust implicitly.

To Izzy and George, who are everything.

To my mum, Pam, for her overwhelming enthusiasm for everything I write.

To Frank, Ruth, Arthur and Tabitha Tope for accompanying the McCleave clan on our various villa holidays. I swear everything in this book is fiction!

To Dave Gaughran for his invaluable support and advice.

And Keira Bowie for her ongoing patience and help.

/

Made in United States
Orlando, FL
24 August 2024

50741594R00200